PRELUDE

London, autumn 1879

S he is not scared yet.

    She has come to the great city because life in the overcrowded slums of Birmingham is hard, dirty, very often brutal and always under the domination of her drunkard of a father and her two loutish older brothers, an unholy triumvirate who rule every moment of her days (at least one is always out of work, often all three) and for whom, despite her efforts, nothing is ever good enough. All through the spring and into the early weeks of summer she employed every iota of her ingenuity and managed to amass a small hoard of coins, largely by such means as telling her father when in his cups that the stale bread and the fatty bacon cost a farthing more than they did, that the pawnbroker paid a penny less than he actually handed out; sometimes by more blatant stealing, when one of the brothers fell into bed so drowned in cheap alcohol that he was unlikely to notice a small, silent shape slipping a careful hand into his pocket and removing a halfpenny.

    She made her escape at the end of June and, arriving in London, tried for an increasingly desperate and terrible five weeks to find work before coming to understand that, uneducated, unworldly, with almost no practical skills and with nobody to champion or help her, only the oldest profession was going to save her from starvation.

    The only small stroke of luck – everything is relative – was to have fallen in with a group of older women who absorbed her into their number and taught her a few brutal facts about her new life. Their companionship – it couldn't really be called friendship – helped a little, but it was no compensation for the awfulness of having sex with a stranger ten or twenty times a week.

    Now on this autumn night as she hurries along the

Embankment towards Battersea Bridge and what for want of a better word could be called home, she is feeling a very small glow of happiness, for the man who has just been holding her up against a wall while he thrust himself inside her was overcome with lust and finished very quickly. In his hurry to be rid of her he overpaid her, and she managed to slip away, still trying to rearrange her skirts, before he noticed.

She is seventeen years old, she has reddish-brown hair so long that she can sit on it, a tiny waist and a shapely bosom and hips. Born into another tranche of society, she would probably be courted by handsome men with good prospects. But she knows better, now, than to dream of Prince Charming seeking her out and sweeping her away. It will not happen.

So, she is lonely, not in good health, barely the right side of destitute and, deep within her soul, ashamed of what she has become.

But she is not scared.

That, however, will soon change.

She has crossed the bridge and is trying to quicken her pace without appearing to run, for she has been told by her mentors that a running woman is a vulnerable woman. Besides, her boots are far too tight and one heel is loose. The other women have also told her to avoid the river late at night if she is alone, hinting at a frightful, lurking danger that, brash and bold though they are, none is prepared to speak aloud. But it *is* late now and she *is* alone; the neat residential streets she hurries through to reach the tenement where she shares a dingy room are deserted, few if any lights showing from behind the tightly drawn curtains.

The fog descends.

She realizes that she has missed a turning. It doesn't matter, she'll take the next, parallel street and double back. No harm done.

But then suddenly she feels a stab of alarm.

Just for an instant it seems that a heavy black veil has descended, and all at once she is viewing the ordinary street and its neat, smug rows of houses through something dark and thick. The air has suddenly turned very cold.

HC

THE WOMAN WHO SPOKE
TO SPIRITS

Recent Titles by Alys Clare from Severn House

A World's End Bureau mystery

THE WOMAN WHO SPOKE TO SPIRITS

The Gabriel Taverner Series

A RUSTLE OF SILK
THE ANGEL IN THE GLASS

The Aelf Fen Series

OUT OF THE DAWN LIGHT
MIST OVER THE WATER
MUSIC OF THE DISTANT STARS
THE WAY BETWEEN THE WORLDS
LAND OF THE SILVER DRAGON
BLOOD OF THE SOUTH
THE NIGHT WANDERER
THE RUFUS SPY

The Hawkenlye Series

THE PATHS OF THE AIR
THE JOYS OF MY LIFE
THE ROSE OF THE WORLD
THE SONG OF THE NIGHTINGALE
THE WINTER KING
A SHADOWED EVIL
THE DEVIL'S CUP

THE WOMAN WHO SPOKE TO SPIRITS

Alys Clare

severn House

This first world edition published 2019
in Great Britain and the USA by
SEVERN HOUSE PUBLISHERS LTD of
Eardley House, 4 Uxbridge Street, London W8 7SY.
Trade paperback edition first published
in Great Britain and the USA 2019 by
SEVERN HOUSE PUBLISHERS LTD.

British Library Cataloguing in Publication Data
A CIP catalogue record for this title is available from the British Library.

ISBN-13: 978-0-7278-8868-6 (cased)
ISBN-13: 978-1-84751-993-1 (trade paper)
ISBN-13: 978-1-4483-0206-2 (e-book)

Typeset by Palimpsest Book Production Ltd.,
Falkirk, Stirlingshire, Scotland.

It is a horrible sensation, full of menace and foreboding. She quickens her steps and, as soon as it began, the sensation stops.

But nevertheless she is shaken, her heart beating too fast, her stays cutting into her ribs as she pants for breath. Despite the other women's warning, despite the tight boots with the loose heel, she breaks into a run.

She comes to a junction, turns, heads off down the next street. Not far away a church looms up out of the fog, big, grey, solid, reassuring. It is not really on her route home but such is its appeal, in this whirl of anxiety and incipient fear, that she decides to make the short detour. The church's door is always open, or so she believes. Maybe she will slip inside and sit for a while in the darkness. Maybe she will try to pray. Maybe – this is a very faint hope – some cheery, avuncular vicar will be kind to her.

There is someone coming towards her, from the direction of the church. Oh, oh, she thinks, if this man (she decides it is probably a man) has been in the church, he'll be nice, and charitable, perhaps even spare her a coin or two.

It is a dangerous assumption.

She hurries towards him.

He gives a little gasp as she approaches, as if he has only just noticed her. He is a very good actor.

'Oh, sorry!' she gasps. 'Didn't mean to make you jump.'

He raises his hat courteously, staring into her face in consternation. He assures her she did no such thing.

He asks one or two questions: where does she live? Why is she out by herself late at night? May he be allowed the pleasure of escorting her to wherever she is going?

His voice is genteel, his tone concerned, and she falls into his trap.

Only when it is far too late does she recall the moment of doubt, when she felt those deep eyes raking her, assessing her, penetrating her, but ignored the instinctive warning.

She should have listened to it, because it would have saved her.

Instead, she is going to die: very unpleasantly. After rather a long time in his hands, her dead, naked body will be slipped into the river, her long reddish-brown hair flowing out behind her in the powerful water like a pennant.

He takes her arm, at first gently but then, pulling her into a dark little high-walled alley as he removes something from his pocket and lifts it towards her mouth, his grip turns to steel, his hard fingers pushing into her soft flesh.

Now she is scared.

ONE

Faced with an unsavoury task which she has no option but to perform, Lily Raynor habitually gets it out of the way at the earliest opportunity. Accordingly, on this bright spring morning in 1880, when the Thames is glittering with spangles and the scent of blossom manages to make itself known above the usual stench of horse shit and sewage, she is drawing on her boots and about to set out to seek audience with Lord Dunorlan.

She knows he will be at home, and also that he will receive her. He is, indeed, desperate to hear what she has to tell him. She is not as keen to reveal it; in fact, she isn't keen at all.

The second boot is on and she stands up. They are inelegant footwear: knee-high and laced, they are work boots, made of well-greased and waterproofed leather, strong yet supple and extremely comfortable. They are low-heeled and Lily can run in them without turning an ankle. Some time after she purchased them, she took the left one to a cobbler in a distant part of town and asked him to sew a long, narrow channel down the inside of it, of a size to accommodate the rigid horn sheath she provided. The cobbler did a neat job and the pocket is hard to spot from the outside, with a shadow of the stitching only just visible. In its sheath inside the channel – she didn't reveal its purpose to the cobbler – lives a long, fine, very sharp boning knife that belonged to her grandmother, worn from years of sharpening, its brass handle bound with red leather.

Lily does not anticipate having to use her knife in her new profession. But if she is ever in a situation where she needs a weapon, she intends to make absolutely sure that she doesn't die for the want of one.

She puts on her coat and hat, picks up the slim file of papers on her desk and crosses the office to the door, closing and locking it behind her. The middle floor of her house is occupied by a tenant – a minute, scruffy and bad-tempered Russian ballet dancer – and Lily is inclined to believe the Little Ballerina may also be incurably nosy and pretty much without conscience. She lets herself out of the front door, locking that too (the Little Ballerina has her own key and, besides, is rehearsing all day today), and steps out into Hob's Court, walking briskly along to where it opens into World's End Passage.

She is tempted, as she always is, to turn right and go down to look at the river. But the swiftest way to Lord Dunorlan's house in Eaton Terrace is in the opposite direction, so she turns left up Riley Street, then right onto the King's Road. Hansom cabs, growlers and several omnibuses pass her, but she keeps walking. Money is tight, and if she can save even the cost of a modest omnibus ride, she does.

She crosses Sloane Square and all too soon is in Eaton Terrace, looking up at the elegant frontage and the smart, glossy black-painted door of Lord Dunorlan's town residence. She does not hesitate, but marches straight up the steps and rings the bell.

She is admitted by the supercilious footman with halitosis who has opened the door to her before. Again without a word, nor indeed any sign other than a faint sneer that he has registered her presence, he stalks off along the corridor and, pausing, taps on a closed door. In answer to some barely audible response from within, he opens the door and says, with the sort of obsequious reverence that a devotee might adopt before a powerful, temperamental and unpredictable god, 'The investigator, my lord.'

He does not grace her with a name and pronounces *investigator* in the tone others might give to *night-soil man* or even *multiple child-killer.*

'Show her in, Forshaw,' says a weary voice.

The footman opens the door a fraction more widely and steps aside. Lily, not a woman to be cowed and refusing to contort herself to get through such a small gap, pushes it fully open and steps into the room. She is aware of Forshaw closing it, rather forcefully, after her.

Lord Dunorlan is standing by one of the long windows that open onto the walled garden. This room is his study and it is beautifully furnished with high-backed leather-covered chairs, elegantly carved bookcases, a deep red Turkey rug in front of the hearth and a wide desk, presently clear of papers, books, writing implements or anything else.

Lord Dunorlan is looking at her. He is an upright man of around the mid-sixties, lean, white-haired, dignified. His expression is a brave smile. He says courteously, 'Let us sit beside the fire, Miss Raynor, for the air is chill and the sunshine deceptive.'

Lily, fresh from her vigorous walk, is already too hot and beside the fire is the last place she wants to sit, but she nods, forcing a reciprocal smile, and, removing her gloves, places the file on her lap.

Lord Dunorlan's faded blue eyes have shot to it. 'You have something to report,' he says dully.

'I have, my lord.' She goes to hold out the file to him, but he shakes his head. 'Am I to read it?'

He makes a vague sound which she takes for assent.

She opens the file.

It is unnecessarily cruel to make him wait, so she clears her throat and starts to read her own words. 'Investigator Y, detailed to observe and record the movements of Subject A, concludes after two weeks of close scrutiny that there is indeed evidence to suggest an inappropriate association, Subject B having been seen in Subject A's company in what cannot reasonably be viewed as innocent circumstances.' She hesitates, but this, too, seems cruel. 'Subject A has been observed to enter Subject B's residence at different times of the day, and invariably when there is nobody except Subject B at home.' She looks up, but Lord Dunorlan's face is hidden by his raised hand. 'Investigator Y was extremely thorough in this respect, my lord, given the sensitivity of this particular aspect.' Lord Dunorlan nods but doesn't speak.

Lily returns to the file. 'On the evening of 24th March, Subjects A and B had been in Subject B's house since just before luncheon, and at half-past eight they emerged and took a hansom to Drury Lane.' There's no need, surely, to add that as the pair stood under the portico of the house waiting for the cab, thinking themselves unobserved, Subject A leaned close to Subject B and slowly and sensuously licked right up his face from chin to ear, in a gesture so fiercely erotic that there was an instant and very evident response within Subject B's close-fitting trousers. 'They attended the theatre,' she continues, 'after which they went to the Café Royal for supper. They returned to Subject B's house afterwards, it being then an hour after midnight, and Subject A did not emerge until ten o'clock the following morning. Nobody but Subjects A and B were within during that time, although a manservant and two lads arrived soon after Subject A had left.'

'As if,' Lord Dunorlan murmurs, 'they had been specifically told the time they might return.'

'Well, one could look at it like that,' Lily agrees.

The hand is dropped and for an instant the faded eyes blaze blue. 'How the devil else could one look at it?' he snaps. Then, instantly contrite, he says, 'I apologize.'

Lily nods her acknowledgement.

After a moment Lord Dunorlan signals for her to go on.

There is quite a lot more to read, but it tells the same incontrovertible story and quite soon Lord Dunorlan says softly, 'Enough, I think.'

He gets to his feet, slowly, levering himself up as if his body has suddenly become an intolerable burden; as if all at once his years have caught him up. He crosses to his desk, leans a hand on it as if in urgent need of support, and then moves to the window to resume his earlier contemplation of the lovely garden, bright with cherry blossom, narcissi, tulips and some brave early irises.

Lily sits perfectly still watching him. His very posture shouts of defeat, despair, grief, and she wants more than anything to go to him, to take his hand, to tell him how very sorry she is. For, although she is not meant to know and discreetly pretends she doesn't, Subject A is, of course, Lady Dunorlan: the beautiful, erratic, self-indulgent Lucia Simpson-Halliday, as she was before her marriage, debutante of the season almost a decade ago and her elderly husband's junior by some thirty-five years. Subject B is the Honourable Jimmy Robertson, playboy, ridiculously wealthy second son of a lord; dilettante and gambler, womanizer; a man who has never had to do a day's work in his life and never will and who thus is free to pursue and bed other men's wives to his heart's content.

Investigator Y is Lily. She is the World's End Bureau's only investigator and, for now, its sole employee, although she is planning to change that imminently. She hasn't revealed her investigator's identity to Lord Dunorlan, and has no idea whether or not he has realized that it is she who has been spying on his wife's movements. She hopes rather fervently not, although really it makes little difference.

Lord Dunorlan has, after what seems a small age, moved to his desk. He is drawing out a cheque book, inking his pen. He writes swiftly, blots the cheque and, rising again, comes across to Lily.

'This is, I believe, the correct amount for the balance I owe you. Thank you, Miss Raynor, for an efficient and discreet service.' He manages a smile, but it is like the grin of teeth in a fleshless skull.

Lily gets to her feet, tucking the cheque inside her file. A swift glance has told her it is right to the penny. She nods her thanks. She cannot think of a thing to say, and every sense tells her that Lord Dunorlan is longing for her to go so that he can give in to his sorrow. He tugs at a long, embroidered bell pull beside the hearth and very swiftly the footman appears. 'Show Miss Raynor out, Forshaw,' says Lord Dunorlan. Lily, needing no second invitation, hurries out of the room. She barely notices Forshaw opening the door onto the street, and for once his superior expression and his attempt to diminish her go entirely unnoticed.

Lily heads left down Chelsea Bridge Road and then right onto the Embankment. It is a longer walk back to Hob's Court this way but she doesn't hesitate to take it. She badly needs the solace that the river always provides.

By the time she leaves the Embankment to turn up World's End Passage, she is feeling calmer. She has been telling herself very firmly that she will be no use in her new profession if she becomes too emotionally involved in the problems of her clients. Lord Dunorlan should have known better, she thinks. He may be elegant, sophisticated, influential, possessor of a country estate in Sussex and an utterly wonderful house in one of the best areas in London and extremely rich, but, when all's said and done, he's old and his wife is young. What, Lily asks silently as she lets herself into No. 3 Hob's Court, did he expect?

She takes off her jacket and hat and files away Lord Dunorlan's papers, having first removed the cheque. She will pay it into the bank this afternoon, before the first of her appointments. She has advertised for clerical assistance, and today is expecting the last two on her shortlist. If the first four are anything to go by she is doomed to disappointment, but she is determined to remain optimistic. She is not in a position to offer much in the way of wages, but then the work that her new assistant will be required to do is not arduous: it will, in short, consist of the myriad small tasks for which Lily doesn't really have time (or, if she's honest, inclination), such as filing, correspondence, tallying the petty cash and taking cheques to the bank, plus making the tea and watering the pot plants.

Lily hears clattering and splashing from the scullery right at the back of the house, at the end of the long passage that runs beside the front and back offices, past the foot of the stairs and through the kitchen. It is, she remembers, one of Mrs Clapper's days. Mrs Clapper comes in three times a week to do the heavy, and it sounds as if she is presently engaged on the weekly wash. Overriding the scents of bleach and soap – and a sort of *wet* smell in the air – is the appetizing aroma of steak and kidney pudding, so Mrs Clapper has clearly had time for a bit of cooking.

Lily has inherited Mrs Clapper from her grandparents, whose house this once was. She is a small, fiery woman of indeterminate age, gunmetal-grey-haired, wiry and strong, and possessed of some of the most extreme opinions Lily has ever come across. She is a hard worker and loyal to Lily as 'the last of the Raynors', as she will insist on depressingly phrasing it. One of her extreme opinions concerns Lily's lodger, the ballet dancer, for there seems to be something about the frail-looking yet steel-cored Avdotya Aleksandrova that just gets under Mrs Clapper's skin.

'I see the Little Ballerina's not had time to tidy up after

herself again,' Mrs Clapper greets her employer in her most censorious tones as Lily goes through to the kitchen in search of some of the steak and kidney pudding. 'Left the necessary in a right state, she did, and her unmentionables soaking in the sink. Downright dirty, I call it.' She gives a violent nod as if in confirmation of her utterance. 'As if the rest of us want to gaze down on you-know-what in the pan and private, personal garments covered in bodily fluids!'

Mrs Clapper's complaints are justified, Lily reflects. She too has wondered why the Little Ballerina can't make use of the stiff-bristled brush that stands soaking in a solution of chloride of lime beside the lavatory and, since Lily herself would not dream of letting anyone else see her own used undergarments, she cannot understand any other woman doing so.

'Yes, I know you do,' she says mildly in reply to Mrs Clapper's angry remark. 'But she pays her rent on time, more or less, and I need the money.'

Mrs Clapper sniffs. She has been known to say that she can't understand for the life of her why Lily gave up the nursing. Mad, she calls it, and she can't see the sense of it, really she can't.

Lily doesn't want to deal with this conversation right now and, since it's clear that Mrs Clapper is winding herself up for it, deflects her by remarking that the steak and kidney pudding smells wonderful and is it ready yet?

It is a little after half-past two. Lily has been to the bank and is now seeing the fifth out of her six interviewees. This one is indeed much like the first four, and Lily mentally rejected her after the first couple of minutes. Mrs Green – she is reluctant to vouchsafe her Christian name – is a timid little widow dressed in musty and mothball-smelling black, her pale face screwed up in an anxious frown and the red patches of psoriasis on her hands, wrists and neck. Lily, while telling herself not to be uncharitable and that poor Mrs Green didn't choose to have the complaint, nevertheless can't help the instinct that makes her pull away from the bleeding cracks on the back of Mrs Green's right hand and the fine shower of skin flakes that flutters down every time she scratches at herself, and she does this with nervous frequency.

But her main reason for deciding not to employ Mrs Green is that she can't spell, her writing is barely legible and the prospect of doing arithmetic, even the simplest of sums, throws her into a bolt-eyed panic. 'I could probably manage the filing,' she offers with pathetic eagerness, 'since I've done that before and I'm all right if I have the halferbet written up somewhere close-handy.' She smiles, revealing rather a lot of gaps between her brownish teeth.

Mentally translating, Lily realizes that *halferbet* means alphabet.

She manages to find an excuse for rejecting this penultimate person on her list – she mutters something about arithmetic really being rather crucial – and, to salve her conscience, presses into Mrs Green's gently bleeding hand the price of the omnibus fare home.

Now she awaits the last applicant.

There is a brisk drum roll of tapping on the office door, and even as Lily calls out, 'Come in!' it is pushed open and the final interviewee stands before her.

The first surprise is that F. Wilbraham is a man.

There is no reason why he should not be, Lily thinks frantically, but all the other applicants (including the seven whose letters didn't encourage her even to invite them for interview) have been female. She knows this because each one either signed their letter with a female Christian name or, like Mrs Green, with the prefix Mrs.

F. Wilbraham, she recalls, signed like that; to be exact, as F. P. D. M. Wilbraham, and, she now appreciates, not one of that imposing series of initials stood for a woman's name. She just didn't expect that a man would have applied for such a lowly and, far more significant, poorly paid post . . .

F. Wilbraham is still standing before her. His smile is growing a little pained. She tries to take him in without its being obvious: he is tall, broad-shouldered, he has dark blond hair worn quite long and, she thinks, trying to peer without making it apparent, hazel eyes. His features are well-formed, with a strong nose, an important jaw and a wide mouth with the sort of curved creases around it that suggest he smiles readily. He is very well dressed – black top coat and trousers, white shirt, neatly tied cravat with a sparkly pin – but, looking more closely, she sees that the garments, while clean, are rather well-worn.

Perhaps the reason why F. Wilbraham is prepared to consider a post of such poor remuneration has just been revealed.

She clears her throat, indicates Mrs Green's recently vacated chair on the opposite side of her desk and says, 'Won't you sit down, Mr Wilbraham?'

Felix Wilbraham pulls the offered chair further from the fair-haired woman's desk – he has long legs – and sits down. She is still staring at him with that frown, as if something about his appearance disturbs her. Has she noticed how worn his cuffs are? Has she spotted the careful darn just above the ankle on his right trouser leg? Has she observed how the good cloth of his coat is shiny from all the pressing? Her blue-green eyes are intent behind the small, round spectacles and he has the feeling she doesn't miss much.

But it is not she who he must impress. 'I have an appointment with Mr Raynor,' he says, 'concerning the post of clerical assistant which you recently advertised. I have the letter here.' He reaches inside his coat but she shakes her head.

'No need to show it to me, Mr Wilbraham, since it was I who wrote it.' Well, of course it is, Felix thinks, you being the clerical assistant and—

Then, about half a minute too late, he understands and straight away wishes as hard as he's ever wished anything that he could call back that reference to *Mr Raynor*.

For if this woman is the clerical assistant, what need has the World's End Bureau of a second one? And, if this putative male proprietor really exists, where is he? There are only the two rooms, and, seated before the desk in the first of them, he can see a similar desk in the second, through the open door, and there's nobody sitting at it.

There is nothing for it but to admit the mistake. 'I apologize,' he says, bowing his head briefly. 'You, of course, are L. G. Raynor.'

'I am,' the fair-haired woman agrees.

She is still frowning. Then she draws forward a file and

opens it to reveal his own letter of application. 'Let us begin with your name, please, Mr Wilbraham. You have four Christian names, I see?'

'Felix Parsifal Derek McIvie,' he supplies unthinkingly. He has been rattling off his burdensome forenames all his life.

She is writing, very neatly and swiftly, as he speaks. He can't be sure but he thinks he sees a tiny twitch of her lips.

She echoes softly, 'Derek.'

'I know, it sits ill, doesn't it?' he agrees. 'It's the name of my grandfather in the Commercial Road who, for want of a more euphemistic term, deals in scrap metal. But he's the one with the money, and my parents were trying to ingratiate themselves.'

She has stopped writing and now raises her head to stare at him. 'The position requires a good hand, numeracy, a certain familiarity with the keeping of accounts and banking procedures in general. Would that be problematic?'

'Not in the least.'

She is making notes. He wishes he could see what she's writing. 'Why, can you tell me, do you wish to be engaged in a clerical post?'

Because I'm hungry, about to be thrown out of my digs, the money's running out and there's very little else for which I'm qualified, is the honest answer. But he can hardly say that. 'I like the idea of a new challenge,' he says brightly. 'The work sounds very interesting, and—'

She holds up a hand to silence him. 'It's clerical work, Mr Wilbraham,' she reproves him gently. 'Correspondence, filing, the preparing of invoices. Necessary to the smooth running of the office, I grant you, but scarcely a challenge, unless the very act of adding figures together and remembering in what order the letters of the alphabet fall are obstacles that must daily be overcome.'

He grins, assuming that the remark about the letters of the alphabet was a joke. Then, noticing her serious expression, he straightens his face.

'I can assure you of my ability in those areas,' he says. 'I had the benefit of a Marlborough College education.' There is no need to add that he'd left under the most thunderous of dark clouds, nor the reason for its having formed. Anyway, it was proved later that the barmaid had been lying.

'Good,' she mutters. She is once more making notes. Looking up, she says, 'Do you have any languages?'

'Latin and a bit of Greek, and I speak French quite well, although I'm not so good with reading and writing it.'

'Good,' she says again, with a little more animation this time. 'Do I take it, then, that you have spent time in France, to have developed a facility with the spoken language?'

'Yes,' he confirms. 'I was secretary cum companion to an elderly, widowed countess –' oh, he thinks, I'm sorry, Solange, for calling you elderly, but if I tell this perceptive and observant woman that you were barely eighteen years older than me, witty, clever, and with those peculiarly attractive looks that make the French call a woman who possesses them a *jolie-laide*, she'll jump to entirely the wrong conclusion, except, of course, that in fact it's entirely the *right* conclusion – 'and, after her death, I cared for her son.'

'If she was elderly, then surely her son was of sufficient years to care for himself?'

Good God, thinks Felix, but she's sharp. 'The son was –' he thinks of the right word to describe the erratic, exciting, wild, self-centred and utterly charming Henri-Josef – 'not entirely responsible,' he says.

She nods. 'I see.'

He is quite sure she does.

She is writing again. She writes for quite some time, giving Felix the opportunity to glance around the office. Apart from the desk, the two chairs and a couple of what he assumes are filing cabinets, there is little else apart from the extensive arrangement of small, square drawers formed into one large item of furniture that virtually fills the length and height of one wall. It is made of glossy wood, obviously old and much used, for the wood has a subtle and attractive patina. He has seen something like it before, and after some thought, realizes it's the sort of thing found in an apothecary's shop; a pharmacy, as they are nowadays called. Now he has come up with this, he realizes that he has been detecting a faint, slightly medicinal, slightly herbal, slightly spicy and alto-gether pleasant aroma since he entered the office.

Without pausing to ask himself if it is wise, he exclaims, 'This used to be an apothecary's shop, didn't it?'

Her head shoots up. There is quite a long pause, and then she says, 'It did. It belonged to my grandparents, and the business had been in the family for a hundred and fifty years.' She points out of the bay window that faces out onto Hob's Court. 'If you look closely, you can still see the darker-coloured brickwork over the window and above the door where the sign saying *Raynor's Pharmacy* was affixed until a few months ago.'

'A hundred and fifty years!' he echoes admiringly. 'You didn't wish to continue the tradition?'

With surely more asperity than the question demands, she says, 'No I did *not*.' And returns to her note-taking.

After a further long time of her writing and him staring around the office, she finally puts down her pen, folds her hands on the desk and says, 'Do you know, Mr Wilbraham, precisely what constitutes the business of the World's End Bureau?'

'No,' he admits. He wonders now why he didn't ask her straight away, hoping very much that it won't count against him. 'A domestic engagement bureau, perhaps? Lady's maids, second footmen and butlers?'

She smiles thinly. 'No, not that.' She pauses. 'It is an investigation bureau.'

'Investigation into what?' He is intrigued.

'To date, I have found a runaway son, returned a very irritating and snappy Pekinese to its distraught owner, discovered that the thefts of small amounts of money in a hardware shop were not in fact done by the youth who had been accused but by the proprietor's wife, who wanted a new bonnet, reassured one man that his wife was not having a love affair and broken the news to two more that their wives were. Oh, and located the father of an illegitimate child born to a woman who very much needed his financial support.' She frowns. 'There are more, but those, I believe, are a representative sample.'

He is studying her with new interest. At first glance he had thought her plain – the fair hair is very firmly secured in its neat bun, the high-necked blouse and the businesslike waistcoat and skirt in fine, dark cloth are well tailored but not very feminine, and just visible under her hem is a very peculiar pair of boots that look like something a stable boy or a gardener might put on for the dirty jobs, although hers shine like glass from careful polishing. Her expression – severe to the point of disapproving – does not flatter.

But once or twice animation has lifted the serious lines of her face, with its broad forehead, sharp cheekbones and firm chin; when she remarked upon the absurd inclusion of Derek among his grandiose Christian names, for example; when she spoke with such enthusiasm of her recent cases. At such moments he has noticed a sparkle in her bright eyes, and her generous mouth has very nearly stretched into a real smile.

'I can see why you have found the need for clerical assist-ance,' he says. He has done his best to come up with the most diplomatic and flattering thing he can think of, for he has decided he really wants this job.

She is studying him again. It really is quite disconcerting, for he has absolutely no idea what she is thinking. Wisely appreciating that any further remark he might make to advance himself as precisely the man for the job would do more harm than good, he keeps quiet.

Then she says – and to his ears the words are like the opening line of the jolliest, happiest song – 'When do you think you would be able to start work?'

He almost says, *Now! Immediately!* But instinct tells him not to look too eager, nor to give the impression that he is worryingly free of responsibilities and commitments. He frowns, as if thinking hard. 'Let me see,' he muses aloud. 'Today is Tuesday . . .' He waits for perhaps twenty seconds, then says, 'I believe it would be convenient to begin next Monday.'

Her eyebrows shoot up and instantly he wonders if he should have said he couldn't start till the following month, or that he'd have to consult his present employer regarding the length of notice required. But it's too late now.

Then she says – and he offers up a brief and sincere little prayer of thanks – 'Oh, of course, you've just been working abroad, you said. In France, so naturally you would not be employed here in England.' She makes another note. He can see from where he sits that the pages headed F. P. D. M. Wilbraham are now covered in her neat, economical hand. She puts down her pen and stands up. She holds out her hand, and he takes it. 'Let us agree to a month's trial, Mr Wilbraham, to determine whether we suit each other. The wage is as set out in the advertisement. I assume that is acceptable?'

'It is.'

She relinquishes his hand and steps round her desk to escort him to the door. 'Until next Monday, then.'

'Until next Monday,' he echoes. 'Good day, Miss Raynor.'

He walks at a sedate pace to the end of Hob's Court and off up World's End Passage. It is only when he is quite sure he is out of her sight and earshot that he punches the air and gives a great shout of glee.

TWO

I t is a Friday afternoon early in Felix's second month of
employment at the World's End Bureau. The preceding
weeks have gone quite well, or so he feels; his rather
enigmatic employer doesn't give very much away, and *quite
well* is as far as he dare go (and this is more because of his
natural and fairly resilient optimism than from any great faith
in his ability as a very new clerical assistant). Lily – he thinks
of her as Lily, although he is careful to be utterly correct and
call her Miss Raynor – is busy at her desk in the inner office,
or the *sanctum sanctorum*, as Felix calls it in the privacy of
his own head. Lacking anything very pressing to do just now,
he mentally reviews his performance. He has been here longer
than the month stipulated for his trial term, so does that mean
he has passed the initial test of his first few weeks?

Filing: yes, pretty good, he's sure he has improved on the
pre-existing system. But this, he admits honestly, is no great
feat, since Lily explained that she hadn't really had the chance
to instigate a system and it was up to Felix to organize the
Bureau's paperwork as he thought best. Anyway, Lily seems
satisfied with what he's done, so, against the first entry in
the report card he sees in his mind's eye, there has to be a
tick.

Preparation of invoices: well, he reflects, there is really very
little room for error here, since he can write neatly, legibly
and rather dashingly, and it is many years since he grew out
of dropping ink blots on the paper. He can spell, he can add
up and he knows how such documents should be set out. He
has also found a tactful way to let his employer know that
there are methods for extracting payment of overdue bills from
even the most recalcitrant debtor, and the Bureau's finances
have accordingly taken a small step for the better. This area
of his work, too, surely warrants a tick.

Correspondence: the same comments about his writing and

his knowledge of laying out documents as above, he tells himself. Since he has largely written letters as directed by his employer, any fault in the content – not that he has detected any – is hers and not his. Moreover, she has acceded to his suggestion that they acquire new stationery printed with the name and details of the Bureau, appreciating his expressed view that it is well worth the cost since these innovations have instantly made the Bureau look a great deal more professional. Once again, a tick.

Plant watering: oh, dear. On his own admission, Felix knows very little about plants, other than the flowering variety found in large, extravagant, fragrant bouquets and in the exquisite corsages pinned to tightly boned bosoms above which soft globes of smooth, creamy flesh spill out . . . All of which, he reproves himself firmly, are a very far cry from Lily Raynor's potted plants. She appears to favour a sage-green-coloured sort of thing with long, spiky leaves that grow up to perhaps a foot or more, four of which are ranged on shelves around the outer office. None of them have responded at all well to Felix's enthusiastic attentions; sadly, it was only with hindsight that he realized they might be related to the cactus family (they are certainly aggressive enough) and therefore should be watered sparingly. Plant-watering, he is sure, has a large cross against it in his imaginary report.

But to counter this failure, he reminds himself cheerfully, his employer appears to be pleasantly surprised by his ability to make a decent pot of tea, toast and butter a teacake and even prepare a plate of ham rolls *with mustard*, all with the minimum of fuss and without leaving a mess in the kitchen. The mustard, indeed, caused Lily to raise her head from whatever matter held her in deep thrall at her desk to give him an appreciative nod and a brief, 'Very tasty, thank you.'

For a man who went to a good public school, there are huge gaps in Felix's academic knowledge. To make up for this, however, he has some surprising talents (his familiarity with the mysteries of the kitchen is a good example), largely because he's been fending for himself since he left school. He has had some unlikely jobs, he has learned from experience that if you're picky about your food then you've never experienced true hunger, he has discovered that when you're really on your uppers (particularly if you speak like he does) you're far more likely to receive a helping hand from the poor than the rich, who, in Felix's experience, tend to cling very tightly to the belief that poverty is largely self-inflicted.

Felix parted company from his wealthy upper-class family not long after he finished with Marlborough College, or rather Marlborough College finished with him. His father, apoplectic at his son's expulsion ('YOU HAVE BROUGHT THE MOST PROFOUND SHAME UPON THIS FAMILY!' – he had definitely been shouting in capital letters – 'HOW *DARE* YOU, BOY?'), immediately set about organizing a tutor, in the hope that it wasn't too late for Felix to make up for lost time and still get the Cambridge (or at worst Oxford) place that his father had set his heart on. Felix refused. They argued, the arguments turned to all-out rows, to increasingly wild and violent threats that, in the end, made Felix burst out laughing: 'You're going to *beat* me, Father? How, may I ask? I am almost a head taller than you and two stone heavier, and I box.'

That laughter signalled the end.

Felix left without saying goodbye to anyone but the cook, who had contrived to get food to him when his father tried to starve him into submission, and the head groom, who had once memorably muttered, not quite far enough under his breath, that Felix's father was an arsehole. Felix packed a small bag, took all the money he could lay his hands on and marched off down the long, lime-tree-lined drive to the majestic old house, and he has not been back.

He prefers not to think of the early months of his self-imposed exile. To begin with he was able to put up with friends who had gone on to varsity, sleeping on floors, surviving on their generosity, relying on the fact that they had liked and admired him as the class clown, the rebel who went his own way. But their tolerance ran out.

He went to London. He learned the cruel ways of the city, and how to survive them (just). He has had terrible times, he has had wonderful times.

And now he is the new clerical assistant at the World's End Bureau.

Something else that Felix has had to fathom out in the course of these first weeks in addition to plant-watering, correspondence and filing is the structure of the household. He has encountered the force of nature that is Mrs Clapper, and learned within the first few minutes of meeting her that his best option is to keep right out of her way on the three days that she comes to 3, Hob's Court. Clearly she is fiercely loyal to Lily, as Felix has learned somewhat dramatically: in those short minutes that constituted their first and, so far, only significant encounter, he was out in the little kitchen and about to pour himself a glass of water. Mrs Clapper, bursting in on him like one of the Eumenides, caught sight of what he was up to – her words – and her small, deep-set eyes widened as if she'd caught him in the act of slitting open his own belly.

'*Put that down!*' she shouted at what he very much hoped was the top of her voice, the incredibly loud, shrill noise making the kitchen window rattle.

Turning, the polite greeting he'd prepared as he heard her approaching footsteps freezing on his lips, he said innocently, 'Put what down?'

She rushed at him like a terrier on a rat and grabbed the glass from his hand. '*This!*' she screeched, right in his face. 'That's cut glass, that is, proper crystal, and it's one of old Mrs Raynor's best, and they was a *wedding present!*' As if further explanation was necessary – as her deeply scathing expression seemed to suggest she thought it must be, he being no more than a mere man – she added, 'There's six of them, see, and Miss Lily, she don't want none of them getting broken!'

Meekly Felix took a chipped tumbler off the wooden draining board and filled that with water instead.

The other occupant of the house is a permanent resident, and Lily has explained briefly that she rents the rooms on the middle floor (Lily, it seems, lives at the top of the house). Her name is Avdotya Aleksandrova, but it appears that Felix won't have to attempt the challenge of pronouncing this as both Lily and Mrs Clapper refer to her as the Little Ballerina; Mrs Clapper, indeed, in such corrosively scathing terms that Felix is shamefully aware of being glad there's someone in the house that Mrs Clapper dislikes more than him.

Unfortunately, he met the Little Ballerina in rather embarrassing circumstances. He had taken advantage of Mrs Clapper's going upstairs to 'turn out your rooms, Miss Lily' to slip along the passage and through the kitchen and the scullery to the lavatory, the door to which is situated just outside the door to the garden. He was opening this door to return inside the house when its handle was pulled sharply out of his grasp and the door flung open from the other side.

He found himself face to face with a tiny woman with the skinny, bony body of a ten-year-old girl who didn't get much to eat. Surely no ten-year-old girl, however, even a very hungry one, could have looked up at him with such venom in her narrow black eyes.

'You use lavatory!' she hissed.

'Er, well, yes –' there was no point in denying it since the Niagara Falls of the flush was clearly audible – 'I've just done so, but I—'

'You *scatter!*' she said furiously. 'Men always scatter, they are so very dirty, I will not share with a *man!*'

'I assure you I never scatter,' Felix replied with as much dignity as he could summon at such short notice.

She leaned towards him, staring hard at him. He noticed several things: first, that her long black hair was very greasy and plastered to her narrow skull; second, that she had been lazy about removing the very pale greasepaint that she must have applied for her last performance, probably several before that too, and it made a sort of crusty tide around the edges of her face; third, that she had a crop of blackheads in the whorls of her left nostril; fourth, that the voluminous but flimsy cotton garment she was clutching to her – he thought it was the sort of indoor robe that the Japanese favour and call a yukata – was far too long and trailed on the ground and had what looked like scrambled egg down the front; fifth, that she stank.

She seemed to be done with her examination of him and she elbowed him out of the way. 'Go,' she said in disgust, making shooing movements with her tiny, skeletal hands as if he were a dog that had just cocked its leg in an inappropriate place. '*Go!*' she repeated.

He went.

Now, on this quiet Friday afternoon, he risks a glance through the partly open door into the inner office. Lily is still absorbed in her task. She absented herself from her desk some half an hour ago, and, although since her return he has heard her muttering to herself, he hasn't actually seen her properly nor spoken to her since her brief absence. Now, though, even as he tries surreptitiously to see what she's up to, suddenly she's on her feet and striding across the room, flinging wide the door and emerging into the front office.

She has changed from the white high-collared shirt and rather severe skirt in black barathea that is her habitual office wear into an outfit that, even if it scarcely warrants the epithet frivolous, at least is considerably more fashionable and *à la mode* – the phrase leaps out of Felix's colourful, cosmopolitan past – than her usual attire. The skirt and matching bodice are in what his experienced eyes inform him is a fine wool and silk mix, and the deep forest-green fabric has a subtle checked pattern of lighter greens and a touch of turquoise blue. The bodice – he can't help noticing both that it fits her extremely well and that she has a figure whose splendour he has not up to now fully appreciated – manages to be both modest and . . . promising, is the best word he can come up with. It is edged with a delicious little frill piped in silk that is exactly the shade of Lily's eyes. She has abandoned those workman's boots in favour of something a lot more delicate in dark green kid, buttoned and heeled, and topping off the outfit she wears a small, neat hat pulled forward over her forehead which has a discreet veil and a dashingly curled feather.

'Miss Raynor, you look magnificent,' he says.

The smile breaks out before she can stop it, but it is swiftly reined in. 'I have been invited to take tea at the Rose Tea Room,' she says. 'I hope this will be suitable.'

She doesn't say this as if it's a question, but he feels sure that it is. Does she believe his knowledge of the mores of the

Rose to be superior to hers? Almost certainly it is, and he rummages around for a way of telling her she's dressed just right without it sounding patronizing.

The Rose Tea Room is situated at the near end of Regent Street, at pavement level beneath the utterly exclusive and astronomically expensive Brougham Club. The Rose is owned by the Club, and it is where the members of the Club – all of them male – are allowed to entertain their female guests, for not a single one of the fair sex is or has ever been permitted to ascend the narrow stairs into the Club itself. The Rose is richly appointed in magenta velvet and dark wood, with swoops and swaggers of curtains at its windows to frustrate the curious eyes of the common man and, all around its walls, a series of little booths with high-backed, padded seating separated by partitions where members of the Brougham may treat their ladies to delicious little teas without anybody necessarily knowing. The Brougham membership knows the meaning of discretion, and the prospect of a fellow member even thinking of gossiping about an afternoon assignation he might accidentally have seen with anyone else, even his accountant or his wife, is as unimaginable as a doctor sharing the secrets of the consulting room or a priest those of the confessional. The staff of the Rose Tea Room might have been deaf and blind for all they appear to notice of the carryings-on over the fine bone-china cups and saucers and the three-tiered cake stands.

Lily is still waiting – somewhat apprehensively, Felix detects – for his comment. 'Eminently suitable,' he pronounces. It would have been enough, but he can't resist. 'As far as I recall,' he adds, 'most of the women there have little or no idea of when to stop, and believe that piling on the jewels and the furs and the latest offerings from Paris only enhances, whereas, as anyone with an ounce of style knows, they simply detract. You, Miss Raynor, will stand out like a diamond on a dung heap.'

She looks quite shocked, and he's not sure if it's because of the vulgarity of the simile or the fact that he's alluded to one of the most prestigious places in London as a dung heap. 'I'm sorry,' he mutters. He genuinely is sorry, for his intention was solely to bolster her confidence and not to alarm her.

But the smile is trying to force its way out again. 'So I was right to leave off the fur tippet, the mummer's streamers, the enormous sunburst brooch and the eight-strand pearl necklace,' she murmurs. Now the smile is winning, but before he can enjoy it she has spun round and gone back into the inner office, from which she returns carrying a very smart little bag in soft green leather.

'The man who has invited me may have a job for the Bureau,' she says. The moment of levity, clearly, is past. She fixes him with a firm glance. 'I shall tell you the details on my return, provided he decides in our favour.'

Our favour. Oh, he likes that.

He nods. 'Very well.'

She looks at his almost bare desk. 'If you have nothing else to do, there is a crate of books in my office which I should like you to unpack and arrange on those shelves.' She points.

'Of course.'

She is smoothing on her gloves. 'I shall return, I hope and expect, before six o'clock.'

He calls out a soft 'Good luck' as she is going out through the street door, but he doesn't think she hears. In any case, she makes no response.

He is all at once struck with the realization that his new employer has just left him alone and in sole charge of the World's End Bureau for at least three and a half hours.

If that doesn't demonstrate her confidence in him, he doesn't know what would. 'Bugger the bloody plants,' he says aloud, thinking back to the one undoubted failure on his imaginary report card, 'I think I've passed!'

He has unpacked, dusted and arranged the crate of books, most of which are heavy and learned tomes on such subjects as the history of London, the British judicial system and the peerage, but with one or two delightful surprises such as a slim volume on poisons and a salacious account of some of the most establishment-rocking divorce cases of recent years. He stands back to view his handiwork. The books look good; some are leather bound and gilt stamped, and his attentions with the duster have given the leather a soft sheen.

He wanders back to his desk. He takes the empty crate out to the yard, where he pauses to make himself a cup of tea. Now, back in his chair, he sips it. He is on the point of fetching that book on hair-raising divorces when he hears the street door open and, after a brief pause, the sound of hesitant footsteps advancing along the hall. One of the shoes making the footsteps squeaks.

There is a timid and apologetic tap on the half-open door to the outer office. A man's face insinuates itself into the gap between door and door frame, and, after a clearing of the throat, a barely audible voice that sounds as if it comes from a mouth made bone-dry with nervous tension says, 'Is this the World's End Bureau?'

Felix gets to his feet. 'Indeed it is,' he replies, forbearing to add to this apparently terrified man that it says so on the discreet brass plaque beside the street door.

'Oh, thank heavens!' the little man breathes fervently, as if against all odds he has succeeded in finding the right place amid a plethora of equally likely but ominously threatening alternatives. 'May I come in?'

'Please do,' Felix says. Stepping forward, he places a chair on the other side of his desk and invites the man to sit down.

While his visitor settles himself rather fussily in the hard, upright chair, removing his gloves, carefully placing them inside the hat that he has already taken off and put on his lap, then smoothing a forefinger over his neatly trimmed moustache, Felix studies him. He is perhaps in his mid-forties, carefully dressed in a dark jacket and trousers that, although clearly not new, have been well cared for. His black boots shine like a guardsman's. He is considerably shorter than Felix but, as Felix is well over six foot, this doesn't make him significantly small. Why, then, Felix asks himself, did I instantly think of him as a *little* man? He has narrow shoulders and a pigeon chest, yes, but that's not it . . . He's apologetic, Felix realizes. He is like a supplicant who has no confidence that his request will be granted. He's nervous, uncertain, and—

At this moment the little man, finished with his self-ministrations, raises his head and meets Felix's eyes. His face is pallid beneath the carefully oiled and combed mid-brown hair, the nose small and straight, the mouth thin and narrow under the moustache. His eyes – a pale, nondescript brown – flicker here and there, reluctant to meet Felix's. Wondering if he's ever going to summon the courage to break the increasingly awkward silence and explain why he's come, Felix decides to help him. He picks up one of the smart little business cards he has persuaded Lily to acquire along with the printed writing paper. As he hands it across the desk, he pauses to have an admiring look at the words, in their elegant script in dark-blue ink on a pale blue background.

World's End Bureau
3, Hob's Court, Chelsea
private enquiry agency
Proprietor: L. G. Raynor

The little man takes it from him. He studies it for a long time; surely, far more than it could take even a novice reader to peruse those four brief lines. Then abruptly, as if he's taken a run at it and must speak before his courage fails, he bursts out, 'Mr Raynor, my name is Stibbins, Ernest Harold Stibbins, and I'm dreadfully afraid someone is threatening to kill my wife.'

Under the circumstances, it hardly seems the moment to correct his misapprehension concerning Felix's identity. It would, Felix reflects, be rather like quibbling over which bucket to use to fetch water when one's house was on fire.

'I think, Mr Stibbins,' he says instead, opening the rather smart black-backed notebook he has purchased especially for his new job and dipping his pen in the inkwell, 'you had better tell me some details.' He thinks rapidly, having little or no idea how to go about this extraordinary business. 'First,' he says with a confidence he is very far from feeling, 'your name, which you have just given me –' he writes it down – 'and that of your wife, and where you live.'

'My wife – well, of course she's my *second* wife, I lost my dear Enid seven years ago – my wife's name is Albertina, and her maiden name was Goodchild.' He goes on to dictate the address, in a south-of-the-river residential area that Felix only knows vaguely, watching intently as Felix writes it down as if checking for misspellings. When Felix has finished and looks up again, wondering what to ask next, Ernest Stibbins leans close and says confidingly, 'Albertina is a good few years my junior, Mr Raynor, but I like to believe that we have been very happy together since we were married two years ago.'

Felix is jotting down *1878 married Albertina*, but more to give himself some thinking time. In the absence of any other bright idea, he leans back and says, 'Why not tell me a little about yourself?'

Ernest Stibbins pauses, takes one or two rather shaky breaths and then says, 'I work as an accounts clerk at Pearson and Mitchell –' it is a large department store a couple of streets behind Oxford Street – 'and I have long been an active member of my Church –' Felix can hear the capital letter – 'which is St Cyprian's, where I have served for many years as church warden and also sing in the choir. The tenors,' he adds. Felix really hadn't envisaged him as a baritone. 'It was through St Cyprian's that I came to marry my first wife, which is why I mention it,' he goes on, leaning forward in his chair. 'My dear Enid, you see, having been left alone in the world and in possession of a modest inheritance, enquired of our then vicar whom to ask for help with investing it, and my name was suggested.' Ernest Stibbins modestly casts his eyes down. 'I like to think my advice was sound. I am a careful man, Mr Raynor, frugal in my habits, and I am not given to frivolity.' His sparse eyebrows draw down into a frown. 'Suffice it to say that, during the eight years of our life together, Enid's little inheritance grew very nicely.'

Felix, busily writing, is startled by what sounds like a suppressed sob. 'Enid drowned, Mr Raynor,' says Ernest Stibbins's muffled voice; when Felix looks up, he sees that his visitor is wiping his eyes and nose with a spotless, carefully ironed handkerchief. 'She fell from Chelsea Bridge and was swept away, and it was not until some time later that I was called upon to identify her poor, broken body.'

Felix murmurs vague words of commiseration, sincerely meant. He has some idea what a body looks like after days or weeks in the Thames.

'I was alone for five years,' Ernest Stibbins goes on, bravely having pulled himself together, 'five sorrowful years, during which time I believed that my chance of love, of happiness, had gone. But then Albertina came to our Church, her youth so fresh upon her, her innocence shining from those lovely blue eyes, an orphan, and quite friendless. She was born and brought up in St Albans, Mr Raynor, and, upon the deaths of her parents, came to London to act as companion to an elderly great-aunt. The lady died, quite unexpectedly, leaving poor Albertina alone in a vast city, desperate not to fall into vice but needing to earn her living. She came to St Cyprian's – and I thank the good Lord every day that she did – because her late father sang in the choir of St Albans Cathedral, and, having become acquainted with our vicar there when he was a young curate, she sought him out in her time of need.' He meets Felix's eyes, and the expression in his is candid. 'I believed her to be far too good for me, Mr Raynor; too young, too beautiful. I could not but treat her with kindness, for she had the vulnerability of a kitten. It was this, I believe, and, not to fool myself with romantic notions, also the security that I could offer, which persuaded Albertina that, despite the seventeen years between us, doing me the great honour of becoming my wife might not be so terrible.' He manages a smile. 'In short, I prayed every night for a fortnight, I gathered every ounce of my courage, I made myself go down on one knee with a modest little engagement ring in my hands and I asked her to marry me, and she said yes. We were married by our own dear vicar, the Reverend James Jellicote, which was most appropriate, he having been the instrument by which we were brought together, and thereafter we set up home in my little house. And there, Mr Raynor, we have been, in simple contentment that I might dare say verges upon happiness, ever since.' His face clouds. 'Until this present unpleasantness.'

And now, Felix thinks, we come to the point. His hand aching from writing so fast, he dips his pen in the inkwell again and prompts, 'Go on, Mr Stibbins.'

His visitor sits thinking for some time. Then he says nervously, 'You must understand, Mr Raynor, that I did not know Albertina all that well when she became my wife, for

we had not the advantage of knowing each other in our childhood and youth, as is the case with some couples, nor were
our families acquainted. So it was that some aspects of her
character came as something of a surprise.'

Wondering what on earth is coming, Felix waits.

'It became apparent, Mr Raynor,' Ernest Stibbins says,
lowering his voice portentously, 'that Albertina has psychic
abilities.'

Whatever Felix expects, it certainly isn't this. 'Psychic?' he
echoes.

Ernest Stibbins nods sagely. 'Yes. She speaks to the spirits.
Ah, I see you are surprised,' he observes. 'As was I, Mr Raynor,
as was I. I will not go into details –' Felix, rather hoping he
would do, is disappointed – 'but will only assure you that
there could be no doubt. When finally I nerved myself to ask
Albertina if she had ever acted as a medium, she instantly
replied, "Oh, for sure, I've been channelling the spirits since
I was a girl!", and, let me tell you, I was hard put to it not to
faint.'

'And then what happened?' Felix, agog, can't hold back
the eager question.

'We began to hold seances,' Ernest Stibbins says, with the
nonchalance of a man saying *We decided to go to Southend
for our holiday.* 'Albertina's gift is strong and true, and very
swiftly we – or I should strictly speaking say *she*, for work
forbids me attending the weekday sessions unless I am
permitted to take the early closing day half-holiday, and it is
after all Albertina who channels the spirits – she built up a
loyal and devoted following. All went well for some time, and
Albertina was able to give comfort to many who mourned the
loss of loved ones and ached to have a reassuring word from
Beyond to let them know all was well. But then something
happened.'

Once again, he pauses. Once again, Felix replenishes his
nib.

'Albertina began to perceive that a sense of threat was
emanating from her spirit guide,' Ernest says, his voice dropping to a whisper, 'and, having eliminated other possibilities,
she has had to conclude that the threat is to her.' Eyes wide

with horror meet Felix's. 'Now I love my Albertina very dearly, Mr Raynor, and to begin with I felt very strongly that it is a man's job to protect his wife and save her from harm.' He pauses, giving a deep sigh. 'But I am not the only one to have witnessed Albertina's fear – her *terror*, I should say – when these threats come through, and others in our Circle who also care about her persuaded me that I should go to the police.'

'And what happened?' Felix asks, although he believes he can guess.

Ernest Stibbins sadly shakes his head. 'One or two notes were taken by a somewhat uninterested sergeant behind the desk at the local police station – not the fulsome sort of notes that *you* have so diligently jotted down, Mr Raynor, oh, dear me, no! – and he said they would keep our case under review, whatever that may mean.' He pauses once more. 'Not being satisfied with that – as, indeed, none of us in our Circle are – I have made up my mind to seek help of a rather different sort, and hence my visit here to you.' He leans forward until his whole upper body seems to hang over Felix's desk. 'Do you think, Mr Raynor, that you can save my beloved Albertina?'

With rather more assurance than perhaps he should give, Felix says stoutly, 'I'm quite sure we can. We shall, in any case,' he adds swiftly, hearing the echo of his impetuous words, 'do our very best.'

The next few minutes pass swiftly by as Felix advises Ernest Stibbins of the World's End Bureau's charges, and Ernest, after blanching a little, agrees that he believes he can meet them. 'Anything to protect my dear wife!' he says somewhat tremulously.

Felix resists his visitor's plea to be told precisely how the investigation will proceed – not hard, since he has absolutely no idea – and presently he sees Ernest Stibbins to the door and watches as he trots anxiously away. Wondering quite what he has taken on and what his employer will say when he tells her, he returns thoughtfully and slightly anxiously to his desk.

THREE

L ily would normally have walked much of the way from World's End to the Brougham Club but today the very smart dark green kid footwear forbids it, for the shoes are nowhere near as comfortable as her workman's boots. She walks along the river to the underground station at Putney Bridge and travels via Earl's Court and South Kensington to St James's Park, where once more she takes to her feet and walks across Pall Mall and Piccadilly, coming out in Piccadilly Circus and turning north into Regent Street, where quite soon she comes upon her destination.

The Rose Tea Rooms and, above, the secretive windows of the Brougham Club exude money, class, exclusivity and, if a building could be said to have a nose down which to look upon the remainder of humanity not sufficiently privileged to gain admittance, then this one does. Lily straightens her shoulders, lifts her chin and strides up to the door, which is opened smoothly by almost invisible hands as she approaches.

'I have an appointment with Lord Berwick,' she says quietly to the uniformed, bewigged – bewigged! – man who is staring at her in vague disapproval. His expression, however, undergoes rather a radical change on hearing the name of the man she is here to see and he murmurs, 'I will enquire as to whether his lordship is ready to receive you. What name?'

'Raynor. Lily Raynor. Miss,' Lily says firmly.

The doorman gives her another odd look, then glides away. Very soon he is back, and is there a light flush to those pale, indoor cheeks? With an attempt at a smile that looks more like a grimace, he says, 'Follow me, Miss Raynor. Please,' he adds in a very obvious afterthought.

He leads the way across what would, were it bare of the clutches of little tables, be a vast expanse of deep rose-madder carpet to a booth on the far side of the room. Situated behind an arrangement of tall, luxuriant potted palms, in a booth hidden on its one open side by a screen, is a table laid for a rather lavish tea. Seated at the table, on his feet even as Lily is shown into the booth, is the man she has come here to see. The doorman bows deeply, murmurs, 'Miss Lily Raynor, my lord,' and, still bowing, backs away.

Lord Berwick steps forward with a smile, holds out a hand – Lily takes it in her kid-gloved one and shakes it – and says in a soft, beautiful voice, 'Miss Raynor, thank you so much for coming. Please, sit down, and I hope you will take tea? Indian or China, I have ordered both.'

Lily sits down, takes off her gloves, sets them down beside her on the soft, velvet-covered banquette and says, 'China, please. No milk, no sugar.'

Is this her first faux pas? Is it not done to take milk or sugar in China tea and ought she to have known? If so, her host gives no sign; indeed, he says, 'Just the way I like it myself,' and gives her another smile.

While he is busy with teapot, strainer and cups – how quaint, she thinks, that he should do this himself rather than summoning a waiter – she studies him. His name is Selwyn Willoughby, and that is what he was known as before he inherited the title from his late father; it is the name by which he became renowned as a decent, hardworking landowner, man of affairs, occasional diplomat and close friend of certain members of the royal family; in particular, of the plump, bearded, middle-aged man who, when Queen Victoria's long reign finally ends, will be king. Selwyn Willoughby is not, however, a member of the Prince of Wales's more salacious circle; quite the contrary, for he is a highly moral, upstanding pillar-of-the-Church sort of man, and not one dark hiss of gossip has ever attached itself to him.

His manners, Lily has noticed, are exquisite, and already she is feeling a great deal more comfortable. He is tall, spare, beautifully dressed; his thick hair is grey, his face is lean and falls readily into lines of sadness. His eyes are dark blue, and presently deeply shadowed underneath with the sort of greyish, purplish semicircles that suggest a chronic lack of sleep.

She sips her tea. It is delicious, and the frail bone-china cup is a work of art. He offers her sandwiches – tiny little triangles set out on the plate in a pattern like a piece of marquetry – and she takes two. She fears, however, that her mouth will prove too dry to eat without the risk of coughing or, worse, choking, and takes only a minuscule bite. They exchange some rather banal remarks about the weather, and then he leans forward and says in a very quiet voice that she strains to hear, 'Miss Raynor, I have asked you here because I am desperately worried about my son and I am very much hoping that you may be able to help.'

Even as he is speaking, she feels herself relax. He needs her services; this is why she is here, she reminds herself. She resolves to do her very best for him.

She pats her mouth with the delicate, lace-edged linen napkin and says, 'Tell me what has happened, Lord Berwick, and I will judge whether assistance is within my power.'

He nods briefly. He refills their cups, then he says, 'I have but the one son, and his name is Julian. Indeed, he is my only child, for my wife is . . . fragile.' The one small word, added to his expression, tells her a great deal. 'Julian is greatly beloved by his mother,' he continues, 'who, I am forced to admit, has over-indulged him. He failed to achieve very much at Harrow and in his first year at Oxford, and it was only with difficulty that I managed to prevent his being rusticated. His mother tells him repeatedly that education is not important, and that he is only young for a few years and should make the very most of it. In addition, she has, I'm afraid, been bailing him out whenever his creditors grow impatient.'

He pauses and sips his tea. She can sense even from across the table how very distressed he is; how agonizing it is to be sharing these shameful family secrets. How desperate he must be that he has been forced to take her into his confidence.

She wishes she could say something to help alleviate his pain, but she knows better than to say a word. She sits, quiet and still, and in time, he is able to continue.

'Now Julian has fallen in love with an actress,' he says baldly. 'Her name, or perhaps it is her professional name, is Violetta da Rosa, and I'm told she is part-Italian and has appeared on the stage in Paris, Rome and elsewhere on the Continent. I do not wish to insult or disparage the lady, but nevertheless I am forced to confess that I mistrust her and have very grave doubts about the sincerity of her feelings for my son. He is in many ways an innocent, Miss Raynor; like many young men of his class, he has had very little experience of the world, although, again like many if not all young men, he believes he knows all there is to know.' He pauses. 'The young lady in question – well, she is not in fact all that young – is, on the face of it, dazzling and fascinating, and she has undoubtedly turned my son's head. I have reason to believe that they have – that they –' to her distress, the pale cheeks blush – 'that he has taken her as his mistress, although he has not yet set her up in her own accommodation.'

They've been signing into the sort of hotels that don't ask too many questions, Lily thinks. It is, she has to agree, a little sordid. How much more so must it seem to this utterly correct and dignified man sitting before her?

'Now you have been recommended to me by my good friend Lord Dunorlan.' His voice has dropped to a whisper. 'He tells me that you acted with efficiency and discretion, and that I would not be likely to find anybody better.'

She bowed her head. 'I am gratified to have been of service to his lordship,' she murmurs.

'What I would like you to do, if you feel it is possible,' Lord Berwick goes on, 'is to perform a very thorough investigation into the lady's background; in particular, whether she has had liaisons before, whether, indeed, she entertains other men even whilst involved with my son, and what she does when she is not with him.' His eyes meet Lily's. His expression is beseeching, full of distress. 'Is this, do you think, the sort of thing that your Bureau could undertake?'

'It is precisely the sort of thing,' she says.

'Then will you agree to take the case?'

'I will.'

He seems to slump a little with relief. As if in celebration, he pushes the tall, many-tiered cake stand her way and now, at last, she thinks she might be able to do the contents justice. When they have each had three little cakes and another cup of tea, Lily takes a very small notebook out of her bag and, writing under cover of the table so that even the long-sighted would not be able to see, she jots down, to Lord Berwick's dictation, the name of the actress (he spells it out), the theatre where she has recently been performing (although he believes that the run is now over and he's not sure what she is doing now), her known haunts and the places to which his son habitually escorts her. She asks one or two questions about Julian Willoughby, to which his father eagerly replies; it touches her that he appears to think that the more he helps her with information, the greater the likelihood of her being able to achieve the result he so badly needs. Which is, of course, the total discrediting of the not-so-young actress and her rapid descent from the pedestal upon which her adoring and besotted young suitor has placed her.

Lily doesn't even let herself think that all the discrediting in the world won't help while young Julian's infatuation remains at its height; while his hot young blood pumps round his body and his lust is focused on only the one woman.

When the Bureau's terms have been discreetly discussed and agreed, there is no more to be said. Lily thanks her host for the delightful tea, draws on her gloves, picks up her bag and, murmuring that she will contact him as soon as there is anything to report, takes her leave.

Making her way home, Lily is wondering whether it might be an idea to entrust this task to her new office assistant. In the weeks he has worked for her, she has begun to see that Felix is far, far more than someone to write letters and do the filing (but she certainly shouldn't have let him anywhere near the plants). It is, after all, a relatively straightforward task, and a handsome man is surely much more likely to persuade an opportunist actress beyond the first flush of youth to open up and tell the truth than someone like herself. Besides, Felix is pawing the ground for something more challenging than the tasks for which she engaged him.

I shall entrust the job to him, she decides. She gives a curt nod, as if to endorse the decision. It will be a test, and I shall judge carefully how he gets on.

She smiles to herself as she heads down into the underground station. She finds she is quite looking forward to telling him the good news.

She can tell as soon as she enters the outer office that something has happened, for there is a sense of suppressed excitement about her new assistant and he is clearly finding it difficult to stop smiling. She nods to him, suggests he makes them a cup of tea and, while he does so, goes into her own office to remove her hat and gloves and take her notebook out of her bag. When he returns with the tea tray she summons him into her office and pulls up a chair.

'Well?' she says, regarding him over her teacup.

He feigns innocence. 'Well what?'

She goes on watching him. 'If I had to guess,' she says, 'I would say someone came to the office, confided some small tale of woe to you, you asked a few questions and then, when this someone asked if the Bureau could help, you said yes and proffered our rates. If I am correct and you have indeed found us a new client, then I congratulate you.'

The rapidly changing expressions that cross his face are highly entertaining, and she is quite hard put to it not to smile. After a moment he puts his cup down and clears his throat.

'You are indeed correct, in all but one detail.' His clear hazel eyes fix on hers. 'If I were to place this small tale of woe, as you call it, somewhere on a scale between lost dogs and illicit love affairs, I would put it very close to, if not at, the top.'

She raises her eyebrows. 'Go on.'

'A man called Stibbins has a young and beautiful wife who he discovered, after a short time of being married to her, is a gifted medium. Seances are now regularly held at their house in the suburbs south of the river, and all went well until the wife, whose name is Albertina, began to be informed by her guides that someone intends to harm her. Mr Stibbins, stoutly uxorial man that he is, wanted to protect his wife himself, but was persuaded by all the seance regulars that the threat was too dangerous and hence he went first to the police, who didn't appear to offer much in the way of protection, and then here to us – er, to the Bureau.'

He corrects himself swiftly, but she rather likes the fact that he said *us*.

'And you said we would investigate?'

'I did,' he agrees. 'I told him what we charge and he swallowed a couple of times but said that would be all right. He asked how we'd go about it and I said I couldn't tell him that. Well, I couldn't have done,' he adds disarmingly, 'since I have absolutely no idea.'

'Well, one thing you should have done is to have asked for a deposit in respect of the engagement of our services, there and then,' she says, 'but that is easily put right by a letter in the post to him tonight.'

He nods an acknowledgement.

She waits, for she is quite sure there is more. 'And?' she prompts when he doesn't speak.

'I gave him one of the business cards and he assumed I was L. G. Raynor and I didn't correct him,' he blurts out. 'I'm sorry, Miss Raynor, I know I ought to have told him, but he was in the middle of spilling his story to me and I didn't want to distract him.'

She nods. She is thinking. After a few moments she says, 'You ought to have told him, yes, but I can appreciate why you didn't.' He looks absurdly grateful. 'And in fact,' she goes on slowly, 'I think it may have been to our advantage that you left the misapprehension uncorrected.' She thinks some more. 'I believe I should be the one to investigate these threats from the spirit world,' she says eventually. His face falls. Wait, she thinks. Just be patient. 'Mr Stibbins doesn't know me, and has no idea of my connection with the World's End Bureau. I think I should discover when the seances are held and present myself at the next one.'

Felix is frowning, but it soon becomes clear that it's not because she has taken over the case. 'I think that you turning up out of the blue the very next time they sit in Circle – that's how they refer to it – would look suspicious. Well, suspicious is the wrong word – I mean that Ernest Stibbins might well guess you've come from the Bureau. Instead, why not observe the comings and goings and select one of the Circle, follow her, get into conversation with her, let it be known you've suffered a recent loss, and let her be the one to suggest you go along to the next seance? That way, you'll be introduced by someone they already know, and the likelihood of Ernest guessing your real reason for being there will be lessened.'

He is right, and he has reasoned well. But, 'Why is it preferable for Mr Stibbins not to know who I am?' she asks.

He frowns in thought. 'Because you need to see them in Circle precisely the way they usually are,' he says. 'If he or anybody else knows there's a private investigator present, it'll be different.' He shakes his head in impatience. 'I can't really explain any better than that, although I do feel strongly that you ought not to reveal who you really are.'

She nods. 'I agree. I will do precisely as you say. When does the Circle meet again?'

He consults a black-backed notebook. 'They almost always sit on Sundays, sometimes on Tuesdays and Thursdays, although Ernest really prefers to be there to support Albertina and it's rare for him to have a half-day holiday. He works at Pearson and Mitchells, off Oxford Street, in the accounts department,' he adds. 'The Sunday session, I imagine, is for the benefit of this who work all the rest of the week. So, the next meeting will be this coming Sunday, I presume.'

'Good. And while I embark on investigating these threats to Albertina Stibbins, there is something I want you to do.' Even when the delighted astonishment is still spreading across his face, she tells him the tale of Julian Willoughby and his actress, and reveals what he is to do about it.

Quite soon, she notices, he has turned to a fresh page in his notebook and is writing rapidly. He asks her several questions, all of them pertinent, one or two of which she cannot in fact answer as she omitted to ask them of Lord Berwick. When she has finished, he sits unspeaking for some time. He is very still, and, uncharacteristically, his mobile face is quite expressionless. This interests her, as she had been starting to wonder how someone whose least emotion seems to be instantly visible in his face could ever hope to succeed as a private investigator. She need wonder no more, for it has suddenly become clear that he has another mode; that, in short, there may well be considerably more to Felix Wilbraham than meets the eye.

Finally he comes out of his reverie. Looking at her, he remarks, 'It's Saturday tomorrow.'

'It is,' she agrees.

'The end of the working week,' he adds softly, 'although probably not if you're an actress . . .'

She waits.

Suddenly he stands up, a swift, quite violent movement as if he can no longer bear to sit still. 'I'm going to do some groundwork tonight,' he says. 'Your Lord Berwick was able to tell you where Violetta da Rosa was last engaged, but he didn't know, apparently, what she's doing now. She'll have an agent, professional actresses always do, and I'm going to begin by finding out who it is.'

Lily looks up at him. 'I didn't necessarily expect you to start immediately,' she says mildly.

He stares at her. 'Didn't you?'

Then, with a grin and a gesture that is almost a salute, he picks up his notebook, calls over his shoulder, 'See you tomorrow,' and is gone.

Lily finishes her tea, then takes the cups through to the scullery, washes and dries them and sets them back on the shelf. Mrs Clapper won't be back until Monday – not that Lily is in the habit of leaving her dirty crocks for anyone else to see to – and it will be up to her to keep the kitchen and the scullery neat and tidy over the next two days. Which will probably mean another argument with the Little Ballerina about the importance of cleaning up after oneself and not expecting one's landlady's hired help to do it for one . . .

Oh, dear.

If Lily could make just one wish and have it fulfilled, it would be to have the necessity of having a lodger removed from her. But it is a wish that cannot yet come true, for running a house as large as 3, Hob's Court is not cheap and she now has the additional cost of employing Felix.

'Who has just demonstrated very plainly,' she says aloud, 'that he is probably worth far more than I am paying him, and

who may very well prove to be the making of the World's
End Bureau.'

On that optimistic thought, she goes upstairs to change out
of her best costume and then returns to the kitchen to set
out a supper tray. Then, passing the hour or so until it is time
to eat, she goes back to her desk, locates the large-scale map
of London and finds the street where Ernest and Albertina
Stibbins live. It is actually quite close, and she can reach it
easily by crossing Battersea Bridge, turning east and going
through Battersea Park, emerging on its south side and diving
down into the maze of streets on the other side of Prince of
Wales Road.

Emulating Felix, she opens her notebook at a new page and
writes down everything he has just told her about the Stibbins
case. The efficient and retentive memory that she developed
during her nursing training flexes its muscles and hastens to
her aid, names, facts and figures flowing from her pen and
onto the clean white paper. After some time, she sits back
and looks at what she has written.

*Ernest Harold Stibbins married first wife Enid (née
Clough) in 1865 when he was 27. She brought a small
inheritance to the marriage, and it was this that caused
the vicar to introduce her to her future husband, it being
his credentials as an accounts clerk (and probably also
a man of modest and frugal habits) that persuaded the
clergyman he was the man for the job of giving considered
and impartial advice.*

Here Lily makes a note to herself that she might consider
trying to discover where the inheritance came from.

*Eight years later, in 1873, Enid Stibbins drowned,
apparently having fallen from Chelsea Bridge. Her body
is not recovered for some time, and her poor husband is
summoned to identify her.*

Lily writes a second note, comprising the details of the river
police, whom she understands to be responsible for bodies

pulled out of the Thames; she believes their headquarters are at Wapping.

Ernest spends several lonely years as a widower before meeting and marrying his second wife, Albertina Goodchild. Considerably younger than he, it is his opinion that she consents to be his wife because he is kind and offers security; he believes, however, that love has since grown. Ernest discovers that she has psychic powers, and—

Lily suddenly sits up straight. It has occurred to her just what a shock it must have been for the correct, upright, frugal-living, excitement-avoiding Ernest to find out just what manner of a young woman he had taken to his bosom and installed, in his carefully neat and tidy little house, as his new wife. Of all things, for a self-confessed stalwart of the local church – churchwarden and long-serving tenor in the choir to boot, she reminds herself – to have married, in all innocence, a gifted medium! What did the fellow members of his congregation think? What about the vicar, the Reverend James Jellicote?

She makes a note: *Speak to vicar.* Then she realizes that this is a job for Felix, for when she presents herself at the seance, she does not want someone piping up, 'Ooh, you're the young woman who was asking the vicar all those questions about Ernest and Albertina!' London may be vast and home to an ever-increasing population but Lily knows full well that most human beings prefer to live in small, tight communities, and that these are formed even – perhaps especially – within the huge impersonality of a city.

She sits perfectly still for a while. Then she realizes that perhaps there is an important fact neither she nor Felix has yet considered, for she doubts very much that Albertina's services as a medium are provided for nothing.

Or, rather, she corrects herself, while it is very unlikely that innocent, unworldly Albertina would expect to be paid for the practising of her gift, what is not so likely is that Ernest would see it that way. If ever called upon by his young wife to justify asking the members of Circle to contribute their thruppence a session, or whatever it is, he would probably say, 'But, my dear, they sit in our house, they take advantage of our fire in the colder months, they drink the tea we offer afterwards and nibble at the biscuits we set out for them. Is it not therefore reasonable to ask a modest sum in recompense? Such is the comfort and the joy that your generous sharing of your gift provides, dear Albertina, that I am perfectly sure none of those who attend would wish us to be out of pocket.'

Although Lily has not yet encountered Ernest Stibbins, she can almost hear him saying the words.

She discovers that she is looking forward very much to meeting Mr and Mrs Stibbins.

She fetches her supper on its tray, lights another lamp, for time has gone by and the darkness is advancing, and, while she takes a first bite, she begins to work on the identity she will assume when she goes to the seance. She cannot, of course, present herself as Lily Raynor or even L. G. Raynor, since, for better or worse, that is the name that Ernest Stibbins associates with Felix.

'I shall be Miss Maud Garrett,' she announces to the empty office, 'gently reared but forced through circumstances to make her own living. A father in the army who died in India, a mother remarried to a man by whom she has several children, so that there is no money to support a grown-up daughter,' she goes on, her imagination fired by this absorbing task of creating an alternative identity, 'and last year cheered enormously by meeting a suitable young man who, after a few months, proposed marriage.'

She writes swiftly, the poached egg on toast forgotten and rapidly cooling.

'My fiancé was called Cecil Sanderson –' she has no idea where the name has sprung from but it will do as well as any – 'and, sadly, it soon transpired that he was not robust. He became pale and ill at the start of the year, with a persistent cough, and all too soon he began to spit blood.'

Oh, poor Cecil Sanderson, she thinks, still writing, to be brought into existence, even if only in somebody's mind, and to be dismissed from it again so soon!

'Despite careful nursing and exorbitant doctor's bills,' she goes on, 'Cecil died a month ago.' She makes a note in the margin to the effect that she must wear mourning when she attends the seance. 'I am finding it very hard to go on without him, and there are one or two particular questions to which I would very much like answers.'

She sucks at the end of her pen, wondering what these questions should be. But slowly, as she sits there deep in the spaces of her own mind, something else arises, pushing aside her preoccupation with the forthcoming seance and the questions she will ask. And it is this: that if by some mystic mechanism she really could turn into Maud Garrett, then the events in her past that still haunt her and give her nightmares would no longer exist . . .

When Lily's father Andrew Owen Raynor died, her mother remarried with unbelievable, hurtful haste and Lily went to live with her paternal grandparents and her spinster aunt Eliza in the rooms above Raynor's Apothecary, later renamed Raynor's Pharmacy. Once she was over the first profound grief, Lily came back to herself from whatever dark, lonely and sad place she had been inhabiting and discovered that her new life suited her rather well.

For a start, she loved the apothecary's shop and everything about it: the smell, the fastidious neatness, cleanliness and order (Lily's mother had never been a good organizer and dismissed routine and order as 'boring'); the perpetual parade of customers and their intriguing requests (although quite often she would be kindly but firmly ushered out of the shop and into the family's private quarters when someone had something of an intimate nature to discuss); the sense that, even at twelve years old, she was a useful and valued member of the family business.

Most of all it was the quiet, habitually undemonstrative love of her grandparents and her aunt that made her smile again. She understood, devastated, grief-stricken child that she was, that her grandparents mourned their son, and her aunt her brother, just as profoundly as Lily mourned her father. Grief, she learned, had many faces and all of them hurt.

Abraham and Martha Raynor were thoughtful, cerebral people, and their daughter Eliza was highly intelligent. It did not even occur to them that Lily would not want to learn everything they could teach her, and fortunately they were quite right because she did.

Aunt Eliza had begun giving her niece lessons even before the death of Andrew Owen Raynor, every morning except Sunday, upstairs in Eliza's book-lined room above the apothecary that always felt much more like a study than a bedroom. To begin with, Eliza had been confident that she could teach her as well as anybody but when Lily was nine, Eliza decided that the child's clear interest in and facility with the sciences deserved a more knowledgeable instructor, and arranged for Lily to have two lessons a week with Eliza's schoolteacher friend, Susan Heale, in biology, chemistry, physics and mathematics.

Back then, when Andrew Owen Raynor was still alive and Lily lived at home with her parents, it was with her mother that she spent most of her time, her father being so often away working. And her flighty, vain, childish, empty-headed, very beautiful but dim mother didn't think girls needed to be educated, but was quite happy for others to take on the responsibility.

Then, in September 1862, after Andrew's death and Lily's move to live with her grandparents and her aunt and just before her thirteenth birthday, Lily became a full-time pupil at Miss Heale's Collegiate School, across the river in Battersea. There she remained for the next five years, leaving in the summer of 1867 and spending the next few months working alongside her grandparents in the pharmacy.

She knew now what she wanted to do, and to her great relief Abraham, Martha and Eliza backed her up. Lily wanted to be a nurse, and on the eve of her twentieth birthday she embarked on five years' training. She developed a particular interest in midwifery, and her hard work in the training hospital earned her a much sought-after place with St Walburga's Nursing Service, an organization of nursing nuns who specialized in midwifery and battlefield medicine. The SWNS – or Swans, as they were affectionately known – were attached to the British army, and, since soldiers very often took their families with them when posted overseas, the two particular skills of the nursing nuns were vital.

Lily worked as hard as she knew how, sometimes exhausting herself to the point of collapse, when the nuns would pack her off back to the rooms above the pharmacy for some of her grandparents' and her aunt's loving care. But the effort was worth it in the end, for Lily graduated with excellent marks and the SWNS offered her a post nursing with the army in India.

During her the years of service in India with the SWNS – looking after pregnant, labouring and nursing mothers and at regular intervals being deployed to strange places with outlandish names to nurse soldiers with horrific wounds and terrifying illnesses – Lily's life was hard but it was also every-thing she had ever wanted. Even the news that her beloved grandparents were dead, dying within three months of each other, did not cast her down for long.

But then something terrible happened.

Lily shut it out, for it was too awful to think about, and referred to it in her mind simply as The Incident.

It had shocked her to her core. She had gone to the defence of the defenceless, believing others would agree with her, fight with her, side with her in the righting of a grievous wrong. But she had gravely misjudged, and those she had trusted to support her and help her had let her down.

She abandoned India, abandoned nursing, and took the first available boat back to England. But it was to find that every-thing was different: she was devastated to find on returning to Raynor's Pharmacy that her beloved Aunt Eliza had succumbed to fever only the previous month. The letter informing Lily of the sad news had arrived in India some time after she had left.

She didn't know what to do. She had to earn her living, but the one thing she knew – nursing – she had quit for ever.

And so the World's End Bureau came into being . . .

Lily comes out of her long reverie. She sighs, stands up and clears away the remains of her abandoned supper. She knows she should return to work on Maud Garrett, but just now she has little heart for it. I shall go to bed, she thinks, and trust that sleep will restore me to myself.

For she *was* herself, will go on being so and has no choice. No matter how alluring it might seem to take on the persona and the history of somebody else, it cannot be done. Or rather, she amends, *she* cannot do it, for if she abandons Lily Raynor it means she must obliterate all the good things along with the bad. Her father. Her good, hard-working grandparents, Abraham and Martha. Aunt Eliza. And how would they react to that, those kind, loving people? How deep would be their hurt if she denied them?

No. Despite everything, despite The Incident, she is Lily Raynor, and so she will remain.

And, eventually, that firm, confident resolve is sufficient to send her to sleep.

FOUR

F elix hears Lily's voice in his head as he walks swiftly
away from Hob's Court towards the King's Road and
transport towards theatre land. *I didn't necessarily expect
you to start immediately*, she just said. Well, he thinks now,
full of the fire of the chase, his legs reacting to the adrenalin
and forcing the pace, that's just what I'm going to do.

He knows his way in the world of actors, the stage, agents,
reviews, trade publications. Solange, bless her, had believed
she was an *artiste manquée*, and after a bottle of champagne
or so she would begin describing outlandish and usually very
risqué incidents in her colourful past on the stage. Felix had
always been pretty sure this past existed solely in Solange's
lively imagination, but she was so entertaining, so funny, that
he never said so. Besides, Solange had the endearing gift of
being able to laugh at herself, and he had sometimes thought
that she knew full well he didn't believe her and it didn't
bother her a jot.

There are two avenues open to him, he thinks as he sits
on the tram heading east. First, he could purchase one of the
theatrical papers and browse through the pages until Violetta
da Rosa's name leaps out. There is the *Era*, commonly known
as the Actor's Bible, but it costs sixpence and, despite now
being in employment, still Felix is being careful with his
pennies. There is also the *Stage Directory*, a new paper which
is rapidly gaining popularity in the theatrical world, but even
that costs thruppence. He can do as he has so often done on
the past, and go to a news stand, pick up the relevant paper
and pretend to be checking that it's the one he wants before
purchasing it, but news vendors are wise to that old trick and
Felix isn't in the mood for verbal abuse.

The second option is to go to the theatre where Violetta
was engaged and simply ask someone for the information he
wants. Julian's father told Lily the location, and Felix knows

it: the Aphrodite Theatre is a pretty little place in a narrow street off the Strand, and there, once, long ago, he seduced a beautiful married woman who very much wanted to be seduced, so much so that it had been she who purchased the tickets for the private box. Until a week ago, Violetta da Rosa has been appearing there in an extremely popular melodrama entitled *Her Father's Beloved.*

The main doors of the Aphrodite are very firmly closed, so Felix makes his way round the back. As he walks along the mean little piss-smelling alley to the workmen's entrance, he hears sounds from within: as he hoped, the stage hands are working on the set for the next production. He opens a battered door and walks soft-footed along a dark, dusty passage that smells of sweat. In a little booth to the right sits a man reading a newspaper. After one or two suspicious glances, this man accepts Felix for what Felix says he is – a devoted fan of Violetta da Rosa who arrived in town too late for the actress's last appearance in *Her Father's Beloved* and is determined to see her in her next production – and provides the information that Felix is after.

As he leaves the theatre a short time later, Felix hurries back to the Strand and then takes out his notebook to record his findings. Violetta's agent has his offices in the New Inn Chambers, Wych Street, but Felix doesn't think he'll need to be bothering the man, whose name is Maurice Isaacs, since the chap at the Aphrodite told him that Violetta da Rosa has landed herself a new role in a Drury Lane theatre, where she will now be busily rehearsing.

'If you'll take my advice,' he added, 'you'll get hold of your ticket straight away, since she's so popular that the show'll soon be sold out for the foreseeable future and you may well already be too late.' He gave a self-satisfied smirk at this, as if Violetta's popularity is somehow directly attributable to the Aphrodite Theatre.

'Oh, I hope not! I'll do as you suggest, and thank you for the good advice,' Felix said sycophantically.

But now, as he hurries along to Drury Lane, he is not in the least perturbed by this latter information, having little wish to watch the lady on stage. He does very much want to see her, but not in her working mode. He finds the Glass Slipper Theatre and unobtrusively merges with the crowd of young – and not-so-young – men, and quite a few women, who are waiting at the stage door in the hope of seeing their beloved Violetta da Rosa as, once rehearsals are finished for the day, she makes her regal way out.

'Did you see *Her Father's Beloved*?' he asks the sandy-haired and bespectacled man standing next to him. The man is forty or so, his suit is shabby, he has dandruff and he smells of fish.

'Of course I did!' he replies indignantly.

'Lucky you,' Felix says, adopting a suitably resentful expression. 'I couldn't get a bloody ticket.'

The sandy-haired man looks smug. 'Yes, I heard it was booked solid.'

'What was she like?' Felix asks wistfully.

'She was wonderful!' breathes the sandy-haired man, his eyes misting. 'She had us all in tears when she leaned over the bed of her dying father, and as for that solo speech she did at the end, my goodness, I don't know how she could do that, night after night!'

'What about this new one?' Felix asks. 'What's it called?'

But this, he instantly realizes, is a mistake, for a true fan would know. The sandy-haired man is eyeing him suspiciously, as if about to demand that he shows his credentials as a true and devoted follower.

'I've only just arrived in town,' Felix says apologetically. 'I haven't caught up with the news.'

Accepting this with a disapproving sniff, the sandy-haired man relents. 'It's called *Miss Sanderson's Fortune*, and she plays a young woman who doesn't realize she's the heiress to a huge fortune, and she spends her life caring for the poor and doing good works, and—'

Felix shuts out the eager voice – the man is all but salivating – for he has no interest in the plot or the details of the lead actress's role. One thing, however, has caught his attention: Violetta, apparently, is still playing the ingenue role.

'She's looking as good as ever, they say,' Felix remarks when the sandy-haired man has at last finished. 'Perhaps a little more mature and stately in *Her Father's Favourite*, I believe I read, but I dare say that was demanded by the role?'

'She's not mature or stately!' the sandy-haired man protests forcefully, a belligerent expression contorting his bland features. For a moment, Felix wonders if he's winding up to punch him. 'She's as fresh and beautiful as she ever was!' But then, with quite a hard and undoubtedly deliberate dig in Felix's ribs, he adds, 'Look sharp, now! She's on her way!'

Glancing round, Felix sees that the crowd has grown. There is a sense of expectation, swiftly escalating. Those present seem to have the theatre's timings in their blood and be aware that rehearsals must now have finished. They are quite right, for, even as Felix is being squeezed by a general push forwards, the stage door opens and the woman they are longing to see stands there at the top of the short flight of steps, bathed in the light from within.

Violetta da Rosa most certainly is not as fresh and beautiful as she ever was, Felix thinks. And he should know, for he saw her on stage thirteen years ago when he was fourteen and, staying with his school friend Humphrey Copland in Hampstead, had sneaked out of Humphrey's parents' home to go to the theatre and see the famous young actress in a salacious little play concerning illicit love affairs and a nun who had to dispose of a baby. Violetta, tightly laced into a very revealing costume, had been every adolescent boy's dream, and the crudely coloured postcards bearing her image that Felix and Humphrey had managed to acquire in the theatre foyer had been sold at many times their face value once the boys were back at Marlborough.

Felix, who has now wormed his way to the front and is taller than most of the crowd, is near enough to see the actress in unforgiving detail. There are lines around her tired eyes, her teeth do not sparkle as once they did, her fine jawline is sagging a little and she is probably a stone or two heavier than when she played the part of the dewy-eyed innocent in the play about the nun and the baby. How old is she? Felix wonders. Thirty-five? Forty? At least, he answers himself.

But still she has the indefinable quality that makes a woman attractive, appealing and adored, despite the passage of time. She is beautifully dressed – mauve gown trimmed with purple that hugs closely and shows off her splendid figure, fur-collared evening cloak, well-fitting gloves in fine calfskin – and her glossy brown hair under the bejewelled headdress with its flirty little veil is dressed to perfection. Her smile is warm and she manages to look modestly surprised by the size of the crowd awaiting her and their obvious devotion.

Felix watches, a smile on his face, as Violetta da Rosa responds like the artist she is to the adulation of the crowd. She is waving, accepting a single rose from one hand, a small (and rather crushed) posy from another. People cry out their appreciation, their admiration, their love, and she responds with a becoming little blush. From his vantage point, Felix observes a tall, swarthy, thick-set man on the far side of the steps draw close, and is near enough to hear him say to her, 'No rehearsal tomorrow, so you coming to the Tom?'

She nods, flashing him a very quick glance. Then she hisses out of the corner of her mouth, 'Don't call for me, because I'll need to shake off Little Jack Horner first. I don't want him seeing you, it always makes him suspicious and querulous and likely to weep. I'll see you there.'

The dark man, grinning, melts away.

Someone is shouting over on the far side of the crowd. A hackney carriage is drawn up beside the pavement, a young man leaning out of the open door. 'Make way, make way!' he cries. Then, since his shrill voice is having absolutely no impact, he jumps down and tries to force a path between the surge of packed humanity. He has a bouquet of mixed roses, lilies and carnations in one hand, so enormous that it is larger than all the other floral offerings put together. The bright orange-gold of the pollen on the lilies' stamens has made a series of marks on his dark lapel. Felix knows from experience that they will be the devil to get out.

He watches, feeling suddenly sad. The man – he's not really a man but a boy in grown-up's clothing – has very fair curly hair, worn daringly long, and a pink and white complexion, at present darkened by a flush of embarrassment or perhaps anger. Everything he wears shouts wealth and privilege, yet not one person present, including, it seems, the actress he has come to meet, has an iota of respect for him.

'Violetta! *Violetta!*' he shouts, and as the tension and the anxiety escalate, his voice breaks into the soprano range. One or two of the men begin to chuckle, and someone says something about it being past his bedtime.

At last Violetta da Rosa takes pity on him. In a first-class impression of only just having noticed him – she is an actress, after all – she shouts, 'Julian! Wait there, I'll make my way to you!'

With queenly grace she looks down on the assembled mass and, as if a queen had indeed spoken, they part for her and she strolls with an elegant, upright carriage towards the young man with the embarrassingly huge bunch of flowers. Now scarlet to the roots of his soft, wavy hair, he shoves them at her. 'I bought these for you,' he manages.

Her dark, carefully drawn eyebrows, as symmetrical as a pair of circumflexes, go up in a parody of amazement. 'Oh, but how sweet! For *me*?'

'No, they're for the cabbie's 'orse!' calls a wag in the crowd, to a gale of laughter.

But Violetta da Rosa knows how to deal with barracking. Thanking Julian prettily – good grief, thinks Felix, she's even managed to conjure up a girlish blush – she precedes him up into the cab, he hurriedly follows, tripping as he does so and all but falling, and then he too is inside and the cabbie is whipping up his horse.

Thoughtfully, Felix sets off for his lodgings. There is little point in trying to follow the cab, for without doubt Violetta and her youthful suitor are bound for some private love-nest where heavily built men with scarred faces and bent noses guard the door.

Felix believes he understands what she's up to. He knows quite a lot about women of Violetta da Rosa's type, although the example of the breed with whom he lived in close proximity for several very enjoyable years was far too honest to play such games.

As he walks home – walking costs nothing, and he tells himself that all this exercise keeps him trim – he is already composing in his mind what he will write in his report for his employer.

'And so I'll go along to the Tom tonight and see what she gets up to,' he says in conclusion to Lily Raynor the following morning, having handed over the report and then made it largely redundant by telling her most of what's in it.

'The Tom?'

'Sorry, there's no reason why you'd know. The Peeping Tom?' Still she looks blank. 'It's a music hall, or so it calls itself, in the Old Kent Road.'

'You know it?' He hears amusement in her voice but she keeps a straight face.

'Yes.' It is not the time to enlighten her about his experiences in the more rackety side of London life. 'It's not exactly high-class, which is why I find it quite interesting that Violetta da Rosa is going there. Moreover that she, presumably in the company of the dark man, is such an habitué of the place that he can call it by its colloquial name and she knows what he means.'

'Indeed,' Lily murmurs. Then: 'Well done. You seem to have made progress towards finding out about this relationship that so worries the young man's father, and so quickly.'

Felix hesitates. Then he thinks, why not tell her what's on my mind? He says, 'I believe I know everything there is to know already, if you'll forgive what sounds like an arrogant boast.'

'Go on,' she says.

'She's amusing herself with him – with young Julian – and, once she's tired of the gifts and the luxuries, she'll throw him over.'

'Yes,' she says. Just that: yes.

All at once, and much to his surprise, he's tempted to tell her about Solange Devaux-Moncontour, about the fun they had, about how they were never anything but honest with each other, about how they understood each other so well, about how they were able to part, with not one single regret on either side, when the time was right. None of which, he knows in his bones, applies to this liaison between the hard-nosed fading actress and the gullible, painfully naive boy . . .

But before he can begin, he realizes Lily is speaking to him. He comes out of his reverie. 'Sorry, what did you say?'

'I was asking you to go and have a few words with the Reverend Mr Jellicote,' she repeats.

'Of St Cyprian's Church, on the corner of St Cyprian's Road and Parkside Road,' he says brightly. He has looked it up on a street map.

'Precisely,' she agrees. 'Apart from the fact that it would be interesting to learn his view of Mr and Mrs Stibbins and this threat to Albertina – if, indeed, he knows of it – I feel it would be to our advantage if word reached Ernest Stibbins that L. G. Raynor – by which of course I mean you – has begun his investigation.'

With a surge of excited pleasure, Felix gets to his feet.

But Lily holds up a detaining hand. 'I would do it myself were it not for the fact that we do not want my identity known,' she says sternly. She stares at him, her eyes narrowed, as if assessing whether or not he is capable of carrying out the interview in the right way. 'You must be cautious, and watch carefully to gauge Mr Jellicote's reaction, and stop immediately if you feel he is taking offence.' She frowns at him.

'I will be careful,' he assures her. 'Really, I will.' He waits, but she doesn't speak. She is still frowning, however.

He decides to get out before she countermands her orders. 'I'll set out straight away,' he says as he strides towards the door.

He finds the vicar of St Cyprian's standing in the aisle of his large, chilly and ugly church, frowning in dismay at some pathetic and already drooping posies of flowers tied rather too tightly to the ends of the front few pews. James Jellicote is a man in early middle age, strongly built and a little above average height, with light brown hair cut neatly, worn but well-brushed jacket and trousers and brilliantly shining black shoes. Half-turning at the sound of Felix's footsteps, he says, 'I really don't know, Mrs Spencer, if they will survive until two o'clock, for the leaves are half-dead and most of the petals already on the floor— oh, I do beg your pardon! I thought you were this afternoon's bride's mother!'

'I'm afraid not,' Felix replies. He holds out one of the Bureau's cards, which the vicar takes and reads. Leaning closer, although it seems that the church is otherwise empty, Felix adds softly, 'The Bureau has been engaged to look into the matter of Mrs Stibbins.'

Straight away he understands that not only does the vicar know about the matter, but is deeply sympathetic and not a little anxious. His kindly face has creased in concern, and the heavy brows have descended above the mild brown eyes. Taking Felix's arm, he murmurs, 'Oh, how relieved I am that somebody is *doing* something! Please, come into the vestry.'

Once inside this small and somewhat depressing room – it smells of damp and just a little of sweat, and everything in it, from paintwork to prayerbooks, appears to be brown – the vicar can no longer hold himself back.

'Poor Albertina must be quite beside herself with dread!' he exclaims. 'I knew her when she was a girl, you know, for I was curate at St Albans, and she and her father sang in the choir. The Goodchilds were a *most* hospitable family, and fellow choir members, among whom I myself numbered, were often invited to their house after Sunday service for sherry and madeira cake. I felt so concerned for her when her elderly great-aunt died and left her all alone, and it was with great delight that I welcomed her here to St Cyprian's. When Ernest Stibbins took her under his wing and eventually made her his wife, I couldn't have been happier!' He beams in delighted recollection, and Felix tells himself he must have imagined the tiny shadow that briefly crossed the smiling face. Leaning closer, his face straightening, the vicar adds, 'The city of London is no place for an innocent young woman on her own, Mr Raynor.' He nods knowingly. 'I cannot bring myself to speak of the shameful, sinful perils of the streets, but I am sure that you, as a man of the world, will know what I mean.' Felix murmurs his agreement. 'Vice is all around us,' James Jellicote goes on, 'and life is cheap. Young girls are seduced into a manner of living whose existence they can scarcely have imagined, and before you know it, they face such troubles, such shame, that sometimes the terrible solution of taking their own lives appears the only road open to them.' He shakes his head sadly. 'Why, even here in our own parish, where many are blessed with relative comfort and security, poverty, desperation and destitution lurk just around the corner, and we have had girls and young women go missing; victims, one must surely conclude, of such a frightful fate.'

'But thankfully Albertina found her saviour,' Felix says brightly, 'and is not of their number.'

'Thankfully indeed!' the vicar says, his smile returning. 'Despite the disparity in their ages, the marriage appears very happy, and Albertina is proving to be an excellent homemaker, encouraging her somewhat conservative husband, if I may so call him, to consider some improvements to the house. But I digress,' he reproves himself. 'Now, Mr Raynor, you have announced your intention of helping in this alarming matter, so please, ask whatever questions you will, and I shall do my best to answer them!'

Felix takes his notebook and pencil out of his pocket and begins.

His second mission of the day could hardly be more of a contrast.

Felix has few illusions about the Peeping Tom Hall of Varieties, which is as rowdy, as lively, as entertaining, as filthy, as sordid and, in a strange way, as captivating as he expected. He is there in very good time, and finds a place from which he can watch new arrivals going through the door that leads to the boxes, which are set in a wide horseshoe around the open area where admittance costs half the price. Violetta da Rosa, he is sure, will settle for nothing less than a box, and he has paid for the more expensive ticket in the hope that he will be able to slip into one next to her. (He makes a careful note of the cost, for Lily has explained to him about how to claim for his expenses.) Few of the boxes are so far occupied.

To pass the time before the performance – he has an idea that his quarry won't arrive until just before it starts – he lets his eyes run around the auditorium, although that is really too grand a name for a space that doesn't look as if it's had a good clean since the Queen, or possibly even her late uncle,

King William, ascended the throne. There are a few rows of seats, set on a gently sloping incline, as well as some large open spaces in which are set out small tables and chairs for three or four people. Along the back row, just below the boxes and partially shadowed by them, there are some double seats. In one of these quite close to where Felix stands, a woman in a crimson bonnet is sitting with her legs spread over the man next to her. Her wide skirts cover their two lower bodies and her right hand is thrust down between them, deep into the man's lap. There is rhythmic movement going on, its pace inexorably increasing, and the man's demeanour – his head thrown back, eyes closed, mouth half-open – indicates the nature of it. He moans softly – 'Hush, can't yer?' the woman scolds – and her hand moves faster. He moans again, and she emits a very fake-sounding cough in an attempt to cover it up. Then it's all over, she is withdrawing her hand and, after wiping it none too surreptitiously on her skirt, holding it out discreetly. Felix hears the chink of coins. She hauls herself up and off him, straightens her skirts and her bonnet, wishes him a cheerful 'Ta-ta, then,' and strolls away.

The theatre is filling up. There is a smell of beer, and once or twice a crash as a bottle or a glass is dropped. Some people have brought food. The temperature rises from the presence of so many people, and the stench of old sweat intensifies. This is the people's entertainment, Felix reflects. It's the release they need from hard lives with little to laugh about in them. Good for them, he says to himself, I hope they enjoy the performance.

There's a shoving and a rustling from just beneath the small stage, part of which projects in a narrow tongue out into the audience, and the band settles itself. They tune up, to loud and derisive comments from the audience. 'Gimme an A, Fred! Oh, fuck it, that's near enough!' Someone throws half a stale bread roll, which hits the man with the baton on the back of the head. He picks it up and hurls it back, to a round of applause.

Then there's a drum roll, a sudden dazzle as lights blaze out, and the master of ceremonies strides across the stage and into his little railed stand at the far side of it. He is a tall, elegant man in full evening dress, pale of cheek, luxuriant of moustache and smooth of hair. 'Here I am, the preacher in the pulpit!' he shouts, to a gale of laughter; it's clearly an old and beloved joke.

Felix has almost forgotten to watch out for Violetta da Rosa. He spins round, trying to look everywhere at once, and just in time he sees her. The swarthy man who muttered to her outside the Glass Slipper is holding her arm. They slip into a box immediately to the left of the master of ceremonies, who looks up and gives her a formal and courteous bow. Felix slips away, sprints along the corridor out of which the boxes open and goes into the one next to the last on the left, which, like at least two-thirds of them, is vacant. There are six red-upholstered gilt chairs inside the box, and he puts one of them right to the front, from where he could, if he wished, peer round and look straight into Violetta's box. But he doesn't. He is here to listen, not to watch.

But for now he can't hear anything except for howls of delight, stamping and thunderous applause, for the master of ceremonies – the Chairman, as he has just introduced himself – has announced the first act, and Sweet Sukie Smith, the Songbird of Stepney, dressed in her usual elegant male evening wear, has taken the stage. The band breaks into the introduction to 'Champagne Charlie', and the evening's programme has begun.

Felix sits with varying degrees of enjoyment, appreciation and occasionally, broad-minded though he is, mild revulsion, through eleven more acts, and then it is the interval. He leans closer to the next box, waiting to see what the occupants will do.

'I'm not going out there, Billy,' Violetta says. 'I don't want the crowds demanding pieces of me tonight. I'm off duty, aren't I?'

'You are,' Billy agrees. 'I'll go and get some champagne. Wait there, love.'

There is the sound of the door to the box opening and closing again. Felix risks a swift glance around the partition between the boxes. Violetta is gazing down at the empty stage, a mild, reminiscent smile on her flushed face. She is fanning herself with a huge feather fan. Felix, very aware of her gusty laughter at some of the cruder acts, is quite sure she's enjoying herself.

Soon the door is opened and closed again, and there is the sound of a cork popping, and of champagne fizzing into glasses. 'Cheers,' says Violetta. There is a pause, then she emits a loud, resonating burp. 'Oh, God, Billy, you don't know how good it feels to be able to do that.'

'Little Jack Horner would piss his pants, I imagine, if you did it in front of him.'

'Piss and shit them,' she replies.

There is a silence, broken only by the sound of the glasses being refilled. Then Billy says, 'You going to go ahead with it?'

'I am.'

Another pause. 'You'll never be able to burp again.'

'Yes I will, Billy old dear. He's going to inherit one of Papa's many properties next year, and it's got about a million rooms, so I can have my own burping suite and he'll never have to know.'

'I suppose I don't have to ask you why,' Billy says. His tone, Felix thinks, is sad.

'You don't,' Violetta says shortly. There's another, longer pause. Then she says in quite a different voice, 'But you know what I just said about that million-room house.'

'You saying what I think you are, girl?'

There are some different sounds now, and Felix, almost sure that he has correctly identified them and that they will be preoccupying the pair in the next-door box to the exclusion of everything else, risks another quick look.

Having pushed a couple of chairs right to the rear of the box, Violetta da Rosa is wrapped in the swarthy man's arms and they are kissing as if they're trying to eat each other.

A little while later, the second half begins. Felix, at least half his mind busy on what he has observed of the goings-on in the next box, sits through a knife-throwing act, a strange sort of dance where small and very supple women bend themselves into extraordinary shapes and are juggled, for want of a better word, by a quartet of burly, muscular men; a couple of animal acts; a trick cycling act, performed by five girls in extremely small costumes; a very blue comedian; a male singer who specializes in putting filthy words to hymn tunes; two women billed as sisters who box each other, once again in skimpy costumes; several more singers and some dancers; an indifferent escapologist, and then, as the penultimate act, a very short man in unbelievably tight trousers who performs a long, word-perfect patter of innuendoes so eye-wateringly crude that Felix can hardly believe what he's hearing. But the intent is made perfectly clear by the midget's lewd body movements, consisting of sharp thrusts with his hips and gestures towards his groin. Felix is all but sure he has pushed a stuffed sock down the front of those skin-tight trousers. No man, surely, is that well-endowed at the hands of nature alone.

The Chairman stands up as the small man takes the last of his many bows, waits for the tumultuous applause, the whistles, the whoops of approval and the stamping feet to die down, then announces that the night will finish with a selection of popular songs in which the audience, many of whom are on the verge of falling-down drunk by now, are invited to join in. 'And you all know the very special Peeping Tom words, don't you?' cries the Chairman.

'*YES!*' thunders the audience, to more yelling and stamping.

As the singers shuffle onstage and the band begins to play 'My Grandfather's Clock', two hundred or more voices start on the salacious first line, which, by the dropping of a single letter from the third word, straight away announces itself as a ditty as different from that written by the songwriter as it's possible to be.

Felix makes a quiet and unobtrusive exit.

FIVE

I t is Sunday afternoon, and Lily has found a spot from which to observe the Stibbins house where she can stand unseen unless somebody is specifically looking out for her, which seems unlikely.

It is a very ordinary-looking suburban dwelling, double-fronted, the front door and the window frames painted an unappealing but practical chocolate brown. It stands in a long row of very similar houses, facing a virtually identical row on the opposite side of the street. Many of the occupants have selected the same chocolate brown as Ernest Stibbins for their paintwork, but here and there one or two braver and more adventurous souls have branched out with dark red and forest green. Two houses further along on this opposite side of the street, a little path dives down between two rows of houses and leads to a pleasant little park, and the entrance to the passage is sheltered by a mature lilac tree. It is beneath its branches that Lily has concealed herself.

Not that concealment has proved all that necessary, for the Sunday afternoon quiet is almost absolute here in Parkside Road, and she has barely seen anybody other than three well-behaved children heading for the park with an older woman, a man walking his dog, three cats and a youth making his furtive way home from the pub and exuding a tell-tale miasma of beer fumes.

Lily waits. And waits.

At last, the chocolate-brown front door of the Stibbins house opens and the men and women who have sat in Circle for Albertina's seance begin to emerge. Drawing back deeper into the foliage, Lily watches.

A man with very neat hair and a small moustache is ushering people out. He speaks quietly and kindly to some of them, and Lily hears him say to an elderly woman with red eyes, 'I'm so glad, Mrs Sullivan, that poor Rodney came through

for you this afternoon.' The woman gives him a grateful look
and nods. 'One of my dear Albertina's best days, wasn't it?'
'Yes!' the old woman agrees fervently, blowing her nose.

So the man is Ernest Stibbins, just as Lily has already
surmised. She would like to study him more closely, but it is
not for this that she has been standing here for the last hour
or more. She turns her attention to the rest of the people
emerging from the house. Two more women, middle-aged this
time, who look like sisters. A young woman dressed in black.
A saturnine-faced man who shakes Ernest Stibbins's hand so
fervently that the poor man winces. Two more men, one with
a soldierly bearing and around the right age to be his older
companion's son. And, last to come out, a pallid, nervous-
looking young man in his early twenties in a dark grey suit
whose knees and elbows shine with long use and whose cheeks
each bear a circle of bright pink, as if from some recently
experienced, strong emotion. Like the old woman who was
first to emerge, he too has red eyes. He is twitchy, staring
rapidly up and down the street as he waits to say goodbye to
his host as if he can't wait to get away.

Lily watches him nod, shake Ernest Stibbins' hand and then
hurry out onto the pavement. He turns to the left and walks
swiftly away. Lily makes herself wait for a few moments and
then follows him.

He keeps up his pace for half a mile or more, crossing
streets, turning to the right and then right again. Then abruptly
he turns down a little alleyway into a row of mean-looking
houses that look as if they are tenanted by a multiplicity of
families and individuals. He draws out a key, goes inside –
Lily is close enough to see a long hallway chequered with
black and white tiles with several doors leading off it – and
closes the door behind him.

What now? she wonders.

She decides to wait.

And her patience is rewarded, for not much more than
twenty-five minutes later the young man comes out again and
makes his way to a rundown cafe two streets away. Lily waits
for a quarter of an hour, long enough for three or four other
people to go in after him, then opens the door and enters.

The twitchy young man is sitting on the far side of the crowded cafe. He is the sole occupant of a table for two and before him there is a cup of tea and a plate containing two poached eggs and a couple of tomatoes on slices of bread. He is eating as if he hasn't seen food for a week.

Lily goes up to the counter and orders tea and a toasted teacake. They are served with swift efficiency and they are cheap. Turning away, she glances round for somewhere to sit. There are other vacant seats, but she edges nearer to the young man's table. She has adopted a woebegone expression, as if the world was already too much for her even before she found that there was no empty table in the cafe.

She is careful not to stare in the young man's direction.

Then she hears a timid voice which she knows without looking is his say, 'Th-th-there's a spare chair here, miss.'

Suppressing a whoop of joy at her success, Lily turns, remembers to look suitably startled and replies, 'Oh, thank you – how very kind!'

She sits down, making a show of nervously arranging her skirts, removing her gloves, looking for a place to put her little handbag before deciding it's safest on her lap. She is aware all the time of the young man's eyes on her. She takes a sip of tea. It's very good. She picks up the small knife that has been supplied with her teacake and cuts it into dainty segments, selecting one. It too is excellent.

He is still looking at her. She senses that he's aching to start a conversation but has not the least idea how. She feels sorry for him, for she also senses that he's a gentle soul.

She emits a tiny sigh, not much more than a soft exhalation of breath with a very slight catch in it. He has noticed: she picks up a new intentness in his watchfulness. She takes a small lace-trimmed handkerchief from her little bag and wipes an imaginary tear from her eye.

He says, 'The t-teacakes are very good here.'

As an opening remark its originality leaves quite a lot to be desired, but it is suitably conventional and non-controversial. She quite admires his restraint, for she has the impression he's just dying to ask her what's the matter and offer her comfort.

She picks up the conversational cue. 'Yes, it's very nice.'

She looks sadly down at the teacake. 'I wish I had more appetite,' she whispers.

He leans closer. 'I could not but observe that you appear d-d-distressed,' he says quietly. 'Are you unwell?'

Now is the moment, she tells herself. She imagines she is straightening her back, summoning her courage to go into battle.

Then she says, 'No, I am not unwell. But—' She breaks off with a little gasp.

'But what?' he prompts.

And, reminding herself that this is the profession she has chosen, that she has committed herself now and must get used to subterfuge and to misrepresenting herself to kind innocents like this young man whose gentle eyes are looking so anxiously into her face, she sighs again, as if only reluctantly allowing herself to be persuaded to tell her tale, and begins.

'I have only recently lost my fiancé,' she whispers. He makes a sound of sympathy, of understanding. 'We were to have been married a month ago, but instead of arranging our wedding I had to watch while his uncle arranged his funeral.'

'How ap-appalling!' the twitchy young man exclaims. His face contorts into a violent tic, as if his distress has to have a physical outlet. 'Was it – did it happen unexpectedly?'

Lily shakes her head. 'No. Poor Cecil had been unwell for a long time, but both of us hoped and prayed that he would get better in time for the wedding. But he didn't.' She hides her face in the very inadequate little handkerchief and says from behind it, 'His uncle paid for him to go to the coast but it was too late.'

Silence descends over the little table. She can feel waves of sympathy coming off the twitchy young man.

'How very sad, for b-both of you,' he says after some time.

She nods. 'Yes.' She draws the word out, hoping to imply uncertainty.

He picks it up. 'You sound doubtful?' he says, his voice rising in a question.

'No!' she protests. Then, after a moment, 'Well, perhaps, but I tell myself I have absolutely no cause and am surely being unfair to my dear Cecil, but . . .' She stops, as if overcome.

'Unfair?' he queries.

'Oh, but I can't!' she cries.

He reaches out a hand as if about to touch hers – his nails, she notices, are bitten fiercely back and the tops of the fingers bulge out over them – but then quickly draws it back. 'Try to t-tell me,' he says.

'It's nothing, I am sure it can be nothing, but it's just that– that—' She pauses, then, as if in a burst of confidence that she just can't hold back, says, 'I am quite certain that it can only have been because of the hardships of his illness and all the anxiety about the future, but latterly it had seemed to me that he became a little off-hand, and I feared that perhaps he was entertaining second thoughts about our marriage.'

'P-perhaps he was unsure of his ability to support you as a husband should, knowing he was so ill,' the twitchy young man suggests. He stares at her, then adds in a fervent whisper, 'That must surely have been all it was!'

She looks up and meets his earnest brown eyes. 'You are very kind,' she says with total honesty.

'I know what it is like to lose someone you dearly love,' he says, so softly that she has to strain to hear. 'My m-m-mother died in February, and I miss her quite dreadfully.'

'I am very sorry,' she says.

He is opening his heart and laying it before me, she thinks. Her guilt at deceiving him is intensifying by the minute. He is being so kind, trying so hard to comfort her. She takes another sip of her tea, once again telling herself very sternly that this is the profession she has chosen and she'll just have to get used to the more troubling aspects.

'W-would it help,' the young man says after a pause, 'if you were to be given one last reassurance of his love?'

She meets his gaze. 'Oh, yes, of *course* it would! But that cannot be, for he left no letter, no message, and—'

'There *is* a way,' says the twitchy young man.

She simply stares at him, not trusting herself to speak.

And he says, 'I am a member of a group who attend meetings with a wonderful young woman named Albertina Stibbins.' His face alight, he leans closer. 'I was there only this afternoon, and she— Well, never mind that for now.' He leans back again.

'Suffice it to say that she has given great comfort to many people, myself included.' He shakes his head in admiration. 'She is truly outstanding, and so very kind and gentle!'

'What does she do?' Lily whispers.

And he says simply, 'She is in touch with the dead.'

Lily's start of alarm is totally genuine, for he has pronounced this extraordinary statement as if he was saying that Albertina made a very good cup of tea. 'She— *what*?' she hisses.

He is smiling, and the reassurance he is offering comes surging towards her. 'Do not be afraid!' he says. 'I felt just like you do when I learned of her special gift, and I told myself I was not the sort of person to believe such nonsense. But then I went along and sat in Circle, and Albertina—' He breaks off. 'It is difficult to explain, but she *sees*, she looks right into your heart and feels the pain, and she understands the cause, and she offers such help, such wonderful reassurance, and—' But he is overcome, and cannot go on.

'Cecil was a God-fearing person and a punctilious church-goer, as indeed am I,' Lily says with appropriate primness.

The twitchy young man shakes his head. 'It makes no difference,' he assures her. 'This – Albertina's gift – surely comes from God. There is nothing to fear, I promise you, and everything to gain.'

She looks at him for a long moment. 'Might I truly hear my dear Cecil's voice? Have his reassurance that he—' She breaks off with a little gasp.

'That he loved you? That he still loves you?' he finishes for her. 'I cannot say for sure, but others have received such reassurances. And you will not know,' he adds, 'unless you try.'

Now, she thinks, is the moment to hang back; to appear uncertain, unconvinced. She stays silent.

He says, 'Why not go along to Albertina's next seance? She lives nearby, I can show you her house.'

Still Lily does not speak.

'Circle isn't having the Tuesday session this week but it sits again on Thursday afternoon,' he says, 'so why not go and see for yourself? She's very good, she helps so many people!'

Lily feigns extreme reluctance. She lets him persuade her

some more, then says very shyly, 'I might find it easier if you were there. Will you be attending on Thursday?'

'No, I can't, for I am at work all week, but I'll be there next Sunday.'

'If I can nerve myself to go, will you—'

'I'll introduce you, of course I will!' He half-rises, holding out his hand. 'My name is Carter, Leonard Carter.'

She takes his hand. 'Maud Garrett.'

'Let us meet here next Sunday at two o'clock, Miss Garrett,' he says, resuming his seat. 'The seance starts at two thirty but Mr Stibbins – that's Albertina's husband, he's really nice – likes us to be there and in our places, sitting quietly, when Albertina takes her seat. We'll go together, shall we?'

And she hears herself saying, 'Very well.'

On Monday morning Felix reports his experiences of Saturday night at the Peeping Tom to Lily, telling her about the incredible vulgarity of some of the songs. 'The remainder of the acts were none too sophisticated, either,' he goes on, 'with double-entendres, brassy women with far too much flesh on display, animal acts, acrobats in skimpy outfits and a great deal of coarseness in the extreme.' He refrains from going into detail, although Lily's interested expression suggests she wouldn't mind.

'You did well,' she says, and he feels a disproportionate amount of pleasure at the brief words of praise. 'And what did Violetta da Rosa think of the evening's entertainment?' she enquires. He has explained about managing to take the next-door box, earning a faint nod of approval.

'Violetta da Rosa lapped it up and became scarlet in the face from laughing,' he replies.

'And you say she was with this man who came to speak to her outside the theatre late on Friday afternoon?'

'She was, and his name's Billy.' He tells her briefly about the kiss, and about Violetta's remarks about finding some sort of place for Billy in her future life.

'So we may surmise that she has very vulgar tastes, and really is serious about marrying Julian,' Lily muses.

But Felix still is far from convinced. 'She may *think* she

wants to marry him,' he demurs. But before she can ask him
to explain – it's only instinct that informs him here and he
doesn't think he *can* explain yet – he hurries on. 'And as to
the vulgar tastes, perhaps it was one single visit. A sort of
mental aberration; a sudden and unrepeated desire to spend
an evening watching the coarsest entertainment that this great
city has to offer,' he says.

'Yet both she and this Billy know the Peeping Tom by its
familiar abbreviation,' Lily reminds him.

'Perhaps I should check,' he says reluctantly.

'Oh, I shouldn't bother,' she says.

He sighs. 'I'm glad you said that. I have to admit to a certain
relief – I think that once was probably enough for me, since
the entertainment value of Philip Maguire and his Amazing
Farting Dachshund would undoubtedly pall rather quickly.'

Lily gets up abruptly and hurries out of the office and
towards the kitchen, muttering something about a cup of tea.
She pulls the door half-closed after her, which is quite unusual,
Felix reflects, as they normally leave it open. But then he hears
a chortle of laughter, swiftly suppressed.

It is in that moment that he realizes he really rather likes
Lily Raynor.

As they drink the tea Lily says, 'We need more insight into
Violetta. I cannot write my report to Lord Berwick based solely
upon your two brief observations of her, useful though they
are.' That puts me in my place, Felix thinks. 'Let me see . . .'
Lily muses.

He spots a way to really impress her. 'She has a theatrical
agent, just as I suspected,' he says.

She fixes him with that cool stare. 'You appear to know
quite a lot about the world of entertainment,' she observes.
'First your familiarity with that music hall, now an awareness
of an actress's professional habits.'

There is the hint of a question in her intonation.

'I worked in a theatre for a while,' he says shortly.
'Backstage.' It was a tiny theatre near Seven Dials and the
work had been awful, consisting mostly of cleaning the stinking
lavatory, mopping up sick (one of the lead actors had a drink

problem) and being sworn at by temperamental artistes of both sexes and everything in between.

'Hm,' Lily says. Then, 'Go and see Violetta's agent, if you can find out who he is.'

'I already know,' Felix says, trying not to sound smug.

Her raised eyebrows suggest he has failed. 'Perhaps you should tell him you're a journalist requiring background for a series of articles,' she suggests.

'Yes,' he says. 'That's a good idea.'

But as soon as he is sitting down facing Maurice Isaacs across an acreage of fine mahogany desk, he is very glad he didn't succumb to the temptation to misrepresent himself. The dark brown eyes in the lean face are extremely shrewd, and Felix knows quite well he lacks sufficient experience in the world of newspaper and magazine reporting to pose convincingly as a journalist. He lacks *any* experience, come to that.

'It's extremely good of you to see me,' he says as Maurice Isaacs pushes a tiny cup of very dark coffee towards him. 'I'm a lifelong fan and I want to compile an account of Violetta's career, and I am very much hoping you can—'

'What do you plan to do with this account?' Maurice Isaacs interrupts.

'Have it printed privately and circulate it among like-minded fans,' Felix replies. He is thinking on his feet and not at all sure of his ground.

'I'll need to see it.'

'Naturally!' Felix says with what he hopes is a disarming smile.

Not quite disarming enough, apparently, for Maurice Isaacs leans forward and says, '*Lifelong* fan?'

One of Felix's maxims for survival in a tricky and often hostile world is that when telling lies, it's best to stay as near as you can to the truth. With total honesty he says, 'I first saw her in *Secrets of the Convent* when I was fourteen. I was staying with a school friend and his parents – it was the holidays, and we were both at Marlborough – and we were supposed to be going to Humphrey's – that's my friend's – godfather's house to play bridge, but the godfather drank quite a lot and was easily outwitted, so Humph and I went to the theatre instead.' Warming to his theme, his mind flooding with happy memories, he goes on, 'It was wonderful! Well, *she* was wonderful, and Humph and I were – er, we were overwhelmed.' He suspects that this clever-eyed man can well imagine the reaction of two sexually frustrated fourteen-year-olds to being in a darkened theatre faced with Violetta's gorgeous, creamy flesh bulging out of her brutally tight corset and knows precisely what Felix means. 'I can still see her in that costume if I close my eyes,' he adds dreamily. 'Burgundy silk really suited her.' He tells Maurice Isaacs about the postcards, hoping that a man who is an astute businessman himself will appreciate another's budding talents.

Maurice nods. 'No harm in that,' he remarks. He gives Felix a man-of-the-world look. 'Some of them got a bit sticky, I'd guess.'

'Yes, but not the ones I was planning to sell,' Felix flashes back.

Maurice Isaacs grins. 'Shame you didn't come and find me back then,' he remarks. 'I might have offered you a job.'

There is quite a long and rather unnerving silence, during which it seems to Felix that Maurice's dark eyes are trying to bore into his head to see what he really wants. He does his best to empty his mind of everything but the most innocent thoughts. Eventually Maurice opens a drawer down to his right and extracts a thick, bulging file which, as he opens it, is revealed to contain playbills. 'You can have a browse through these if you like,' he says laconically. He nods towards the door that leads to the outer office. 'Out there.'

This is clearly the best Felix is going to get but, since it's a great deal more than he was hoping for and will save him the labour of looking up the details of Violetta's past performances in dozens if not hundreds of old publications, he is extremely grateful. Thanking Maurice Isaacs profusely – he even finds himself bowing – he backs out and finds himself a quiet corner in the outer office.

An hour later, some dozen pages of his notebook are covered with his neat handwriting and he has the full story of Violetta's performances – and hence her whereabouts when working, which seems to be the majority of the time – for the past fifteen years. Most of the time she seems to have been in or close to London, but there was a brief season in Brighton – perhaps the play was not a hit – and another in Guildford, and several periods in Tunbridge Wells, the most recent of which was earlier this year.

Felix knows what he must do next.

Lily is frustrated, for she must wait for almost a week before presenting herself before Albertina Stibbins for her first seance. Her frustration is increased by constantly having to observe Felix, who is not only working very diligently at the task of exploring Violetta da Rosa's background but apparently absorbed and utterly fascinated by it. When they pause to eat their lunchtime bread, cheese and pickles on Wednesday, he brings her up to date on his progress. He announces that since the actress appears to be a frequent visitor to the Kent town of Tunbridge Wells, he plans to go there, if Lily agrees, to see what he can unearth. 'It almost seems,' he adds persuasively, 'that she looks for excuses to go down there, since she's even appeared in one or two amateur efforts that surely weren't worthy of an actress of her quality.'

'Perhaps she takes the waters,' Lily remarks. Felix looks blank, so she explains. 'Tunbridge Wells is a spa town. People drink the water from a spring there, and it is said to be beneficial for the health.'

'Oh.' For a moment he looks crestfallen. Then, brightening, he says, 'Even if that was what took her to the town originally, it may not entirely explain why she keeps going back.'

Lily nods. 'I suppose not,' she allows.

He is flipping through his notebook. 'Seven plays in fifteen years, the first nearly a decade ago and the most recent at the start of the year,' he says eagerly.

Lily smiles. 'I think it's well worth investigating,' she says.

With Felix heading out of the office the next day and into the bright spring day, Lily decides she must do likewise and she sets off down the river to Wapping. She was right, and it is indeed where the river police have their headquarters. She finds a bored-looking officer only too pleased to pass half an hour by chatting to a pretty woman.

'There's the five of us plus me on my regular shift,' he tells her, 'and we call ourselves the Disciples.' He has an anticipatory smile hovering around his mouth.

'Fishers of men,' Lily says unthinkingly.

His face falls. She realizes her mistake, for she should have played dumb and let him explain; should have let him have his moment.

'Yeah, that's right,' he says huffily. 'The stiffs often end up here, see – well, they're not so much stiff as bloated if they've been in the water any length of time – and we hook them out.'

Belatedly she adopts the demeanour of horrified member of the weaker sex on the point of fainting. 'How frightful!' she breathes.

'Sit down, miss, there, that's better,' he says solicitously, pulling out a chair for her. They are in a very small, cramped office crowded with far too many objects in it, and the river is slapping repetitively and persistently against the wooden pilings supporting the platform on which it sits. 'Yeah, well, you have to have nerve in this business,' he goes on. 'Me and the Disciples, we can take it, see, we can handle anything.'

'And you have to suffer the poor relatives coming to identify the dead!' she exclaims.

'Yeah, that's quite right, miss, and it's not pretty, but what me and the Disciples say is that it's a comfort, see, because once people know, once they've seen their dead with their own eyes, they start to accept.'

She nods. 'Yes, I do see,' she says. After a respectful pause she asks, 'Do many people fall in and drown?'

He laughs shortly. 'Well, everyone what falls in drowns, miss, there's no escaping your fate once you're in the water. And it's not always whole bodies as ends up here, what with the battering they get, even assuming they were whole when they went in.' He looks at her. 'Good place to discard a body, whole or in bits, is the Thames,' he mutters darkly.

'I see.' The tremor in her voice is by no means entirely fake.

'Trouble is,' he goes on, resuming his cheerful tone, 'it's no longer just people missing their footing on bridges and falling in, not any more, because we're seeing different sorts of mishaps now, what with so many people taking to the river in pleasure craft and that and not knowing what they're about on the water. And there's suicides too, don't forget that. As to numbers –' he pauses, drawing in breath over clenched teeth to make a whistling noise – 'ooh, we're talking a good hundred, maybe a hundred and fifty or even more, per annum. That's per year,' he adds helpfully.

One of whom, Lily thinks, was the first Mrs Stibbins. Saddened, and guilty all over again because she's about to trespass into two people's private tragedy when it's really none of her business – except that of course it *is* her business – she forces herself to go on.

'Would a body that fell from Chelsea Bridge end up here?'

He shoots her a glance. 'Why d'you want to know?'

She has prepared for this. 'Somebody I know lost his wife,' she replies. 'She drowned, having slipped and gone in the water under Chelsea Bridge, and he had to identify her body. I do not wish my ignorance of such matters to inadvertently cause offence.'

He frowns as he tries to work out exactly what she means, and she adopts a prim and slightly disapproving expression, as if it is he who is being insensitive. Taken in, he flushes slightly and says, 'Right, miss, yes, I see,' although she is quite sure he doesn't. 'Yeah, well, she'd have ended up with us, likely as not, so the poor bugg— the poor man would probably have come here to view the body.'

'Thank you,' she says quietly.

They chat for a while longer, although no longer about drowned bodies, and Lily discovers that her new friend's name is Alf Wilson. He seems to have forgiven her for spoiling his little joke and even provides a cup of amazingly strong tea, and, after managing to drink it without wincing, Lily takes her leave.

In the late afternoon Lily goes to observe the people who attend the Thursday seance at the Stibbins house. But it is poorly attended, and Leonard Carter, just as he had said, isn't there. She recognizes a couple of faces from the Sunday seance: the older man who came with his soldier son, and the old woman, Mrs Sullivan, who on Sunday had some sort of message from poor Rodney, whoever he is. Was, she corrects herself. There are two more women, black-clad, one with a cloud of gauze obscuring her face. They are elderly; too old to still be in employment and thus free to seek out other activities on a weekday afternoon. Including, thinks Lily as she watches Mrs Sullivan totter away, going to a modest and very ordinary-looking suburban house and trying to get in touch with the dead.

She waits a little longer, giving them a chance to get away before she sets off. The sky is overcast and darkness is already falling. She looks across at the Stibbins house and sees a figure at a ground-floor window. It is a woman – Albertina, no doubt – and she is reaching up to draw the curtains.

Just for an instant it seems to Lily that a heavy black veil descends between the two of them, and it is as if she is viewing Albertina through something dark and thick. The air has suddenly turned very cold.

It is a horrible sensation, full of ancient menace and foreboding.

Lily shrugs it off.

She sets off briskly down the road, her heels ringing on the pavement. It was nothing but an illusion, she tells herself, brought about by the late afternoon gloom and her own fatigue.

Nevertheless, the chill and the foreboding seem to walk beside her for quite a long way before they eventually dissipate.

In the morning there is a telegram from Felix.

Request approval to stay in TW until Sunday night stop.

That is all, and it poses far more questions than it answers. It doesn't answer any questions at all, in fact, except that Felix appears to have discovered something worth pursuing.

The telegraph boy is waiting for her reply. Lily stands in the doorway, thinking.

She will have to pay the additional expense of two more nights' accommodation, which will not be cheap because of the sort of town that Tunbridge Wells is. But if Felix really has found a lead, then surely she must give him his head and allow him to follow it?

It comes down to how much she is willing to trust his judgement.

And, after the briefest of pauses, she reaches in her purse for a coin and tells the boy, 'Just send back *Approved.*'

Lily is ready far too early on Sunday. The morning has had its fill of frustrations, however, and she makes up her mind to get out of the house and be on her way.

It's all because of the Little Ballerina, of course.

She is at present in a production of *Coppélia*, and, although still only a member of the chorus, it seems she has advanced by a row or two into a position of greater prominence, and this has been sufficient to elevate her sense of her own importance by a factor of ten. She managed to annoy Mrs Clapper to boiling point on Friday morning by airily informing her that she expected her personal laundry to be rinsed out and put out on the line now that more time spent at rehearsals meant there was less available for seeing to her own washing. Mrs Clapper's reply left the Little Ballerina in no doubt that this was unlikely to happen. This morning, Lily's own request was that the dancer, coming home so late after evening performances, might try to make a little less noise.

The Little Ballerina had drawn herself up to her full height, which seemed more than it was because she held herself so well. 'I am *artiste,*' she said in a scandalized gasp. 'I perform, I give all of myself, then afterwards there is still so much excitement, and this cannot go away quick!'

There was a lot more in this vein, and eventually Lily had had enough. 'Yes, I understand,' she said curtly, interrupting the Little Ballerina in mid-sentence. 'Just stop slamming the doors, please, and try to be a little lighter on your feet as you go upstairs.'

The Little Ballerina, shocked at this slur on her professional qualities, called Lily something in Russian that Lily was quite sure was no compliment.

*   *   *

Now it is a little before one o'clock and Lily, clad in black, is striding across Battersea Bridge, deliberately putting thoughts of temperamental ballet dancers right out of her mind and thinking ahead to her own performance, which will start in just over an hour when she meets Leonard Carter at the cafe. Reaching the south side of the river, she walks along to the park and finds a bench, where she sits down and watches a family entertain their four children with a picnic. Then at a quarter to two, she sets off for the cafe.

Leonard Carter is waiting for her outside, and he looks as nervous as she feels. But I need not disguise my anxiety, she thinks, for what is more natural when setting off for one's first seance?

Leonard greets her courteously, and he turns to lead the way to the Stibbins house on Parkside Road. She remembers just in time that she's not meant to know where it is, and lets him walk slightly ahead. He makes one or two remarks about the weather, to which she struggles to respond. Then, mercifully, he lapses into an understanding silence. Lily, repeating to herself *Maud Garrett, I'm Maud Garrett*, follows him right up to the chocolate-brown front door.

Impressions crowd in on her swiftly and relentlessly. A modest little house, clean and tidy, the rooms reasonably sized and filled with slightly too much furniture. A door to a rear room – the kitchen? – quickly closed by Ernest Stibbins, as if he, like his guests, has suddenly noticed the smell of cabbage and gravy. A room to the right of the narrow, dark hall, its curtains drawn and lit by a couple of oil lamps on the big round table, and six chairs set around it. Ernest Stibbins counts heads and hurries away to fetch a seventh. The chair beneath the window is left vacant, and Ernest settles the six people in the remainder.

'May I introduce Miss Maud Garrett?' Leonard says once they are all seated. 'She is a friend of mine, and would very much like to sit in Circle with us today.'

There are some polite murmurs of acquiescence. Ernest Stibbins comes to stand beside Lily's chair and says, 'Welcome, Miss Garrett, to our house and to our Circle. I hope you will find that which you seek.' He gives a kindly and encouraging little smile, as if this is really a foregone conclusion. Lily is just framing a reply when there is a movement in the shadowy doorway as a young woman walks into the room and quietly takes the last seat.

Leonard Carter, seated to Lily's right, draws in his breath. Lily risks a swift glance at him and sees his face alive with devotion and admiration. Ah, she thinks.

Under cover of the dim light, Lily stares at Albertina Stibbins. She is young; perhaps as much as eighteen or twenty years younger than her husband. No, seventeen, she corrects herself, recalling that it was in Felix's notes. Albertina is quite short, with a curvaceous figure dressed sombrely in a dark shade, with white at the collar and cuffs. Her hair is reddish-fair and dressed decorously, parted in the centre and swept down over her ears and into a bun at the nape. Her neck is long, and curves gracefully into sloping shoulders.

Her face is quite lovely. Her eyes are wide and light-coloured, fringed with thick lashes. Her nose tips up at the end, her skin is creamy, with a slight flush to the plump cheeks. Her deep-lipped mouth curves up in a smile as she looks at the people around the table. 'Good afternoon, Mrs Sullivan, Mr Haverford, Mr Sutherland and Robert, how nice to see you all today.' After a quick glance at Leonard, seated on her immediate left, her eyes have gone widdershins round the table and now they rest on Lily. 'And welcome to our new friend!' she says, her smile widening.

And then, before Lily has a chance to prepare herself – even had she known what to do – one lamp is extinguished and the other turned down to the dimmest of lights and removed to a sideboard in the corner of the room, and her first seance begins.

She has no idea what to expect.

She realizes, as Albertina Stibbins gets into her stride and speaks with gentleness, with affection, sometimes with love, to people around the table, that she hadn't expected it to be like this.

For, to begin with at least, it seems to be all about kindness.

'Oh, of course poor dear Rodney didn't suffer, Mrs Sullivan!' she says, holding the tearful old woman's hand. 'He says to remind you that you were there with him right to the end, that you witnessed how peaceful he was, that you saw the lines of pain ease from his face as death took him.' Mrs Sullivan nods, and a weak little smile tweaks at her thin lips. 'He loved you very much, and he doesn't want you to torment yourself like this, for he can see that it is not good for you, and he wants you to try to eat a little more if you can.'

Poor dear Rodney is right, Lily thinks, for the lines of suffering on Mrs Sullivan's face are clear to see, and, to judge by the loose jowls under her chin, it does indeed look as if she has lost weight recently.

After some more words of comfort and encouragement, Albertina's attention is suddenly jerked away and she is looking straight at the soldierly man's father, sitting on the far side of his son, who is to Lily's left. 'George, George,' she says in a voice that's not quite her own, 'now you know what happened on Thursday, don't you?' George Sutherland mutters something inaudible. Lily senses his son stiffen slightly, as if wondering if to leap to his father's defence. 'It is not a matter for you to be so worried about, and you must really try to allow time to do its work.'

And then there is something else in the room with them.

Lily, uneasy, has a surreptitious look around. The light of the single lamp in the corner makes deep shadows, and Lily thinks she sees movement . . . But it's all right, it's only Ernest, who is standing just inside the door, quietly watching his wife with an expression of tenderness.

What is it? Why can Lily sense menace?

For menace there undoubtedly is, and all at once Lily is very afraid.

Ernest said that Albertina's spirit guides were warning her that she was in danger. Can it be that Lily is picking up a little of what Albertina senses? Oh, but if this . . . this *horror* is directing its full force at the poor woman, how can she sit there and not leap up to flee to safety?

Lily's skin is crawling. She can almost *see* the menace, smell it, creeping over the walls and down from the ceiling as if black mould was suddenly spreading, far too quickly and profusely to have anything but supernatural origins . . .

Stop it, she commands herself.

She forces her attention back to what is happening around the table.

There is a brief message of bland reassurance for Mr Haverford – Lily recognizes him as the man who shook Ernest Stibbins's hand rather too powerfully last Sunday – and a longer one for Leonard Carter, whose grief for his mother produces tears which Albertina wipes away with a clean handkerchief and a gentle hand. She is in the middle of saying something about loss being the inevitable result of love when, as if somebody has reached down and twisted her head, all at once she is staring past Leonard and straight at Lily.

She darts a hand across the table and grasps hold of Lily's. Her grip is very tight, her hand hot and slightly moist.

And she cries, 'I see him falling! Oh, *oh*, and the water is so far below!' She has gone very pale, and there are beads of sweat on her upper lip. 'Oh, it's *terrible*! And you, poor, poor you, you loved him so much and of course he loved you too, and it was far, far too soon to leave you!'

Shaken to her soul, Lily shakes her head as if mystified, for it is difficult to see how this image can possibly relate to the story of Miss Maud Garrett and her fiancé Cecil, because she has hinted to Leonard Carter that he succumbed to TB. Risking a very quick glance to her right, she sees Leonard's perplexed face. All she can do is shake her head and mutter, 'He used to say how he liked to sit looking down at the sea . . .' and then, reclaiming her hand and reaching in her little bag for a handkerchief, she presses it to her face and pretends to be overcome.

And all the time, like the threat of darkness creeping closer and intent on harm, she feels the menace . . .

Leonard is holding her up, supporting her as she slumps. She has no idea what has happened; why she's leaning against him; why she feels cold with dread.

The second lamp has been rekindled and both of them are now on the table, casting a glowing circle of light. Ernest is drawing back the curtains. Albertina has left the room, and as if from a long way away Lily hears the sound of water filling a kettle, the lighting of the gas.

They are all very kind to her. 'Your first time, dearie! It's only to be expected,' says old Mrs Sullivan, and, 'Brace up, Miss Garrett, it can only be beneficial in the long run to have received such a powerful message,' says the soldierly young man called Robert Sutherland. Ernest Stibbins hands her a wonderfully welcome cup of tea, and watches anxiously as she sips it. 'Drink it up,' he says, his face creased with kindly concern. 'That's the way!'

At last the tea is drunk, the cups handed in to be stacked on the tray, the thruppences discreetly dropped into an empty sugar bowl and the session is over. Ernest sees them to the door, bids them goodbye until next time.

Leonard seems on the point of escorting Lily back to the cafe where they met, but she cannot take any more for now. With an apologetic smile and muttering about a headache, she turns the other way, about to hurry off.

Mrs Sullivan catches her sleeve, edging very close. Her face is lined with distress. 'Oh, take care, Miss Garrett!' she says quietly.

'I'm quite all right now, thank you,' Lily manages.

But Mrs Sullivan shakes her head. 'I do not refer to what went on within,' she whispers, glancing back towards the Stibbins house. Then, her face right up against Lily's, she says, 'Have you far to go? Shall you be home before dusk?'

'Not far, just over the bridge,' Lily says, trying to sound confident; not easy, for, what with her recent experience and these alarming mutterings, she isn't feeling confident at all.

'Hurry home, and do not tarry!' Mrs Sullivan says in a sort of strangled hiss. 'It is not safe, Miss Garrett, for a young woman on her own! There have been far too many—' Abruptly she stops. Watching her closely, Lily thinks that it is as if she has forced herself to bite back the words that were about to spill out. With a curt little nod, Mrs Sullivan turns away and, falling into step with George and Robert Sutherland, who have courteously been waiting for her, trots away.

Lily takes her advice. By the time she reaches the river she is all but running. She doesn't even begin to feel safe until she is back on the north side of Battersea Bridge and hurrying into Hob's Court.

SIX

The house is empty and it looks likely to remain so for the rest of the evening. The Little Ballerina won't be back until the small hours, and in any case Lily would have to feel a good deal more desperate before turning to *her* for company. Felix is in, or at best on his way back from, Tunbridge Wells, and anyway it's Sunday, and not a working day.

Lily is alone.

She pretended not to recognize the meaning of Albertina's terrible words, but she does and she is shocked to the very heart of her.

It was her father, Andrew Owen Raynor, who fell.

He was a civil engineer and when Lily was twelve he worked away from home for many months on the construction of a bridge high above a Scottish firth. He was killed when he fell hundreds of feet into the sea below.

Very few people know of the tragedy and none of them is now in Lily's life. Her mother, almost as swiftly as it could be arranged, married the man with whom she had been having an affair and by whom she was already pregnant at the time of her husband's death. She, her husband and the two sons she bore him live in Argentina, where the husband has interests in beef.

Lily's grandparents and her aunt are dead.

Who, then, told Albertina Stibbins that, nearly nineteen years later, Lily is still haunted by her father's death?

The distress is refusing to dissipate; in fact, it is intensifying. Lily needs help, for she doesn't think she can deal with this alone.

She knows who she needs to talk to.

She puts her hat and jacket on again and leaves the house. She walks down to the river and turns west, hurrying along until she reaches the small basin where the boats tie up. Four or five craft lie along the little quay. One of them she recognizes. She approaches it and calls out softly to attract the boatman's attention. He opens the hatch and his head and shoulders appear. He gives her a smile. She says, 'Please, have you seen *The Dawning of the Day* recently?'

He nods. 'Aye. He'll be on his way down from Oxford.' They both know who the boatman means by *he*. 'Want me to pass on a message? He'll be here later, like as not.'

Thank God, Lily thinks. 'Yes, if you please. Just that Lily wishes to see him.'

He nods again. 'Right.'

Then he descends below deck again and quietly shuts the hatch.

The master of *The Dawning of the Day* is called Tamáz Edey. His mother was from Galicia, his father a Fensman. One night in the autumn of the previous year, he and Lily met in a way that seems to have thrown them straight into the sort of friendship, if that is what it is, that will probably endure for a lifetime.

It was late at night, and Lily knew she wouldn't sleep. She had only recently returned from India, and The Incident was still so fresh and so horrific in her mind that she found it very difficult ever to sleep. In addition, her panicky dash back to England brought dreadful news, learning on arrival as she did that her beloved Aunt Eliza had died soon after Lily had boarded the ship bringing her home.

In her shocked and panicked state she had acted with uncharacteristic precipitateness, closing the shop, packing away and disposing of most of the stock, finding workmen to take down the sign that said Raynor's Pharmacy.

None of which made her feel any better.

She was about to make her weary way up to bed, sick at heart, grieving – for not only had she lost her aunt but she had also been forced to flee from her life as a nurse – and knowing sleep was still far away, when she heard a soft tap at the street door.

She wasn't aware of being afraid, or even apprehensive. So much had happened to her recently that she sometimes felt all emotion was dead. She opened the door a crack and said dully, 'Yes?'

'I have need of the apothecary,' said a low-pitched male voice. Lily was aware of a bulky silhouette, above average height, made taller by the battered top hat.

'The apothecary has gone,' Lily replied.

'But this is Raynor's Apothecary? Raynor's Pharmacy, as it became?'

'It was,' she corrected. 'My grandparents are dead, as is my aunt, and the pharmacy is no more.' She had given too much away by letting him know of her blood connection to the erstwhile apothecaries and, suddenly defensive, she clutched at the door. 'I am unable to help you.'

But the low voice said urgently, 'A young woman – a girl – lies on my boat and she is in labour. I have done what I can for her but something is gravely amiss.'

Something in Lily shrivelled away as if it had been scorched with acid. She had turned her back on nursing, put that life behind her; and, of all things, obstetrics and the care of women in their reproductive role was the very thing she could not bear to think about.

'I'm sorry,' she said. 'As I said, I cannot help you. You must find someone else.' She closed the door.

But it stopped about five inches from the jam, because the low-voiced man's foot in its big boot was in the gap. 'I believe you can,' he said. *How did he know?* 'If you don't come she may very well die. If you have the skill and yet you do not try to help, will you be able to live with that?'

You have no idea what I'm already living with, she thought.

But she didn't think she could bear to add to those burdens.

With a curt, 'Wait there,' she rushed into the room that had once housed the shop counter and, from the very bottom of the corner cupboard where she thought she had hidden it away for ever, took out her medical bag. She grabbed a cloak, put the door key on its chain around her neck and followed the man into the night.

He led the way out of Hob's Court and turned right towards the river. Then right again, past the ends of rows of houses and on beyond the patch of waste ground, on the far side of which was a basin in which the river and canal boats moored. He strode on to the last boat, and she had an impression of a long, low craft, its foredeck shrouded in tarpaulin and the living quarters at the stern. A lantern shone from a tall post and in its soft light she saw that there was a name written in cursive script beneath the gunwale: *The Dawning of the Day*. He jumped aboard, held out a hand to help her, then opened the hatch and led her below.

She had heard the screams as they hurried along the quay. Now, in this small but, she noticed, extremely clean and well-arranged space, the sound was deafening. Two young men stood awkwardly against the far wall of the cabin, their expressions saying very clearly that they wished they were anywhere but there. On the single bed along the opposite wall lay a girl.

And girl was right, Lily thought as she approached, for the straining, sweating, grossly swollen figure could have been no more than fifteen and perhaps less.

The big man said right in her ear, 'It is not my child.'

Lily nodded. She turned to him, and seeing him properly in the lamplight and without his hat, she saw short brown hair, deep eyes, good features and a beard in which his teeth looked very white. 'I am Tamáz Edey,' he added.

'Lily Raynor,' she replied. Then, turning with her eyes and all of her attention to her patient, she said quite firmly to the girl, 'Now, I want you to stop screaming and together we shall calm your breathing, make you a little more comfortable and then, when you are ready, you will talk to me.' The girl stared up at her wide-eyed, mouth open. But the screaming had stopped.

Lily propped her up, straightened her body out of its grotesque twisting and laid her straight. Then she said over her shoulder, 'Please ask the young men to leave.'

The bearded man – Tamáz – muttered some soft words and the two youngsters fled up the steps and away. Tamáz had begun to climb after them but Lily said, 'No, not you, for I shall need you.'

'Very well,' he said calmly.

'I require water,' Lily said, 'and a wash cloth.'

Tamáz fetched a basin of warm water – there was a kettle on top of the stove – and handed her a piece of flannel. Like everything else in the cabin, it was clean. It smelt faintly of lavender and herbs.

'Now,' Lily said to the girl in a matter-of-fact tone, 'I am going to examine you.' The girl shrank away, but Lily went on, 'I am sorry but I have to see what is happening with the baby, for quite soon you will feel the need to push – you will, my love,' she added, for the girl was frantically shaking her head – 'it's nature's way and cannot be gainsaid. My job is to make sure that your body is sufficiently open for this pushing to begin.'

She wasn't sure the girl understood but she had no option, for the contractions were coming quickly now and birth was surely close.

Swiftly she sponged the girl's face, pushed back the sweat-soaked hair, and wiped her neck and throat. She wanted this first touch to be of a less intimate nature than what she must do next, and even as she ministered to her patient, she felt her relax a little. Then she said gently, 'Now, bend your knees and let your legs drop apart. Yes, good, very good, that's right! I'm going to look inside you.'

She acted as she spoke and found that, as she had thought, the girl's cervix was well dilated. 'Very good,' she repeated cheerfully, 'I don't think it will be too long now, and you're doing splendidly.'

But as she withdrew her fingers she touched something that surely shouldn't have been there: a raised line of scarred flesh . . .

Questions flew into her mind and she began to suspect what had happened. But she put it aside, for the girl was pleading for her help and needed all her skill and concentration.

After a short while Lily said to Tamáz, 'You need to put water on to boil. Oh, and have you a knife?'

Looking slightly surprised, he reached behind him and drew from his belt a twelve-inch knife with a broad, wicked-looking blade. 'This?'

'Good God, have you nothing smaller?' she hissed. 'It's to cut the cord!'

She caught a brief flash of white teeth amid the heavy beard as Tamáz grinned. 'I will find something,' he said. She heard him refilling the kettle and returning it to the stove, then rummaging in a drawer. He held up for her approval what looked like a small vegetable knife.

'Perfect,' she said. 'When the water's boiling hard, put the knife in it and leave it there for several minutes.' He nodded.

Lily knew some time before the baby emerged that it must surely be dead.

Labour continued for a while without very much progress, then, as sometimes happened, suddenly the contractions merged into one long contraction, the girl drew her legs right up to her chest, clenched her teeth, then screamed and yelled a curse, and the baby's head crowned. Calling instructions – 'Stop pushing till I tell you' – 'Now. *Now!*' – Lily eased out the bulge of the head, turned the shoulders, and the rest of the still little body followed. The baby – it was a boy – was grey-blue and lifeless and lay like a perfect little statue between the girl's thighs. Then a gush of blood burst from her, showering the tiny corpse.

Tamáz, right behind her, said some soft, quiet words that sounded like a prayer. 'Is there nothing you can do?' he whispered, his mouth so close to her ear that his beard tickled her.

'Nothing,' she whispered back. Tamáz handed her the knife, its handle wrapped in a piece of cloth against the heat, and she cut the cord. 'This little boy has been dead for some time.'

Her hands flew as she tried to stem the haemorrhage. Tamáz, understanding, said, 'I will take him. Do not worry,' he added, 'I will care for him.'

She stood back briefly and he reached down and took the body from the bed.

Lily returned to the girl.

Some time later, she became aware of soft singing.

She stood up – she had slumped onto the other, wider bed at the rear of the cabin, half-concealed by a curtain – and was taking a short rest, for her back was aching. The girl was asleep. Lily had delivered the afterbirth, checked that it was entire and managed to stem the bleeding. She had washed the girl, told her gently that the baby had died and done what she could to comfort her. She had dressed her in a clean nightshirt – a man's garment, very obviously, and a large man at that – and removed the blood-soaked sheets. Then she helped her to lie down, drew up the blankets and, with a deep sigh, the girl closed her eyes. Within moments, the deep, regular breathing told its own story.

Now, intrigued by the singing, Lily got up and very quietly climbed the short flight of steps to the deck.

Tamáz Edey was pacing slowly up and down on a patch of shingly beach that was gradually being taken by the last few inches of the incoming tide. The tiny shape of the dead baby was cradled in his strong arms. Noticing for the first time, Lily saw that, despite the chill of the night, he wore no coat or jacket but merely a shirt with its sleeves rolled up, beneath a waistcoat. His breeches were tucked into boots very similar to her own.

The baby's little body was wrapped snugly in one of the soft cloths that Lily had brought with her. Its head lay against Tamáz's heart. She recognized the song now; he was singing the child a lullaby.

She couldn't look away and, as she watched, he reached down and selected a large, round stone. He slipped it inside the shroud, wrapping a fold of cloth round it and tying it firmly. The singing went on. Then, slowly, gracefully, he crouched down and laid the infant in the rising water. He supported its small weight for quite a long time, then, as all but imperceptibly the tide turned, gradually lowered his hands until the body sank. She hadn't realized, but there must be deep water just beyond the narrow stretch of beach, for the pale shape of the wrapped body swiftly dropped down and out of sight.

Tamáz straightened and stood up. He had tears streaming down his face. He walked slowly back to his boat and, coming aboard and noticing her eyes on him, nodded. 'I have given him to the water,' he said.

She stayed with Tamáz and the girl for the rest of the night, checking on her patient regularly to make sure she wasn't bleeding again, comforting her once or twice when she woke and cried.

Then, towards dawn, noticing her rubbing at her back, Tamáz said to Lily, 'Go back and lie in my crib for a while. I will watch.'

She realized, from the direction in which he was nodding, that he was referring to the larger bed, behind its curtain. 'Are you sure?'

'Yes.'

Very gratefully she crept onto the bed, and he drew up a soft woollen blanket to cover her. The pillow under her cheek was rough linen, and it too smelt of lavender and herbs. The pain in her back eased and she slipped into a doze.

When she opened her eyes, dawn was beginning to lighten the eastern sky. She pushed back the blanket and sat up. Tamáz, coming to sit on the edge of the bed, handed her a mug of tea, and she didn't think she'd ever tasted anything more welcome.

'Is she still asleep?' she asked, nodding at the girl.

'Yes.' Moving closer, dropping his voice to a soft whisper, he said, 'I will tell you about her. She is from Ireland, and she is of the kin of my paternal grandmother, although we are but distantly related and, until very recently, had never met. She was raped by one of her father's good friends and when she managed to tell her mother what had happened, and that she thought she had been damaged inside, she was not believed. Her father accused her of having lain with some village lad and told her she would be sent to the laundries. You understand about the laundries?'

'I do,' Lily murmured, for she knew and abhorred the system by which young girls in repressively Catholic Ireland who were sometimes pregnant outside marriage, sometimes guilty of no more than being lively and flirtatious, were dispatched to the Magdalene Laundries where, under the stern eyes of nuns, they worked, sometimes for years, and where, if they had been sent there pregnant, they gave birth and had their babies taken away from them.

'You will understand, then, why Maeve preferred to run away,' Tamáz said.

Maeve, Lily thought, her name is Maeve. In all the drama and the fierce emotion of the night, she hadn't thought to ask. 'Of course I do,' she said.

'She stole money and paid her fare to Liverpool,' Tamáz went on, 'and there she managed to contact a cousin who had also run away, some years back, and who now like me lives on a boat. The cousin wanted to help but her man refused to allow it, it seems because he carries the fear of the priesthood with him yet and will not go against what has been deemed to be right. Maeve, he said, was a fallen woman and he'd have no truck with her and her bastard.' He sighed. 'The woman – Maeve's cousin – is my friend, as well as also being a distant relation of mine. She asked me to take Maeve with me, for her man was threatening to write home and tell the family she was here. So I did.' He sighed again, rubbing his hand through his beard. 'That was two months ago, and she's been with us on the *Dawning* ever since.'

After quite a long time Lily said, 'What will happen to her now?'

'Now, with no illegitimate child to hamper her, she will return to her cousin, who has promised to find a position for her. In service,' he added. 'The cousin has done the same for other young relations who have made their way to England from Ireland. She'll be all right,' he assured her.

'Will she?' Lily said bleakly.

'Yes,' he replied very firmly. 'Can you not see that any life is better than what she would have had? To be in service will seem like freedom to her, in comparison.'

'Yet it's not freedom,' she said.

He looked at her for some time. 'Which of us is free?' he asked softly.

Later he saw her home.

He stood with her outside her house. It was early still, and nobody was about. 'Lily Raynor. Lillibullero,' he said quietly, smiling down her.

'What did you say?'

His smile broadened. 'Lillibullero. It's the name of an ancient Irish song.'

She turned, reaching for her door key. He caught hold of her hand, detaining her, and dropped a soft kiss on her cheek. 'Goodbye, Lily Raynor,' he said. 'Until we meet again.'

Then he turned and strode away, and the white mist of an autumn morning that was rising off the water soon swallowed him up.

She has seen Tamáz twice since then. The first time was heralded by the arrival of a letter, with her name and address written in a very beautiful hand which looked like a work of art. The letter said:

> *I have news of Maeve and if you would like to know how she does, I shall be moored in the boat basin tomorrow evening.*

It was signed, as she knew even as she had looked down at that stylish handwriting, Tamáz.

The month was January, and it was a cold night. Something warned Lily against leaving for her assignation via the front door of 3, Hob's Court, although she could not have said what it was. Not for fear of the Little Ballerina, newly installed as her lodger, overseeing her movements; for she was at the theatre and would be until after midnight. She wrapped herself warmly, went through the house to the rear door, locking it behind her, stepped hurriedly down the garden and, unfastening the heavy padlock, went into the shed at the far end. The shed was very large, running the width of the narrow garden, and her grandparents had used it for the preparation of remedies. Accordingly, it was very secure: the rear door, opening into a narrow little passage that ran along between the back of Hob's Court and a muddle of old sheds and warehouses on the river, not only had a lock and bolts top and bottom, but had also been fitted with two heavy wooden planks that slotted into iron brackets set into the wall on either side.

Lily let herself out, re-locked the door and, as quiet and unnoticed as a shadow, slipped along the passage and towards the riverside.

Tamáz was waiting for her at the end of the passage.

She gave a shocked little cry. 'How did you know I was on my way?'

'I guessed.' She couldn't make out his features very well in the dim light, but she knew from his voice that he was smiling. 'Thank you for coming,' he went on. 'The stove is warm on the *Dawning*, so we'll go there.'

Then they were back on his boat, drinking hot tea, cosy, and so comfortable with each other that it was as if she had known him all her life.

He told her his news.

'Maeve has recovered well. She has put her experience from her mind, and she is working hard to make a success of her new life. Her cousin was as good as her word, and found her a position as a scullery maid in a fine house in the countryside to the north of Manchester. Maeve has written to say that she has made friends, that her employees are good people, that those who have charge of her days are adequately kind to her and, to begin with, were reasonably tolerant of her ignorance of their ways.' He looked up, as if he had sensed the protest that Lily would utter. 'Yes, I know,' he murmured, 'but it's as good a life as very many people have or aspire to, a great deal better than many.'

He was right. Lily bowed her head and kept her silence.

After quite a long pause, Tamáz said very softly, 'What did you discover when you were tending her?'

Her head shot up. She was very surprised that he had noticed. But then, because he was who he was, she wasn't. 'She was in my care,' she demurred. 'The bond between nurse and patient is sacrosanct.'

'Yes. But you and I are already complicit, and you know that what is said here remains between us.'

She *did* know.

'There was an injury, fairly recent, suggesting very strongly that she had tried to procure an abortion.'

He nodded, as if he had suspected it. 'Fairly recent, you said?'

'Yes. If Maeve had hoped to bring about a relatively pain-less slipping of the products of conception, she was wrong.'

'She knew nothing,' Tamáz said. 'She was ignorant of the facts of life, of how birth happens, of the workings of the human body. When her father's friend raped her she had no idea what he was doing, and when afterwards she found her own blood on her body, she believed he had punctured her innards. Those were her very words.'

Lily said after a moment, 'Then she probably does not mourn the death of her baby.'

But he said, 'Oh yes, she does.'

And then there seemed nothing more to say.

Presently he took her back to the passage, and the door into the shed, and once again he bade her goodbye and kissed her cheek.

The second time she saw him after their initial meeting was at the end of March, on the date of what she later learned was the spring equinox. Then she was alerted to his presence because she saw him.

Or, more accurately, she heard him. She thought she could hear music, coming from the riverside. Summoned by something so strong that it was irresistible she went to her bedroom window, at the back up on the top floor, and stared out. It was night, and she could see soft lights, shadows. She knew one of the shadows was his.

Hurrying out through the back garden and the door into the passage, she ran all the way to the riverside, and there they were, twenty, thirty people, men, women, children, circling round a fire that burned bright and cheerful, dancing to the music played by two men and a woman on fiddle, squeezebox and banjo, twirling, twisting, now linking hands, now dancing alone. She watched for a while, her smile spreading across her face, and after a time – as if he'd been giving her the chance to understand the steps – Tamáz emerged from the darkness, took her hand and led her into the dance.

She had no idea how long she was there. Sometimes the pace slowed, and he took her in his arms in a waltz, holding her so close that, like the poor, dead baby boy, her head was held to his heart. That night, when he saw her back to her door, he whispered, 'Goodnight, cushla macree.'

Or that was what it sounded like.

*   *   *

Now it is Tamáz that Lily must speak to.

Tamáz, with his strange mixture of forebears and his early life with the Irish boatmen and women who took him in for love of his late paternal grandmother the Irish matriarch, is the man to ask about messages from beyond, for without ever having asked, she is quite sure he is well versed in the ways of the spirit world.

Now, on this night of fear after her first seance, Lily goes home and waits for him to find her.

She is watching from her bedroom window and she sees his dark shape in the alley behind the house. She hurries down, grabbing her shawl, and emerges through the shed. He nods to her in greeting and they walk together back to *The Dawning of the Day*. He tells her to sit down and he makes tea. Then he says, 'You have felt a strong emotion this night. Fear, I think, and deep, deep sorrow.'

'Yes,' she says.

She tells him about the seance. About the extraordinary way that Albertina picked up on the death of her father. She also admits to the very strong sense of menace that she felt.

He lets her talk without interruption, and it takes some time. When she has finished, he sits in thought for a further time.

'Did she describe your father's death accurately, in the precise way that it happened?' he asks eventually.

'I don't know how it happened, not in any detail,' she replies. 'Nobody would tell me. They said I would be too upset, which was incomprehensible because I couldn't possibly have been more upset than I was.' She takes a steadying breath. 'But she – Albertina – described it in just the way I see it in my imagination.'

He nods slowly, a faint smile on his lips, as if she has just confirmed something.

After a long silence, he says, 'I cannot say for sure what is the truth of it. I do not believe that those we love are able to contact us after death, for all that a clever and skilled medium may try to convince us of it. Yet I too have experienced the inexplicable.'

She feels the very faintest brush of dread, and sees again

that image of spreading black mould. But he says swiftly, 'There is nothing to fear, Lily, not here and now.' He pauses again, then says, 'I believe there may be a way in which men and women communicate without speech. It usually occurs only where there is great love, and it is perhaps the love that opens the channel.' He pauses again. 'This I have experienced for myself. Once I wished to ask my grandmother a question, and when next I saw her, she told me the answer before I had spoken. Another time, I knew when a boy I was close to as a child had been in an accident and I went to find him.'

She nods. She knows there's no use asking for more details because he won't give them. Tamáz is a man who only tells you things when he is ready.

He sighs, turns his inner eye from whatever events in his history he has been contemplating and says, 'If you wish me to give an opinion, Lily, then I will tell you only this: that I believe all of us carry the major events of our past with us for the rest of our lives, and that there are some people who are able to look into our minds and pick up these memories.'

She murmurs, 'Yes.' It makes sense to her.

'And the woman who saw the image of your father falling to his death was able to perceive it not because of a message from the other side, but because *you* had it in your mind, as you always do.'

She does. He is quite right. She mutters, 'Yes,' again, more softly.

'You say you felt a threat? A menace?' he goes on.

'Yes.'

'And you will, I assume, be returning to this place?'

'Yes.'

He nods. He doesn't try to dissuade her. He reaches inside his waistcoat and shirt and extracts something on a long silver chain, lifting the chain over his head and holding the object out to her. It is a little bottle, about the length of a forefinger, and some two fingers in breadth. It appears to contain nails, pieces of wire . . . One long nail, several shorter ones, some barbs, a coil of wire sharpened to a point.

'This is a witch's bottle,' he says very softly. 'My grand-mother Mary Bridey made it for me when I was small and afraid of the night walkers of the Fenlands. It keeps all harm away.' He puts the bottle on its silver chain – both still warm from his body – over her head.

She touches the little bottle cautiously. 'Don't you need it?'

He smiles. 'I no longer fear the night walkers. Besides, just now I believe that the darkness is more of a threat to you.' He puts his big, warm hand around hers, closing hers tightly around the bottle. 'Stay safe, cushla.'

SEVEN

Felix decides quite soon upon arriving in Tunbridge Wells that he rather likes the town. He follows a sign to the left-luggage office, situated across a bridge and on the 'up' line, and deposits his small overnight bag. Then he re-crosses the bridge and walks out of the railway station, where he sees the road climb up a steep hill to his left. In the opposite direction, this same road curves round to the right, slightly downhill, and the High Street branches off it. Felix goes back inside the station and asks the station master how to find the Dippers' Steps Theatre.

'Ah, now, you want to make your way to the Parade!' the station master exclaims with such abundant cheerfulness that it's as if Felix's request is precisely what has been lacking to make his day. 'You go straight down the High Street – that's over there, where it says High Street – then cross the road at the end and go into Chapel Place. Don't you turn right or left, mind!' Felix assures him that he won't. 'Then at the far end of Chapel Place you'll go round the back of King Charles the Martyr's chapel – that was Charles the First, the one what had his head cut off – and go straight across the road, and the Parade will be just in front of you. You'll find the Dippers' Steps Theatre on your right, and a pretty little place it is too!'

Felix thanks him and sets off.

The High Street is busy with Thursday morning shoppers, strollers, delivery boys and gossips, and there is a pleasant buzz of activity. Felix crosses Chapel Place, having remembered not to deviate to right or left, then hurries over another busy road, and he finds himself in the Parade.

The Dippers' Steps Theatre is just where the station master said it would be, and it is equally as pretty as he promised. Intrigued by the name, Felix stops to read a notice set in the wall beside a recessed space – a sort of well – where reddish-coloured water bubbles up. The notice informs him that if he wishes to take the waters, a Dipper will be in attendance between the hours of 2 and 5pm every Tuesday and Friday. There is a further sign that urges him to do so, the waters from the chalybeate spring being extremely beneficial in the treatment of a wide array of ailments. Looking at this water, Felix is quite glad that today is Thursday.

He turns his attention to the theatre. The entrance is framed by two elegant pillars at the top of a short flight of shallow steps. The walls are painted white and the roof is made of small red tiles. There are framed posters to right and left of the doors, one advertising the present production and one next week's offering. The taste of the citizenry of Tunbridge Wells appears to be for light melodrama.

He runs up the steps and tries the door, which opens. He can hear sounds of activity from within: loud voices from the auditorium, straight ahead – or perhaps, he thinks, that should be *well-projected* voices, for these surely are members of the company rehearsing the next production. To the left is the ticket office, at present unoccupied, and to the right a little passage leads off into darkness. Felix follows it and presently comes to the open door of an incredibly busy-looking office. At second glance he realizes that in fact there's only one occupant, shouting at someone invisible who is apparently somewhere further along the passage, and that the impression of busyness has come about because the office is filled to bursting with papers, books, files, a vast desk, too many chairs, a battered chaise-longue and a large rubber plant.

'You'll just have to tell them if it's not here by tomorrow morning I'll place the order elsewhere. What can I do for you?'

Since the man in the office has only marginally decreased the volume for the last six words, Felix does not immediately realize that these are addressed to him. He steps into the office, smiles, extends his hand and says, 'My name's Felix Wilbraham, I'm trying to compile a full account of the career of Violetta da Rosa, and I understand that this wonderful theatre is one of her favourites and that she has often appeared here?'

The combination of earnest admiration of the actress and

overt flattery of the theatre seems to work. The man shakes the proffered hand and then, puffing out his chest and sticking his thumbs in his braces, says, 'Oh, you've come to the right place if you want to know about our beloved Violetta.'

A tray of tea is commanded, Felix is offered a seat and even as he sits down and takes out his notebook and pencil, the man – who has introduced himself as Clement Smith and who tells Felix with only a hint of pride that he is the manager – is already rummaging in an overflowing cupboard for details of the history of Violetta da Rosa's long association with the Dippers' Steps Theatre.

An hour and a quarter later, his right hand cramping, Felix is once more outside in the sunshine.

He finds a bench and sits down, considering his next move. Clement Smith has given him a full – an *over*-full – account of all the roles Violetta has performed in his theatre, as well as sheaves of newspaper and magazine clippings with very favourable reviews, but this is only a part of what Felix is after. Yes, he now has a picture of when, and for how long, Violetta has been in the town for each professional engagement, but his instincts are shouting out to him that there is more to it than this.

'What I require,' he says softly to himself, 'is one of those gossips I saw in the High Street earlier; one whose favourite subject is the private lives of actors and actresses, and one actress in particular.'

He sits there for some time. He hears voices from inside the theatre – a woman calls out 'I'm off then, Perce,' and Perce answers, 'See you on Monday, Beryl!' – and then the door is flung open and the woman emerges. She is around the late forties, early fifties, she is dressed in a clean but mended gown of dark blue Lindsay wool and a particularly unflattering hat, her hands are red and chapped and over her arm she carries a large and bulging cloth bag.

A cleaner? A dresser? A sempstress? Felix is on the point of jumping up, repeating his story of preparing an account of Violetta's professional life and asking if she can provide any information, but the woman turns and shoots him a very suspicious look. Perceiving that if he approaches her she is more than likely to reply belligerently, 'Who wants to know?' he decides he will need a change of tactic.

He bends his head and pretends to be absorbed in the contents of his notebook. He hears her footsteps as she draws level, and just then a voice calls out from the open doorway of the theatre, 'Beryl! *Beryl!* You forgot these!'

Surreptitiously glancing up, Felix sees the figure of a small, bald man in a very large and much-pocketed apron standing on the steps of the Dippers' Steps Theatre, a huge bunch of spring flowers over one arm. With a tut, Beryl turns and hurries back just as he trots towards her.

'Thanks, Perce. I'd forget my own head if it was loose,' she says.

'Madam coming down, then?' Perce enquires in a low voice.

'No,' Beryl replies shortly. Perce sends a very obvious glance in the direction of the flowers, his sparse eyebrows raised in question. 'Someone left them for her, didn't they?' Beryl says. 'People – men – are always doing that, as well as baskets of fruit and what-have-you, and what I always say is, given what they must spend on their offerings, you think they'd have the sense to make sure she was going to be here to appreciate them. Missed her by half a day, this latest devoted fan did. She nipped down late Tuesday but was off again first thing Wednesday. She's rehearsing,' she adds.

'So you're taking them home for Florrie, then?' Perce says, nodding towards the flowers. Beryl shoots him a narrow-eyed glance. 'Shame to waste them, eh?' he says.

Beryl turns smartly on her heel. 'Goodbye, Perce,' she says with a clear air of finality.

She strides away. Felix, hurriedly putting away his notebook, sees her disappear round the corner, in the direction of Chapel Place.

It is distinctly possible, he decides, that *Madam* may very well be Violetta da Rosa; it's surely worth following up on this unexpected lead. If she is, he thinks as he gets up to follow in Beryl's footsteps, then who on earth is Florrie?

Felix is well versed in the art of tracking people without their noticing him. It is the result of a life lived among quite a lot of risks and hazards. To begin with, the bustling streets of Tunbridge Wells make his task easy, and he trails his quarry along the High Street and up the hill on the far side of the railway station without incident. All goes well, in fact, until the woman – Beryl – clears the congested areas and sets off at quite a lick along a road leading out of the town. It goes along between pleasant parkland and what looks like the estate of a wealthy landowner, and Felix is obliged to hang back some way to avoid being spotted. Pausing in the shade of a huge lime tree, he sees the woman come to a sharp bend in the road, where she turns to her left. Waiting until she is out of sight, he breaks into a run.

He reaches the corner and turns into a narrow lane. The sign at the corner reads Marlpits Lane. The woman is now some fifty yards ahead, but now she is slowing her steps and turning off down a path towards one of the group of eight or ten farm cottages on the left of the lane. Cautiously Felix goes after her, hurrying on a few paces beyond the path and crossing the lane to conceal himself in the shade of the big oak tree growing in the hedge.

A girl of perhaps thirteen or fourteen comes out to meet her, exclaiming with delight as she sees the flowers. The two of them greet each other with a brief hug. The older woman's stern expression has softened, and she reaches up her rough red hand and gently touches the girl's smooth, dark hair. She hands over the flowers, and makes some remark that makes the girl laugh. They exchange a few more words. They are clearly close but Felix does not believe they are mother and daughter. Their body shapes are totally different – the older woman is sturdy, narrow-shouldered and not very tall whereas the girl is willowy with a width to her shoulders and a depth to her chest that promise a fine figure – and besides he already has an idea about the girl's identity.

A woman pokes her head out of the door of the neighbouring house. 'It was looking like rain earlier, Mrs Twort, so I fetched your washing in, what with you and Florrie both being at work.'

The woman – whose name Felix now knows to be Beryl Twort; what a wonderful name, he thinks – turns to give her neighbour a cool glance and nods her thanks.

From the brief exchange Felix detects that the neighbour is an interfering gossip who can't keep her nose out of other people's business, and that Beryl Twort knows this and does what she can to block her at every turn. Both of which, he reflects, could perhaps also be applied to Perce.

Now the girl – Florrie – turns towards the door of their own cottage and for a moment Felix can see her face very clearly. She is so very like Violetta da Rosa that there can surely be little doubt that she is her daughter.

He slips deeper into the shadow of the oak tree. When he hears the door of Beryl Twort's cottage close, he emerges and walks away.

Back in the centre of the town, he finds a tea room and orders a pot of tea and a ham sandwich. It is now mid-afternoon and he forgot to have any lunch. He opens his notebook and sits thinking.

If he is right in his approximation of her age, Florrie was born around 1866 or 1867. It is perfectly possible that Violetta became pregnant outside matrimony, and indeed as far as Felix knows there has never been any mention of a husband. (It is also perfectly possible that he's quite wrong about Florrie being her daughter, but he has to start somewhere, and if he forces himself to forget that fascinating hypothesis, he's not quite sure where else to begin.) But supposing Violetta did marry? Supposing she had a lover in this appealing town where she comes so often to perform, and supposing she became pregnant and told him he had to marry her? Perhaps he was longing to do so, and it was she, the beautiful and adored actress with the burgeoning career, who didn't want to marry and only did so to avoid the stigma and the shame of an illegitimate child.

With some reluctance, for while he is not at all sure how to go about it he's quite certain it'll mean an awful lot of work, Felix accepts what his next task must be.

He begins with the town churches. That takes him the rest of the day, and he is still turning the pages of well-thumbed ledgers with grumpy clerics waiting for him to finish when darkness falls. He finds a cheap commercial hotel tucked away behind the railway station which, apart from persistent snoring from the room next door and a very indifferent breakfast, he finds adequate; he has most assuredly experienced far worse. Resuming his hunt, he realizes that the task – which may well be futile – is going to take a long time, so he goes to the telegraph office and sends a wire to Lily requesting permission to stay until Sunday. After a brief wait, her approval arrives.

He spends all Friday tramping from church to church, gradually widening the circle whose centre is in the middle of the town. He knows full well that he is probably wasting his time and Lily's money, but having begun he feels there is no option but to go on.

On Saturday he begins tramping out to the nearby settlements; the villages that are large enough to have a church. His feet are very sore by the time he goes to bed. On Sunday morning he sets out for the next church on his list, in a small village called Frant that lies on the road going south out of the town. If his blisters weren't so sore he would have enjoyed the walk, for the countryside is beautiful and the air tastes delicious. There is little traffic on the road: a couple of carts, a fine carriage and pair, a man on a bay who tips his hat to Felix as he passes, considerately riding around a puddle so as not to splash him.

The church in the small village is full of Sunday worshippers when he arrives, so he finds a very old grave in a far corner of the churchyard, sits down on it and removes his boots and his hose. Instantly he wishes he hadn't, for the largest blister on his left foot has burst and the fine wool of his hose is soaked with fluid and blood. He cools his feet in the long grass, listening to the sound of the congregation singing hymns and the vicar's penetrating voice leading them in the prayers. Presently the organist begins on a very accomplished voluntary, and, guessing this heralds the end of the service, Felix puts his hose and his boots back on and stands up.

It takes some time for the worshippers to disperse, for their minister appears to be a friendly soul and he has a word or two to say to almost everyone. At last the church has emptied and the last of the congregation has gone. Felix approaches the vicar as he turns to go back inside his church.

'Good morning!' he says brightly. The vicar, a man in his sixties with a round, cheerful face and a coronet of fluffy white hair surrounding a bald pate, turns with a politely enquiring expression and returns the greeting. 'You're the vicar?'

'In fact I am the rector,' the man responds.

Felix is uncertain of the distinction, but he mutters an apology.

'I'm sorry to bother you when I'm sure your well-earned meal awaits you,' Felix goes on – he suspects the minister likes his food, for there is a large bulge of belly beneath the snowy surplice – 'but I wonder if I might have a look through your parish records?'

The rector looks startled. 'We don't usually have people wishing to do so on a Sunday,' he says with mild reproof.

'Yes, I do understand, and I appreciate it's not really right,' Felix replies earnestly. 'I wouldn't ask, except I have to return to London this evening and my employer will not like it at all if I have not completed my researches and am forced to return to the area.' He smiles ruefully, as if to say, you know how it is.

The rector nods, as if he does indeed know all about the vagaries of unreasonable employers. 'Well, I suppose it wouldn't hurt . . .' he begins.

Pretending he thinks this is unqualified approval, Felix says gushingly, 'Oh, thank you! How kind you are. Lead the way!'

With one last dubious look, the rector does as he's told.

Some ten minutes later, Felix is alone in the vestry, one fat book of records open on a small table in front of him and the remainder – in an ancient and vast oak cupboard whose five shelves are absolutely crammed with leather-bound volumes – at his disposal. The rector has obeyed the urgings not to let his dinner get cold, and has said he will return later to lock up.

Felix sets his pocket watch on the table beside the first ledger. He has an idea he is going to strike lucky, and he is interested in how long it's going to take.

Fifty-five minutes later, he finds what he is looking for.

In late September 1866, in this church, Violet Ross, spinster of the parish, married Archibald Twort, bachelor.

Flipping the pages with manic speed, Felix comes to April 1867, when a baby girl named Florence Violet Twort was baptized.

He sits quite still for some time.

He is almost sorry that his ruthless searching has succeeded. He's pleased for Lily's sake, of course, and for his own, for she must surely be impressed by his hard work and his dedication, not to mention his blistered feet.

But he can't help regretting that he has winkled out Violetta's secret. He can't help liking her, and if she's prepared to take on a life of boredom with her childlike little lordling for the sake of luxury and security, then he almost admires her.

He returns to the two entries, carefully copying all the details into his notebook. Then he closes the book, puts it back in its place on the shelf, shuts and locks the cupboard and emerges from the vestry into the church. There's no sign of the rector, so he makes his way to the rectory, situated almost next to the church behind a sign usefully saying *The Rectory*, and taps at the door.

The rector answers his knock still chewing and with a drop of custard on his chin.

'I've finished,' Felix says with a smile, holding up the keys. 'I've locked up the cupboard but you said you would see to the vestry door.'

The rector swallows, taking the keys. 'You were very quick,' he observes. 'Did you find what you were looking for?'

'I did,' Felix says with a sigh.

The rector looks intrigued. 'I was about to make a pot of tea,' he says. 'I always have one after luncheon. Will you come in and take a cup?'

Thinking of the long walk back into the town on his blistered feet, Felix says honestly, 'There's nothing I'd like more.'

'I suppose,' says the rector as he carefully sets down the tea tray, 'I should have asked you your business with my parish records before I let you loose upon them.' There is a faint note of inquisition in his tone. 'But I confess I was hungry and looking forward to my roast, and I did not,' he adds disarmingly. 'Let me introduce myself: Pilbury, Arnold Pilbury.'

'Felix Wilbraham.' Felix rises to take the rector's hand. He sits down again very carefully, for Arnold Pilbury has just placed a very delicate bone-china teacup and saucer down on a very insubstantial-looking little table. He is wondering how much he should reveal about his business, and the answer pops into his head: as little as possible.

'I needed to look up a marriage record,' he says. He reaches in his pocket and takes out one of the World's End Bureau's cards, which he hands over.

The rector stares at it for some moments. 'Private enquiry,' he says softly. 'That's usually divorce cases, isn't it?' He looks straight at Felix out of candid blue eyes. He hasn't voiced his disapproval but nevertheless Felix feels it.

'Sometimes,' he says. 'It's also lost dogs and cats, the placing of blame for crimes such as small degrees of theft in the place where it belongs and occasionally –' he thinks of the Stibbins case – 'trying to find out who is distressing a young woman by threatening her.'

Arnold Pilbury nods. 'I see. And your present investigation?'

Sensing that he's going to have to be rather more open, Felix says, 'I was looking into the records for the name of Violetta da Rosa, possibly connected with a man by the name of Twort, and I found Violet Ross. Who was married to Archibald Twort in your church in September 1866.'

The rector leans back in his wing chair and expels a gusty sigh. 'It was I who conducted the service,' he says. His expression is sad, perhaps even a little guilty. 'Poor Violet.'

Wondering if this unexpected reaction is because Violetta – Violet – was pregnant at the time of the marriage and possibly it was apparent, Felix says, 'There was a child, a daughter.'

'Florence, yes I know,' Arnold Pilbury says. 'A delightful girl, or young woman now, I suppose.'

'She's thirteen,' Felix says.

'Ah.'

'She doesn't live with her mother,' Felix observes.

'No, indeed,' the rector agrees. Felix waits. 'She's looked after by her great-aunt, the widow of her grandfather's younger brother.' Felix does his best to commit this to memory, for it doesn't seem the moment to take out his notebook and jot it down. 'I say looked after,' Arnold Pilbury is saying, 'but in truth I sense that nowadays they look after one another, for Beryl Twort does not enjoy the best of health and Florence is now also working.'

'What does she do?'

The rector shoots him a glance. 'She works in the brickworks up the road from Beryl Twort's house,' he says expressionlessly. If, like Felix, he is thinking it's a hard life for such a beautiful young girl with a famous actress for a mother, he refrains from saying so.

But Felix is desperate to know. Instead of a direct question, he remarks instead, 'Just now you said *poor* Violet.'

It is Arnold Pilbury's turn to look as if he's deciding how much he can reveal. After a short silence he nods to himself, as if in response to some privately posed question, and mutters, 'It is all in the records, anyway.' Then he looks up, meets Felix's eyes once more and says, 'Archie Twort was already married.'

Poor Violet indeed, thinks Felix.

He waits.

'Archie Twort was a conscienceless man,' Arnold Pilbury pronounces eventually. 'He was handsome, charming, and he had a way with the fair sex. He was a local man but he went away to sea when he was young, and his family heard not a word from him for years. He'd been in the Royal Navy, the rumours said, and at some point his disregard for rules and regulations must have caught up with him, for the story goes that he was dismissed. He returned to the area, which was when he met Violet – Violetta, I suppose I should say – when she was appearing in a delightful little comedy at the Dippers' Steps Theatre. Do you know it?'

'I do,' Felix says.

'He swept her off her feet, as the saying goes, and there must have been intimacy between them, for when they came to see me to ask me to marry them Violet admitted that she was expecting a child.'

'I do not believe that anybody in her professional life knows of Florence's existence, nor that Violet is married.'

'In fact she is *not* married,' the rector corrects him gently, 'for, with Archie already wed, the marriage is bigamous and thus invalid.'

Felix sits back, trying to work out the ramifications of this. He wonders if Violetta is aware of her true marital state. He's about to ask when Arnold Pilbury says, 'She came down here, of course, for her confinement. She had always got on well with Beryl Twort, who of course is her aunt by marriage, only of course she isn't.' He smiles sadly.

So that is how Violetta has kept her secret, Felix thinks. And also, he supposes, why she keeps returning to the town to perform in a pretty but surely not very important little theatre. Because this is where her daughter lives.

Her beautiful thirteen-year-old daughter, who labours in a brickworks. Oh, Violetta, he thinks, was there not something better you could have come up with for her? Once again, his heart is struck with pity. This time, it's for both mother and daughter.

Silence falls. There is a post prandial sense of torpor, and Felix guesses that the Reverend Mr Pilbury is keen for his unexpected guest to go so that he can slump into his Sunday afternoon nap.

Felix puts his empty cup back on the tray and stands up. 'Thank you very much, sir, for the information and for the very welcome cup of tea,' he says.

The rector looks up at him. 'I expect,' he says with surprising shrewdness, 'that Violet is wishing to marry, and that is why you have come chasing after my parish records.'

Felix doesn't answer, which is a way of agreeing.

'Well, there is nothing to prevent her,' Arnold Pilbury goes on. 'Unless, of course,' he adds with a smile, 'she has taken another husband in the meantime. I would think that unlikely, however –' his expression is sombre again – 'for she truly loved Archie Twort, and I believe it broke her heart when she found out he had deceived her.'

'So she knows?' Felix says.

The rector nods. 'Oh, yes. The first wife tracked him down and came looking for him. He fled,' he concludes succinctly.

'I see,' murmurs Felix.

'Yes, that was the last we saw of Archie Twort,' the rector says as he escorts him to the door. 'I heard a rumour that he is dead – killed in a fight up in Birmingham, or it could have been Manchester . . . Liverpool! It was Liverpool.' He nods.

Felix thanks him again and steps outside. Just as he is about to walk away, Arnold Pilbury calls him back. 'She is more sinned against than sinner,' he says softly. 'She has suffered, and it would be nice to think she might now find some happiness.'

Felix meets his concerned eyes. 'Rather how I feel too,' he says.

Then he tips his hat and strides away.

EIGHT

It is Monday morning, very early. Lily wakes soon after dawn, and out of consideration for the Little Ballerina – would that such consideration were reciprocated – she moves very soft-footedly around her top-floor rooms as she washes and dresses, conscious of her tenant on the floor below and aware that this tenant didn't get home until the small hours.

Monday is a Mrs Clapper day and washday to boot, and there will be steam, wet clothing and constant activity out in the little brick outhouse where the copper is. Mrs Clapper will still undoubtedly find the time to make something tasty for Lily's midday meal. Lily has tried to persuade her to include Felix in her reckoning, and there are the first signs that Mrs Clapper's fortifications may be beginning to crumble a little. She said grudgingly to Lily only last week as she set about preparing a steamed pudding, 'Suppose he doesn't turn his nose up at belly pork,' which was definitely promising.

But it is too soon even for the early bird Mrs Clapper to be here yet, and, if you ignore the Little Ballerina (easy to do when she's asleep, for she sleeps very soundly for hours at a time; no doubt being a ballet dancer is extremely draining), Lily has the house to herself.

She sits at her desk reading through her notes on the seance. She is secretly impressed by Felix's smart black book and his note-taking habit and has made up her mind to emulate it. Now she has a list of those who attended Circle at the Stibbins house, and a neat diagram indicating where they all sat. She has recorded as well as she can everything that was said, and to whom.

Now she tries to describe the sense of menace, but as she writes the hesitant words she realizes with dismay that she doesn't seem to have been watching the one person whose reaction to it she should have observed the most closely:

Albertina Stibbins. She is cross with herself. She has already planned to return on Tuesday – tomorrow – and she makes a firm resolve not to allow herself to be distracted, whatever happens, but to keep her focus firmly on Albertina.

As she makes one or two further notes on what she intends to do next – she believes she should find out more about Albertina's background, for example – she discovers how much she is looking forward to going over it all with Felix. And he, she thinks with a definite lift of the spirits, will be bursting to tell her how he got on in Tunbridge Wells, and exactly what it was that necessitated staying in the town for the best part of four days.

She glances at her watch. It is a small gold half-hunter, and belonged to her Aunt Eliza. It's rather a mannish item, and Lily, like Eliza before her, wears it on a long chain around her neck. She is often tempted to purchase a waistcoat with pockets and a suitably placed button on which to secure the larger link in the chain, but possibly her work attire is quite unfeminine enough already. She goes through into the outer office, for it is a little after eight fifteen and Felix will be here any minute.

The next minute, as it turns out.

The outer door is flung open, she hears his tread in the hall – his footfalls slightly uneven – and then there he is, the vivid colour in his face and the bright shine in his eyes suggesting he has been hurrying. She is taken aback by how pleased she is to see him.

He opens his mouth to speak but she says, 'Sit down, for you look a little out of breath. The kettle has only just boiled, so I will not be long making tea.'

As she glides out of the office she catches a brief glimpse of his crestfallen expression, and instantly wonders if he thinks she was being overly repressive. If so, she regrets it.

Returning with two mugs of tea, she says, 'Come through into my office and pull up a chair. Now,' she goes on when he has done so, 'I would like you to tell me everything you have discovered.' She sits down opposite him and smiles. He looks quite surprised – perhaps she doesn't smile often enough – but recovers, takes a sip of his tea and takes out his notebook. Then he tells her.

*   *   *

Some time later, as she absorbs the details of Violetta da Rosa's private past, Lily is struck by how hard Felix has worked. He has revealed how he walked round what seems like an endless list of churches in and around Tunbridge Wells, and now she understands his odd gait: she guesses he has rather sore feet.

After a few moments' reflection, she says, 'So she became pregnant out of wedlock by this Archie Twort, but married him in plenty of time to make their daughter legitimate. Only, of course, she did no such thing, the marriage not being valid because he already had a wife.'

'Yes, but she didn't know!' Felix protests.

'I appreciate that.' She smiles at him. She is impressed by his championship of Violetta. Such a forgiving attitude is rare in men, in Lily's experience. 'She was a victim of Archie Twort's deception, of course she was, but our job is not to apportion blame.' He opens his mouth as if to protest but she talks over him. 'Mr Wilbraham, we have been employed by her young suitor's father to determine what sort of a woman she is; in short, whether she is fit to be the wife of a man who will one day inherit a title, considerable wealth and several estates. Our job is to relate the facts to the man who is paying us to find them out, and I very much doubt that he will appreciate our marginal comments and footnotes explaining why Violetta acted as she did and why this does not detract from her good character.'

Felix has a rebellious look in his eyes. 'What sort of a woman she is,' he repeats. 'Your very words. She has suffered by another's dishonesty, and in all innocence borne an illegitimate child, who she has hidden in that little cottage on the outskirts of the town. She visits her daughter as often as she can, and presumably, since Florence works in the brickworks and her great-aunt is a laundress and seamstress in a very small theatre, she supports the household. Surely that all speaks in her favour and suggests she is a fine woman!'

Lily, moved by his passion, nods. 'I quite agree,' she says gently. 'But then I am not Lord Berwick.'

He begins to say something but then, as if her words and her tone have only just penetrated to his brain, he stops. 'I do not wish to stab her in the back,' he says mutinously.

'No, and I applaud your sentiments,' she replies. 'But we are in business as investigators. If we allow our own strong emotional responses to colour our conclusions, if we gain a reputation for being anything but totally impartial, it will not be long before word spreads and the World's End Bureau will have failed before it has had a chance to succeed.'

'So what are we to do?' he demands.

'We do what we must always do. We tell the truth, hold nothing back, and leave the facts to speak for themselves.'

He bows his head, and she thinks he has accepted her judgement. After a short silence he stands up, gives her a sort of bow and says, 'Then I shall draft my report.'

'Before you do,' she replies quickly, 'I would like to talk to you about what I found out in the Stibbins household.'

He looks down at her. 'You want to share it with me?' Me and my strong emotional responses, hangs unspoken between them.

'I do,' she says.

He draws in a breath and sits down again, and she relates to him almost all of what happened at the seance. She tells him what Albertina said to her, but she doesn't reveal that the vision of the falling man described precisely how Lily saw her father's death. She isn't sure why she holds this back, but she finds she cannot confide it to him.

He has been busy with his notebook and pencil while she has been speaking. She had thought perhaps he was doodling, but when she finishes speaking he waits for a few moments and then says, 'So, Leonard Carter is in love with her, old Mrs Sullivan depends on her providing a link to her beloved late husband in order to go on with life, and the Sutherland father and son have some distressing mystery to sort out for which they need help from beyond the grave, which they believe she can relay to them, and we have no idea as to the nature of Mr Haverford's reasons for attending.'

'Er – yes,' she says. It is a succinct but essentially accurate summation. 'I should add that there are others who were not there yesterday but whom I observed on Thursday. There was a young woman dressed in unrelieved black and two middle-aged women whose resemblance to each other suggests they are sisters.'

He makes some more notes. 'And you felt that another entity was in the room,' he says very softly, 'one that you could not see but from which you felt a strong sense of menace.'

'Yes,' she whispers.

He looks straight at her. 'Of course you'll be going back,' he says tonelessly. Then, a fleeting expression too swift to read crossing his face, he says, 'Be careful, Miss Raynor.'

It is the second time somebody has cautioned her that she needs to take care.

Not wishing to dwell on this, she says hurriedly, 'I believe that our next step is to discover all that we can about these regular Circle members, for our first hypothesis must surely be that Albertina's strong sense of being threatened originates in one of them.' She stares out across the office, frowning. 'I know Ernest Stibbins told you it was her spirit guides who were warning her of the danger, and that this meant the peril could emanate from anyone anywhere, but—'

'But we have to begin somewhere,' Felix, writing again, is nodding. 'Yes, I agree.'

'At the same time,' she goes on, feeling a definite sense of pleasurable satisfaction that he sees it the same way, 'I believe it is necessary to look into Albertina's background. She came to London from St Albans on the death of her parents, so that seems a good place to begin.'

Again he nods, but this time doesn't speak.

Lily waits until his pencil is still. Then she says, 'I would like you to pursue the enquiries here, because—'

Once again he leaps in. 'Because they think you're Miss Maud Garrett and we need them to go on thinking it,' he says. 'Furthermore, it was I to whom Ernest Stibbins first spoke, and by now he's probably expecting some sort of a report from me.' His face eager, he adds, 'He'll be at work but I'll go this evening, shall I?'

'Yes.'

There is a moment of silence. Then he says, 'What do I tell him when he asks Mr Raynor what progress he has made?'

She smiles briefly. 'I suggest you mention that there are

several areas of enquiry but you don't want to reveal them as yet because if and when any of them turn out to be invalid, you prefer not to have cast suspicion where there was no need.'

He nods again. 'Yes. I like that.' He makes another note. 'Then I go through all the regular Circle members – I'll just describe them and wait for them to provide names to fit, since it'd be stretching my abilities a little if I had somehow managed to find out all the identities – and ask them to tell me what they know about each one.' He glances up and meets her eyes. 'Do you think they'll be forthcoming, or will some sort of professional confidentiality apply?'

'I don't know,' she replies honestly. 'If they are reluctant, you'll simply have to remind them what's at stake.'

'Albertina's safety,' he says softly. 'Yes. I'll do that.'

'And I think I shall go to St Albans,' she goes on. 'I cannot see how it can possibly get back to Ernest or Albertina that I have done so, her kin there being dead.'

He is watching her. 'Do you truly think that some dark shadow of her past is reaching out its malice to do her harm?'

His words give her a sense of alarm, for the image he has unwittingly drawn is far too close to what she has seen. What she thought she saw, she corrects herself. She shakes off the sudden fear and says briskly, 'I have no idea. That is why I am going to do what I can to find out.'

He is getting to his feet, tucking away his notebook. 'Very well,' he says. 'Now, if you'll excuse me, I'm going to get down to work on my preparations for this evening's meeting. I'll need a full description of all the Circle members, in due course, if that's all right?'

'Of course,' she says. 'I will prepare them directly.'

She watches him return to the front office and his own desk. She had been going to go on to say that she is also going to take over the investigation into Violetta da Rosa and her suitability as a wife to Julian, believing as she does that Felix is not being entirely objective in his assessment of the actress. But, although her conscience whispers to her that she's being cowardly, she elects to postpone that command.

*   *   *

Shortly afterwards, leaving Felix studying her list of Circle regulars and working on his preparatory notes, Lily sets off for King's Cross station and a train to St Albans.

The journey takes under an hour, and she arrives in a pleasant town where a helpful woman tells her the way to the cathedral. Noticing its bell tower soaring into the blue sky just as the woman finishes, Lily quite admires the forbearance which held back the comment, 'Use your eyes!'

Lily pauses to look briefly at a noticeboard just inside the entrance, which tells her amongst other things that the Cathedral and Abbey Church of St Alban has the longest nave in England, as well as the saint's shrine and its own Watching Tower above it and some fine medieval paintings.

None of which, interesting facts though they are, has anything to do with the reason for her visit.

She introduces herself to one of the vergers. After a brief exchange of pleasantries and an admiring comment or two from Lily on the longest nave in England, she admits that she has a purpose in coming here. She shows him one of the Bureau's cards, and he raises his eyebrows in an unspoken question.

'I am making enquiries on behalf of a man named Ernest Stibbins,' she says, 'who is anxious about the safety of his wife, Albertina. Now I understand her to be a former member of the cathedral's congregation, and—'

'Albertina!' the verger cries, interrupting her. 'Yes, of course, I do indeed recall that Albertina Goodchild went to London and subsequently was married. One or two of her friends were invited to her wedding, although it was by no means a grand affair.' And then, as if the full portent of her remarks has only just penetrated to his understanding, his expression of polite enquiry turns to one of mild shock and he says, 'But you say her husband fears for her *safety*? My goodness, how frightful! In what way?'

Deciding in an instant that she will learn more from the man if she plays down the danger element, Lily says calmingly, 'I sense it may be no more than a deeply uxorious man worrying about his young wife, but nevertheless these matters should not be lightly dismissed.'

'No indeed!' agrees the verger. Then he takes Lily lightly by the elbow and, escorting her across to a pew, invites her to sit down and settles beside her. 'My name is Pepperson, Francis Pepperson, Miss –' he glances down at the card – 'Miss Raynor. Now, since all of us here hold the Goodchild family in high esteem and would hate to see any harm come to Albertina, please tell me what I can do to help.'

'Albertina has sensed that she is being threatened,' she says, once again maintaining a matter-of-fact tone. 'As far as can be ascertained, she has met with nothing but friendship in her married life. She met her husband, Ernest Stibbins, when she began attending services at St Cyprian's, where—'

Once again the verger interrupts. 'Where young James Jellicote went to take up his first incumbency! Yes, of course, I remember now. He was curate here, you know.'

'So I've been told,' Lily murmurs.

Francis Pepperson smiles. 'Which, of course, is why you are here.' Before she can concur, he says, 'Well, from what I know of Joshua and Grace Goodchild, I can imagine not a single element of their past that could lead to anybody now wishing to threaten Albertina.' He speaks for some time of the little family's fine qualities, and Lily takes it all in.

'Albertina was an only child?' she asks.

'Indeed.'

'And when her parents died, she went to be companion to an elderly relation?'

'Yes, yes, her spinster great-aunt Millicent Snell, sister of her maternal grandmother.'

'Who also died?'

'She did, she did, and we were all rather concerned when the news made its way back to us, meaning as it did that Albertina was all at once quite alone among strangers.' He lowers his eyes. 'Many good intentions were expressed concerning venturing all the way down to London –' he speaks of the city as if it were on far distant shores rather than twenty-five miles away – 'to ensure that Albertina was not about to become homeless and destitute, but sadly good intentions are not deeds, and time elapsed, and then came the welcome news first that she had found her way to St Cyprian's and the guiding hand of James Jellicote, and, soon afterwards, of her pending nuptials.' He raises his head again. 'All's well that ends well, eh, Miss Raynor?' Then, as if recalling her mission, he blushes and adds, 'Except that of course all may not be well.'

Sensing that she has discovered all there is to discover about Albertina from this particular source, Lily stands up and thanks him. As she prepares to depart, she says, as if it is an after-thought, 'You mentioned that some of Albertina's friends had attended her wedding. Would it be possible, do you think, to direct me to them? I would very much like to speak to them.'

It seems to take Francis Pepperson some time to work out whether or not to comply, and while Lily waits, she notices that he seems to be studying her intently, as if trying to look inside her mind. Eventually, apparently not alarmed by what he sees, he says, 'I am sure the two young women in ques-tion would be pleased to speak to someone who has Albertina's welfare at heart,' and provides the information Lily has asked for.

Conveniently for Lily, these two young women both work in a milliner's shop, situated in a little side street some five minutes' walk from the cathedral. The glass-panelled door is set back between two small bow windows, in each of which is a display of bonnets trimmed with flowers, ribbons and feathers. The display on the right is in shades of green, turquoise and blue; that on the left, red, yellow, vermilion and orange. Apart from the fact that there is rather too much of everything, the displays are quite artistic. Two young women are standing behind the counter when Lily walks in, and they interrupt their intense conversation to give her bright smiles.

'I'm afraid I haven't come to buy a hat,' Lily says, returning the smiles.

The faces fall. 'Some ribbon? A feather? We've some lovely peacock feathers in the back, and they're proving very popular, for all that some folks say they're terrible bad luck,' says the plumper of the two girls.

Lily shakes her head. 'I'm not looking to purchase anything,' she says firmly. She extracts another of her cards and puts it on the counter. The smaller girl reads it, her lips moving, then looks up at Lily with bright, interested eyes. 'Private enquiry!' she whispers. 'Coo!'

'It's nothing to be alarmed about,' Lily says calmly, 'merely a small matter concerning a young lady who I'm led to believe is a friend of yours, Albertina Stibbins, née Goodchild. Assuming, that is, that I am right in believing you to be Florence Barton and Rose Jordan?'

They confirm that they are, the plump one being Rose Jordan. Perhaps it is a dull day in the millinery business, but both girls prove to be the perfect informants, chattering away about Albertina as if this is the very thing they've been longing to do since she left St Albans.

It soon becomes clear that they both liked Albertina, although the fulsome way in which they describe her looks, her temperament and her winning ways has, to Lily's alert ears, a very slight touch of spite, and she suspects both young women might have been a little jealous of their popular, and now married, friend. 'Her late parents and she attended services at the cathedral?' Lily prompts when the flurry of comments begins to run dry.

'Yes, that's right, they—' Rose begins.

But, 'That Mr Jellicote what was curate, he really liked her,' Florence interrupts. 'He used to wait behind after choir practice and help her tidy away the scores, and I heard him offer to walk her home more than once, for all that her own father would be waiting outside for her to do that very thing!'

'No, and he was very sorry when he left here and went to be a vicar in London,' adds Rose. 'Word was he didn't really want to go, but vicars and that can't say no, can they?'

'No, I don't suppose they can,' agrees Lily, who really has no idea. 'Still, it was a good thing he had gone to London, wasn't it, when Albertina's great-aunt died and, left alone, she was in dire need of a friend?'

Florence glances at Rose as Lily says *friend*, and both girls snigger. 'Yes, it was, of course it was,' Florence says.

'You went to her wedding, I'm told?' Lily asks.

'Yes, that's right, and he – the curate, only he wasn't, he was the vicar then – did the service,' Rose says. Again the glance between the two young women. 'He's *old*, her husband. Much older than her,' Rose adds.

'But kind, and solicitous; perhaps providing a modicum of security to a woman on her own,' Lily replies, a slight note of reproof in her tone.

The two young women look at her blankly. 'He's still old,' mutters Florence.

On the train back to London, Lily makes up her notes. She has discovered pretty much what she expected to discover from her visit to Albertina's former residence, amounting to a picture of utter respectability. The two young milliners were able to direct her to the house where the Goodchilds lived, and it, too, proved to be much as Lily expected. She has discovered nothing that could constitute a threat to Albertina in her new life in Battersea.

She does, however, write as a footnote: find out about James Jellicote and his feelings for Albertina.

Very soon after Lily's departure, Felix realizes that he has done all he can do on the list of Circle regulars. He has memorized names and descriptions and is confident of knowing which belongs to whom, if necessary. While appreciating that there are not a few useful clerical and general office jobs he could be getting on with, his mind is full of Albertina Stibbins and the danger she may be in and he has not the least enthusiasm for anything else.

He sits quite still for a few moments, then gets up and strides to the bookshelf that he himself arranged during his first weeks (which, he notices in passing, seem an awfully long time ago). Reaching up a hand in exactly the right place, he draws out *Kelly's Directory* for the area.

The directory, comprising as it does the names and street addresses of local businesses, tradesmen, landowners, charitable institutions and other varied information, seems a good place to begin. Assuming, of course, that the people who attend Albertina's Circle are reasonably local . . . He decides he'll worry about that once the intriguing possibilities of Kelly's have been exhausted. He has transcribed Lily's list into alphabetical order, and the first name is Carter, Leonard. Lily describes him as *pale, brown hair and eyes, nervous and twitchy, early twenties, recently lost his mother, lives in lowly digs about half a mile from Parkside Road* (here Lily had included a street name with a question mark), *in full-time work*. If Leonard is renting his modest accommodation, Felix thinks, then his name will not appear as the owner. But Lily had a putative name for the street, Beulah Road, and so Felix looks it up on his map. At least two of the houses in the road appear large enough for multiple occupancy, and he makes a note of their numbers. Not at all sure how, or even if, it will advance him to know where Leonard lives, he moves on.

Next is Haverford, Arthur. *Saturnine complexion, strong handshake*, is all Lily has to say. The directory is considerably more helpful, informing Felix not only of Arthur Haverford's address – in a close just off Battersea Park – but that he is an officer in Her Majesty's Excise. Translating, Felix thinks: reasonably well-off, respectable occupation, lives in a pleasant area. By himself, he notes: Arthur Haverford is the sole occupant of his house.

Whether anything among those facts could possibly lead to his making menacing threats against Albertina remains to be seen.

Next are two names bracketed together, the word 'sisters' written beside the bracket. The first is Hobson, Eileen, Miss, the second Philpott, Agnes, Mrs. Reasoning that a married woman might be the more likely to own her own house, Felix tries the latter first, but soon has to revise his thinking when he discovers that both sisters in fact live in a large house close to the river in the possession of Miss Hobson. Perhaps it is a case of a widowed sister returning to live with the last surviving sibling inhabiting the family home, for the area is prestigious and Felix thinks it unlikely that a spinster would have afforded such a dwelling by her own efforts. Is it at all likely that either of these women – *middle-aged*, according to Lily – has malicious designs upon Albertina?

Malloy, Richenda, Miss, is next, described by Lily as young, perhaps seventeen or eighteen, and dressed in unrelieved black. Flipping through Kelly's pages Felix comes across several households of Malloys, but since without more information he cannot tell which one is home to Richenda, he leaves her and moves on.

Sutherland, George, and Sutherland, Robert are father and son, the son described as *of soldierly bearing*. Lily has added a note to the effect that George has a serious anxiety, concerning which Albertina – or, more correctly, Albertina's guide from the spirit world – advises waiting for time to do its work. Father and son appear to share George Sutherland's house on the Chelsea Embankment, and so far among those on the list have the longest journey to seances in Parkside Road. George is a solicitor with a firm whose name Felix recognizes as being on the King's Road, and Robert, as Lily has perceptively detected, is a soldier. Felix makes a note to ask Lily to try to find out more about this anxiety. On the face of it, Albertina appears to be helping George Sutherland, perhaps his son too, and so why should either of them want to harm her?

Sullivan, Dorothy, Mrs (widow) is the last name. According to Lily, she is elderly, kindly, has recently lost her husband (?) Rodney and misses him sorely, to the extent of not eating. *Much comforted by A*, Lily has noted. Again, thinks Felix as he thumbs through the directory, why would Mrs Sullivan entertain dark and menacing thoughts towards the very person able to give comfort?

He sits back in his chair, frowning. He lets all that he has just learned filter into his mind, for, tonight, he is going to be talking to Albertina herself, and he wants to be as well prepared as it is possible to be.

NINE

Felix waits with some impatience for Lily to return because there is something he urgently wants to raise with her; something, indeed, that he is quite surprised neither of them has mentioned before.

As soon as she is inside the door, even as she is taking off her hat, he says, 'I've been thinking, and I imagine you have too, about this business of Albertina being warned by her spirit guides of the danger to her.' Lily's greenish eyes watch him closely but he can't read their expression. 'I mean, I don't know your feelings on the matter, but I don't believe there is any such thing. As spirit guides, I mean. Voices from beyond the grave. Messages from the dead that imply they are still involved with the living. All that.'

There is quite a long pause, and then – somewhat to his relief – she says, 'I agree with you.' He is just about to express this relief when she adds, 'But I have the advantage over you in that I have sat in that room in the house on Parkside Road, and I have felt a little of what I understand Albertina feels. The menace. The darkness.' She pauses. 'The danger.'

He has always felt there were aspects of the seance that she has not revealed to him. This, however, is a bit of a surprise. 'You didn't say,' he says quietly.

She shakes her head, a small, rueful smile on her wide mouth. 'No, I didn't.' He thinks that is her only comment but then she adds, 'I really didn't know how to. It was so strange. Disturbing. And also she—'

But this time she doesn't go on, and he is left wondering.

After a moment she says, 'I do not, however, believe that this is any reason not to pursue the line upon which we have embarked, by which I mean the backgrounds of the regular Circle members, for it still seems most likely – most logical – that the threat comes from one of them.'

'But—'

'Someone I know said—' She stops and begins again. 'I have heard it said that some people have the ability to pick up the thoughts of others, in particular their most powerful, persistent and emotional memories.' As if she knows full well he is bursting to interrupt, she says quickly, 'I believe it is possible that Albertina has this ability; that she detects what is distressing the members of her Circle, understands their pain and, because she is a good and kind-hearted young woman, tries to assuage it. By dressing up her ability as hearing the voices of her spirit guides, perhaps, unconsciously, she believes her reassurance and comfort will be the more powerful.'

He thinks about this for a moment but does not speak. The words he would have uttered, he realizes, are perhaps a little too forceful in their scepticism. Instead, after a while, he says mildly, 'You may well be right. I shall go to see Mr and Mrs Stibbins this evening with an open mind.'

There is a small and, Felix feels, slightly awkward silence. Fortuitously, she comes up with something to fill it. 'I spoke to two of Albertina's friends today,' she says. He raises his eyebrows in query. 'They were invited to her wedding, and remember her fondly, although they don't envy her her husband, he being much older than her, to quote one of them. They were not able to provide much in the way of useful information, except for the fact that they both believed James Jellicote was sweet on her.'

'On Albertina?' This is unexpected.

'Yes.'

He senses her watching him and he has a fair idea what is going through her mind. It would, he feels, be insulting if she were to tell him not to raise this inappropriately with Mr and Mrs Stibbins when he meets them later, and happily she doesn't.

He makes a note in his book. Then, looking up he says, 'I find it hard to conceive the mild vicar could be having malicious thoughts about her, and, even if he has, then why should they be made manifest to her during the seances, since he doesn't attend them, and not at any other time?'

'But do we know they are not?' she counters.

It's something he hasn't thought of before and, to judge by Lily's expression, neither has she.

He makes another note.

He walks across Battersea Bridge an hour before he is due at the Stibbins house. He wishes to spend this time walking around the neighbourhood, since he finds his mind works better when he can visualize the scene and, so far, he has only been to the vicinity immediately surrounding St Cyprian's Church.

Around the park there is a large residential area, street after intersecting street of houses which in the main are in terraces or sometimes in semi-detached pairs. There is an air of respectability in the majority of these tightly packed streets. However, as so often happens in London, there are also one or two streets of more exclusive dwellings, especially in favoured locations such as facing the cricket ground or the river. And, within a short walk of these, are a few examples of the over-crowded, stinking slums of the poor. Felix stands at the end of one dank, dark court, watching two near-naked children filling a pail from a standpipe at the near end. He counts ten doors opening into the court, whose cobbled surface slopes down to a gully flowing through the middle of it which, from both the sight and the stench, is filled with sundry waste, including animal and human. He can hear raised voices coming from one of the doors: a man's and two women's, and they are far from having a cheery chat about the happenings of the day. There is a crash, a scream and a man comes running out of the door, shouting a stream of obscenities over his shoulder. One of the children at the standpipe – he is, Felix estimates, about six – notices Felix and yells, 'Oi, you, what yer staring at? Fuck off out of it!'

Felix turns and strides away.

He locates Parkside Road, which leads on to St Cyprian's Road, with the church at the junction of the two. He walks on, managing to locate what he thinks must be the cafe to which Lily followed Leonard Carter and also, he believes, the dwelling house where Leonard rents a room. He finds an observation point where he can stand unobserved in the shade of a plane tree and watches this house for some time. He counts two couples, one with a small child, an elderly man, two middle-aged men and an old couple, the man crippled and walking with a stick, going into the house. He wonders how many rooms there are. He hopes the crippled old man lives on the ground floor.

His mind is busy with many thoughts. As the hour of his appointment approaches, deliberately he clears it. Then he turns, walks back to Parkside Road and knocks on the door.

Ernest and Albertina welcome him warmly. He is led into the room to the left of the front door, which is furnished with a small drop-leaf table set against a wall with four chairs pushed under it, a sideboard, a tall cupboard with glass-fronted doors that is sparsely filled with brilliantly patterned plates and a large number of small ornaments on various delicate little tables and tassel-edged shelves. Many of these ornaments have an Egyptian flavour – sphinxes, models of the pyramids, a camel or two, some rather amateurish framed watercolours depicting gods and goddesses – and there is a book on the table about the Egyptian deities. 'My little hobby,' says Ernest Stibbins, noticing Felix looking. 'My beloved wife would say it is closer to being an obsession,' he adds with a smile, 'but the world of those ancient people was such a vibrant and colourful one, was it not?' Felix agrees that it was.

Ernest picks up an object, box-like with three compartments. It has the ghostly shapes of old painted illustrations on its sides. 'This is a shabti box,' he says. He holds it in delicate hands as if it is very precious. 'Empty now, sadly, but once it would have held little statues of a dead person's servants, to ensure he or she was as well looked after in death as in life.' He sighs, a rueful smile on his face. 'It was sold to me as genuinely old, but I think it is not very likely that it is.'

Felix nods, mentally altering *not very likely* to *totally unlikely*. He feels a stab of pity for Ernest, who is carefully replacing the box on its shelf. Felix resumes his scrutiny. In addition to the many ornaments, and making the modestly proportioned room appear even more cramped, some tea chests stand stacked against the wall behind the door.

'We are a little short of space,' Albertina says, waving an apologetic hand around the room. 'But quite soon that will cease to be the case, for my husband has agreed to carry out some much-needed alterations downstairs, which will make a great deal more room and enable us finally to sort ourselves out.'

Ernest Stibbins gives his young wife the sort of kindly and indulgent smile that husbands tend to bestow when they believe they are being magnanimous in the extreme by acceding to their wives' more extravagant requests. He says meekly, 'That's quite right, dear.'

Felix is invited to sit down in a wing chair beside the empty grate. Ernest sits opposite in the chair's pair and Albertina, after pouring tea for all of them and handing round a plate of biscuits, sits on a low stool at her husband's side. From Lily's description, Felix knows this is not the room in which the seances are held. Somewhat to his surprise, he is quite relieved.

After a few courteous remarks about the weather – 'Warm for the time of year,' opines Ernest, which probably explains the lack of a fire – Felix puts down his cup and saucer, takes his notebook and pencil from his pocket and says, 'Now, I should like you to tell me the names of everyone who regularly attends your meetings, Mrs Stibbins, and, if you feel it is not betraying their confidence, something of the reasons why they need your help.'

Not wanting either of them to notice his already extensive notes on the seance regulars, he has turned to a clean page.

Albertina has leaned close to Ernest, and they are having a whispered conversation. Felix tries not to listen. After several exchanges, Ernest says more loudly, 'But, my dear, we have asked for Mr Raynor's help, and I do feel we must try to comply with his request! Besides, are not our friends as concerned as I that you might be in danger?'

Slowly Albertina nods.

Then, turning to Felix, she begins to speak.

Half an hour later, Felix has learned quite a lot that he didn't know. It is indeed her late husband whom 'Dear Mrs Sullivan' wishes so fervently to hear from, since she is very anxious that she may not have done enough to ease his sufferings in the last days and weeks of life and desperately wants reassurance that she did. Mentally Felix crosses Dorothy Sullivan off the list of suspects, it clearly being vitally important to her to keep Albertina alive. And reassuring. Miss Hobson and her widowed sister attend from largely mercenary reasons, believing as they do that their late father had private means not discovered at his death. These include a savings account with an unknown bank and a jewellery box that he is supposed to have hidden somewhere in the large house in which the sisters live. Since it is clearly in their interest to keep Albertina alive and fully functioning until the dead father has made contact via the spirit guides and informed his daughters of all that they wish to know, it seems very unlikely that either of them are responsible for menacing her either.

Miss Richenda Malloy is interesting.

'She sings soprano in the choir at St Cyprian's,' Ernest supplies. 'She sang a beautiful solo at Easter, didn't she, my love?' Albertina nods. Ernest rests his eyes upon his wife for a moment, eyebrows raised, and she gives another little nod. This appears to be one of permission, for, leaning closer, Ernest says, 'Dear Richenda is, we believe, a little sweet upon James. James Jellicote. Our vicar,' he adds.

'Really?' Felix tries to inject the right amount of interest into his voice, so as to appear somewhere between coolly disinterested and pruriently fascinated. It's quite a wide spectrum, and he feels he has done all right.

'Oh, yes.' Ernest smiles. 'Now this has at times proved a little awkward, since, although my modest wife would not dream of mentioning it, I as her husband feel able to reveal that James Jellicote was in fact more than a little sweet on *her* before I was lucky enough to make her my wife!' He leans back, his smile widening, as if to say, what do you think of that?

Felix, who already knows this, makes suitably astonished noises and makes another note. As he writes he listens to Albertina, muttering in an undertone to her husband. He looks up, meeting her anxious eyes, and notices a soft and becoming flush on her cheeks.

'Mr Stibbins exaggerates,' she says, 'for Mr Jellicote was

always the perfect gentleman. While it is true that he was courteous, considerate and kindly, he was no more so towards me than to any of the other young women of our acquaintance. Truly!' The blush intensifies, and Felix, murmuring that he quite understands, remembers the quotation about the lady protesting too much.

Her small moment of embarrassment over, Albertina next speaks of 'poor young Leonard' who misses his mother so acutely – Ernest smiles to himself as she speaks – and of George and Robert Sutherland, the soldier son so dutiful in his attempts to help his father overcome the memories of 'something very distressing' that happened in his past.

'Now this is a matter upon which my wife really cannot be as frank as she might wish,' Ernest interjects, 'for George Sutherland is a professional man, and client confidentiality is involved.' He nods solemnly.

'I understand,' Felix says. He makes a note to try to find out if the senior Mr Sutherland's firm of solicitors has been involved in some dreadful case, and then listens as Albertina begins to speak again.

Arthur Haverford, it appears, is a bit of a mystery. He has been attending for nearly a year, yet no clue has been given as to why he comes, nor whether or not he is finding solace in the sessions. Felix draws a large question mark beside the name. Albertina then speaks of several others but, just as he is about to ask her to repeat the names more slowly and tell him something about each one, she says, 'But none of them attend Circle very often, and I have the strongest sense that the . . . the you-know-what –' her face has paled and it seems she can't bring herself to mention the menace by name – 'must surely emanate from somebody closer to me. I don't know any of these irregulars, not like I know the regulars,' she adds plaintively, 'so why should they wish me harm?'

Felix makes a brief note, then, looking up, once again meets Albertina's big, frightened eyes. 'Why indeed,' he says gently, smiling at her and receiving a very faint but still lovely smile in return.

'And lastly there is the newcomer, Miss Maud Garrett, who was introduced by our faithful Leonard Carter,' Albertina says after a moment to recover herself. Once again Ernest, at this second mention of Leonard's name, gives his gentle smile and says teasingly to his wife, 'Your young swain, my dear,' to which comment Albertina blushes prettily and shakes her head in modest denial. 'But since Miss Garrett has only just joined us,' she resumes, 'and the – er, the *threat* has been apparent for some time now, I do not believe she can have anything whatever to do with it.'

Felix is relieved to hear this.

He makes one or two more notes, but they are unnecessary and he is merely playing for time. The moment has come, and he must ask Albertina the question which is at the root of this visit: at the root, perhaps, of the entire investigation.

He says, 'Mrs Stibbins, I appreciate that this will not be easy for you and I regret causing you distress, but please will you tell me just how it is that you perceive this sense of threat?'

She flinches. Her husband, aware of this for all that it is a tiny movement, puts a hand on her shoulder and she reaches up her own hand to take hold of it. Then she sits up a little straighter and says, 'I see blackness, Mr Raynor. It is as if a pall of thick black tar, or something like it, is slowly drawn down over me, over my face, my body. I sense chill, desolation, desperate loneliness, a sort of dank, ancient breath. I see myself lying alone on cold stone, and in some strange way that I do not begin to understand I am both alive yet dead. It is as if—' But the horror overcomes her, and she can't go on. Her face falls, tears fill her eyes and she turns in mute distress to her husband. He wraps her in his arms, one hand gently patting her shoulder while he whispers soft reassurances.

Felix waits for a while, then, as she appears to gather herself together and sits up straight again, says, 'Mrs Stibbins, please forgive me. It was not my wish to cause you such anguish.'

She dries her eyes and gives him a brave smile. 'I realize that, Mr Raynor.' She pauses, then goes on in a small voice, 'Did it help?'

He has no idea if it helped or nor. But, since he would not have her suffer for nothing, he says stoutly, 'Oh, yes, indeed it did.'

*   *   *

The following morning, Lily and Felix sit in her inner office, either side of her desk. Lily has asked him to join her in order that together they may review the Stibbins case. And decide what on earth to do next concerning Violetta da Rosa and Julian, she adds silently to herself.

Felix has made tea for them and now sits with an expectant look on his face, his notebook open. Realizing that it is up to her to begin the proceedings, Lily says, 'In the light of your conversation with Albertina and Ernest yesterday evening, I believe we now should go through the list of Circle regulars and decide which of them, if any, could be behind the threat to Albertina.'

Surprisingly he doesn't instantly begin. Instead he looks at her with almost an abashed expression and, after a moment, says, 'I do truly believe there is a threat. Whether it comes via her spirit guide is altogether a different matter, but the poor woman is genuinely afraid. She sees a thick pall of darkness, and herself lying on something made of cold stone that sounds horribly like a sarcophagus.'

Lily does not even try to speak, for she knows that, just now, she is incapable. For what Felix has just described echoed far too closely what she herself felt as she walked past the Stibbins house and saw Albertina reach up to draw the curtains. The heavy black veil descending, the icy chill.

Felix has picked up that something is wrong. He leans forward, his face concerned. 'What is it?'

She is clutching Tamáz's little bottle, concealed on its long chain under her shirt and her mannish waistcoat. She forces her hand to unclench and release it.

'I experienced something similar,' she says, trying to affect nonchalance.

Unsuccessfully, it seems, for he is on his feet and round on her side of the desk. He picks up her teacup, holding it to her lips. This is silly! she thinks, and takes it from him, nodding her thanks. He resumes his seat.

'Sorry,' he says gruffly. 'You went so pale I thought you were about to faint.'

'I don't faint,' she says repressively.

'So, this similar experience,' he ploughs on. 'Was it at the seance? Was it the thing you're not telling me?'

'Not at the seance, no.' Deliberately she doesn't answer his second question. 'It was after I had been to observe the house on the Thursday.' She tells him what she experienced.

'Very similar to what Albertina described,' he murmurs. Then: 'Do you think you were picking it up from her? In the way you mentioned the other day, whereby some people are able to listen in to what's at the forefront of others' minds?'

But Lily can only shrug. 'I have no idea.'

There is silence for a while. Then he says quietly, 'Shall we proceed with the list of names?'

Some time later they have finished. Felix has returned to his own desk and Lily is staring down at her notes. They have eliminated Mrs Sullivan, Miss Henshaw and Mrs Philpott, for now at least, and provisionally done the same for the Sutherland father and son, although Felix says he will see if he can find out what this disturbing professional matter could have been. Their list of Circle members with a question mark beside their names comprises Richenda Malloy (on the somewhat slim grounds that she resents Albertina because the man of her dreams, James Jellicote, is sweet on her), Arthur Haverford (because nobody seems to have a clue what he is doing attending the seances) and Leonard Carter.

Lily reflects that it came as a surprise to both herself and Felix when the other did not rule Leonard out. Lily, who has the advantage of having met and talked to the young man, is uneasy purely because *he* is so uneasy, with his twitches, his stammer, his pallor and his viciously bitten nails. Felix, when she asked him his reasons for suspicion, said succinctly, 'If he's in love with Albertina, he's under the sway of a very powerful emotion. And she's married.'

Lily does not entirely understand why these two factors should make Leonard wish to menace and terrify the object of his love. But then Felix is a man and she isn't, so, for now anyway she is prepared to take his word for it.

She hears Felix get to his feet. He comes to stand in the doorway. 'I'm off to the *King's Road Chronicle and Gazette*'s office,' he announces. It is their local newspaper. 'I'm going

to browse through their back numbers searching for the name
of Spencer, Caldicot and Brown, which is—'

'The firm of solicitors where George Sutherland is engaged,'
she finishes for him, just to show she's digested his notes.

He nods. 'See you later.'

He doesn't ask what she will be doing, which she
appreciates because, for one thing, she is his employer and
not answerable to him and, for another, she's planning to see
if she can do a little surveillance of her own on Violetta da
Rosa and she's not going to tell him.

TEN

S he waits until he has gone and then realizes that she can't remember the name of the theatre where Violetta is currently rehearsing. It is written down in Felix's notebook, which is in his inside pocket and by now probably a hundred yards up the road.

She glances across at the filing cabinet, still shining with newness. She recalls telling Felix at the start of their association that one of his duties would be to transcribe notes taken whilst in the field – she was rather pleased with the term – into the files that would be kept on each client, but she is quite sure that she has kept him much too busy for him to be anywhere near up to date. Nevertheless, she walks across to the cabinet and opens the lower, N to Z, drawer. There is no file in the R section. She checks the upper drawer and under D, finds Da Rosa, Violetta.

The cardboard file contains quite a lot of papers. Somehow, Felix has found the time to write out every single thing he has discovered. Her reaction to this discovery is complex, and she does not want to stop and investigate it (in no small part because she is already feeling guilty that she's not paying him nearly enough). She finds what she needs: it is the Glass Slipper Theatre, the play is called *Miss Sanderson's Fortune*, and Violetta plays the part of an innocent young heiress who, unsuspecting of her good fortune, occupies herself helping the poor. Lily copies out the bare bones of this and, putting on her hat and picking up her bag, sets out.

She has been worrying, all the way to Drury Lane, how she will gain admittance to the Glass Slipper Theatre. In the event, it is ridiculously easy, for, observing a sweating man trying to open the double doors whilst bearing a large armchair, she hurries to hold the left-hand door open for him. 'Thanks, miss,' he pants, 'this chair's a right heavy bugger, and they're all pissing their pants in there because it's needed for this afternoon's rehearsal.'

'Wouldn't it be easier to take it through the stage door?' she asks, trying to sound like a theatre professional.

He shakes his head. 'Tried that. Won't go through, it's too wide.' He gives the chair, which he has set down while he recovers his breath, a look of sheer hatred. Then, picking it up again, he says, 'Ah, well, no rest for the wicked!', gives her a grin and staggers away.

There are two women having an argument in the box office, which is to Lily's right and opposite the doorway through which the man and the armchair have just disappeared. They are too intent on hurling thinly veiled abuse at each other to take any notice of Lily, so she walks purposefully across the foyer and through the large doors marked 'STALLS'. Inside the lights are quite subdued, so she waits a moment to let her eyes adjust. Then she strides down the left-hand aisle until she is some twenty rows from the front, and takes a seat near the end of the row. She takes out her notebook and pencil, having already spotted that most of the fifteen or so other people sitting in front of her are busy scribbling.

She lets her heartbeat slow down, then studies these other people. In the second row and immediately in front of the stage – brightly lit, occupied by two young men and an older woman and a set that looks as if it's meant to be the dwelling of someone quite poor – sits a fat, bald-headed man in shirt-sleeves and scarlet braces. He has two people sitting on each side of him, and periodically he leans over to speak to one of the quartet, an action which is followed by a furious flurry of scribbling. He is, Lily concludes, in charge, so he's probably the director. Or is it the producer? She doesn't know. Felix would, she thinks. It's quite an annoying thought.

Presently another actor enters from the left. It is Violetta, and she strides to the front of the stage, where there is a bundle of rags presumably meant to be a baby; Lily discerns this because it's lying in a cot. Violetta lifts up the pretend infant, clasps it dramatically to her breast and instantly begins declaiming forcefully and, Lily admits, quite movingly to the auditorium, the gist of her long speech being that life is pretty unfair and rotten and something must be done to alleviate a situation in which the rich are far too rich and the poor far too poor. It isn't exactly Shakespeare, but Lily can see how it would go down well with an audience, provided, of course, none of them were hugely wealthy, in which case they would probably resent the slur.

Violetta has finished, and she has replaced the baby in its cot. She wipes away a tear or two, and there is an embrace with a downtrodden-looking young woman, presumably the infant's mother. The scene winds to its conclusion, and the director calls, 'That's enough, we'll stop it there. Polly, not bad but you need to move to your right a shade because Violetta's blocking you half the time and we need to see your face when she's talking. Violetta, lovely.' But in case his leading lady runs away with the idea that there's no more work to do on the scene, he adds, 'A few small points, but they can wait till this evening.'

Violetta gives him a curt nod and strides offstage.

Lily notices a movement down on her right, where, a couple of rows in front of her, a fair-haired young man has been watching entranced, gazing down at the stage and sitting right on the edge of his seat, his folded arms resting on the back of the one on front. He looks so like a small child at his first pantomime that Lily has already decided this must be Julian Willoughby. 'Little Jack Horner, she calls him,' Lily murmurs to herself. Now that she has seen him, she can see why.

She goes on studying him. Now he is staring intently at a door to the right of the stage through which, after some ten or fifteen minutes, Violetta da Rosa appears. She looks out at the rows of stalls, and instantly Julian stands up and silently waves his arms in huge windmilling circles. If he had thought that he wouldn't distract the ongoing rehearsal as long as he didn't speak, he is clearly wrong, since the two actors going through a tense piece of dialogue both notice the arm-waving and stop to stare out into the dimly lit auditorium.

'Tell that silly arse 'ole to sit down,' comes an all too audible growl from the direction of the second row. Even from where she is sitting, Lily can see the hot blush of embarrassment flow up the young man's long, thin neck and across his smooth cheeks. She feels a stab of pity.

Violetta is hurrying to join her young man, making sit-down gestures as she edges along the row and settles beside him. 'Sorry, oh, sorry!' he whispers, catching hold of her hands and bending over them. 'I keep forgetting I have to be still as well as quiet, but it's all so thrilling, and, my darling, you're *so good*!'

Violetta murmurs something, her words cut off because Julian has grabbed her by the shoulders and is kissing her passionately. She breaks away after a moment, and Lily hears her gentle reproof: 'Not here, sweetie! Wait until later.'

Julian emits a sort of groan.

'Actually,' Violetta goes on, keeping her voice down and shooting glances towards the fat bald man, 'I won't be able to see you this evening after all, my love, as I have to go out of town and I won't be back until late.'

There is a short silence. Then in a hoarse whisper Julian says, his hurt and distress very evident in his voice, 'Where are you going? Can't I come with you? You should let me escort you, you know darling, especially if you're going to be out till late. I could have Father's carriage again, and we could—'

Violetta puts a long, beautifully manicured finger to his lips, stopping the spill of eager words. '*Sssh!*' The fat man has shot them an angry glare. 'Now we've been through all this before, haven't we?' she murmurs gently. 'You have my word that I will not work as hard as I do now once we're married, but for now, you have agreed that I must be free to pursue my career as I think fit.' There is a subtle but unmissable stress on the last *I*.

'But I want to be with you,' Julian says sulkily.

'I know.' Is there a hint of weariness in the two short words? 'Provided it all works out as you've planned, you will be.'

There is a brief, laden silence. 'You are involved in the planning too, Violetta,' Julian says. 'Are you trying to say that—'

But once again she stops him, for she, like Lily, must have sensed the potential danger in the words he was surely about to say. This time, it is her own lips rather than her finger that she puts to his mouth. 'Hush, sweetheart,' she whispers as she draws back. 'Let's just wait and see, shall we?'

'But—' he begins. She shoots a look at him, and he stops. Then, after a pause, he says, 'May I meet you after rehearsals tomorrow?'

He has spoken with quiet dignity, and Lily admires him for it. So, it seems, does Violetta, for she says warmly, 'Yes, that would be lovely.'

As if he knows when it's wise to stop pushing, Julian gets up, gives her a formal little bow and leaves.

Violetta goes on sitting exactly where she is. So does Lily. After about a quarter of an hour, and during the rehearsal of a particularly noisy fight scene on stage, someone else comes to take up Julian's abandoned seat. He is big, broad, dark-haired and dark-complexioned, and he gives the impression that his shoulders are too wide for his coat. Lily is in no doubt that this is Billy.

Without a word, without even looking up to verify his identity, Violetta leans her head on his shoulder. It is the familiar intimacy of this gesture that tells Lily they are very old acquaintances and probably lovers of long standing.

'All right?' Billy says quietly after a while.

'Suppose so,' Violetta replies. She sounds downcast.

'Little Jack Horner still acting like a twelve-year-old?'

'Yes. He can't help it, Billy, it's the way they all are.'

'The wealthy and the sons of privilege, you mean?' Billy says. 'The class who have it all provided for them from birth onwards?'

'He hasn't been provided with much love,' Violetta murmurs.

'Don't give me that!' Billy protests in an angry whisper. 'That mother of his dotes on him. You've told me yourself she can't say no to his requests, no matter how extravagant and outlandish!'

'Yes, that's true,' Violetta agrees. 'But she doesn't know, never has done, how to be his mother; how to guide him, how to let him know she's always there, supporting him, watching him. *Loving* him.'

'So that's what you're going to be, is it?' Billy asks sadly. 'His mother?' She doesn't answer. 'You're not going to let him fuck you whenever he feels like it, then, I suppose?' There is a harsh edge to his voice now.

'I am. I do,' she admits. She too sounds sad.

As if wringing this confession from her is too much for them both, Billy falls silent.

After a while she says, 'I'm going to see Florrie tonight. Want to come?'

And, putting his arm round her and drawing her close, he says, 'Course I do.'

Felix strides along the King's Road – so called, he has discovered, because until 1830 it was reserved for the use of the sovereign, and later for a privileged few of his favoured friends and cronies who were issued with special metal tickets – until he reaches the offices of the *King's Road Chronicle and Gazette*. There is a small reception area with an office leading off it, and the door to this office stands open. A further door, ajar, appears to lead to more offices, from which there is the sound of male voices. A woman sits very straight-backed at a desk in the office with the open door and she looks disapprovingly at Felix as, with a smile on his face, he approaches.

'Yes?' she demands.

Felix's smile fades in the face of her disapproval. She is about fifty, he estimates, tall, very skinny, her face yellowish and her teeth even more so. Her sparse silver-grey hair is drawn back and up into a ruthless little topknot on the crown of her head, and behind the small spectacles her eyes are pale brown. Her small, thin-lipped mouth is surrounded with deep lines radiating out like the spokes of a wheel. Felix is irresist-ibly reminded of a cat's anus. 'What do you want?' she snaps, as Felix doesn't speak.

'I would like to look through your newspaper's back numbers, please,' he says pleasantly.

The woman glares at him. 'Which ones? They are very numerous, you know.'

He suppresses a sigh. 'I am looking for a news item which may or may not have been covered in the *King's Road Chronicle and Gazette*, and I don't know when it was. Shall we begin with the last couple of years?' He manages to stretch his face into a renewed smile.

'Two *years*?' She looks thunderstruck. 'This is a weekly newspaper!'

'Yes, I know,' Felix says, 'so that's very roughly a hundred and four copies.'

She is still glaring at him. 'I can only let you see fifty at a time,' she says coldly.

'Then for both our sakes, let us hope that the item I'm after crops up within the last twelve months.' He is rapidly tiring of her prevarication. 'Shall I sit over there while you bring them, or do you want me to carry them?'

Her sparse eyebrows have descended in a thunderous scowl. She rises to her feet – Felix can almost hear the creak of protesting stays – and stands erect before him. She is very scrawny and seems to have no bottom. 'Sit,' she commands. 'I will have them brought.'

He makes himself comfortable at a long table on the far side of the reception area. He waits for some time, and then a young man with red hair and a rebellious look in his blue eyes comes staggering towards him, his arms full of newspapers. 'Miss Mundy told me you want to look at back numbers,' he says with a grin. 'Must be your lucky day,' he adds, 'since normally she makes people sign their names in their own blood before they'll even be allowed a sniff at them.' He dumps the stack of paper on the table beside Felix. 'Let me know when you're ready for more.'

There is the sound of footsteps tapping across the floor: Miss Mundy, returning to her desk. Even her footfalls sound condemnatory.

'Don't mind her,' says the red-headed young man. 'Arabella Mundy was once pinched on the bum by one of the Queen's more distant and disreputable relations and she's never got over the outrage.'

'I'm surprised he could find anything to pinch,' Felix mutters.

The young man's grin widens. 'Good luck!' he says, and strolls away.

Felix gets down to work.

The *King's Road Chronicle and Gazette* is a typical local newspaper of the penny-illustrated type, with a front cover devoted to a drawing of whatever topic is covered by the week's headlines, underneath which are a few lines of explanatory text. Inside there are several leaders, all written in various states of disgruntlement, some commentaries on recent local events, quite a lot of commercial advertising, much of it for patent medicines, several more illustrations and a letters page. At the back are the small, private advertisements, everything from appeals for lost cats to unwanted articles of furniture and personal items for sale.

The actual news content is thankfully, from Felix's point of view, relatively sparse.

He works through several months of editions. One or two items catch his eye, but they are not what he is looking for. Nevertheless, he leaves the copies in which these items appear sticking out from the pile so that he can find them again. He works on, and he is just starting to think that he will have to ask the disobliging Miss Mundy of the pinched bottom to release more back numbers when, in the edition for July of the previous year, he finds it.

ASSAULT ON THE COURT STEPS! yells the headline on the front page, beneath a drawing of a furious and distraught old woman appearing to be on the point of thumping a fat and cowering middle-aged man with her umbrella. Felix turns hurriedly to the full article on the inside page, and reads the full story.

> *Well-known barrister to the rich and the influential, William Fleurival Hart today won freedom for another wealthy client when his persuasive tongue convinced the jury to find Granville Roberts, 54, owner and managing director of Roberts and Sons, boiler manufacturers, not guilty of negligence. The case was brought by Mr Gregory Amberley, 36, who lost a hand and was blinded in a terrible accident at the firm's Middlesex works in January this year. Mr Amberley maintained that he and others had complained many times at the lack of proper maintenance of the large and potentially hazardous machines with which he worked, but that management – by which it was clear he meant Mr Roberts – did nothing. 'It's all*

about profit with Granville Roberts!' he shouted when giving evidence. 'He won't stop the machines, not ever, not even when we all tell him they're dangerous.' The mellifluous-voiced William Fleurival Hart, however, indignantly defended his client, portraying him as a good and honourable employer whose concern for the welfare of his employees was demonstrated by such measures as a scheme for providing sickness benefits and an annual seaside outing to Clacton.

The contretemps on the steps of the courthouse was between the recently exonerated Mr Roberts and Mrs Gladys Amberley, the 68-year-old mother of the crippled man. 'You're a wicked, greedy man,' she screeched at him, 'and you've hoodwinked all of them! But I know the truth!'

Then there is a sub-heading: *GRAVE ACCUSATION.* Felix reads on.

Mrs Amberley went on to make a most grave accusation, which was that as Mr Roberts left the courtroom with his solicitor, Mr George Sutherland of local firm Spencer, Caldicot and Brown, she was walking close behind them and heard Mr Roberts mutter very quietly to Mr Sutherland, 'Thanks for all your hard work, old boy, it certainly got me out of a tight spot! I'd been meaning to see to those d****d machines for months, and you'll be pleased to know that repairs are now in hand.'

DID MRS AMBERLEY HEAR CORRECTLY? shrieks another sub-heading.

The plaintiff's mother was clearly in a highly emotional state after the verdict, and if she believed she overheard a conversation that did not in fact take place, it is understandable. Under English law, a man cannot be tried twice for the same crime, so if there was indeed any tiny kernel of truth in what Mrs Amberley maintained, then Mr Roberts need not worry unduly that the authorities will once more come knocking on his door.

Felix goes on staring down at the newspaper. There is another, smaller illustration, this one showing the fat man leaning close to a tall, spare man walking beside him who he imagines to be George Sutherland. With a sigh, he begins to make his notes.

When he has written down every detail that is at all likely to be pertinent, he puts the paper back in its place in the pile and sits in thought for several moments. Then, making up his mind, he returns to the ones he left sticking out and makes several more pages of notes. When he has finished doing that, he checks through the rest of the fifty copies that the ginger-haired young man brought. He finds one more similar story.

'I've finished with these,' he calls out to Miss Mundy. 'I'll have the next fifty, please, and I shall require another fifty after that.'

She leaps up as if stung and hurries over to him. She stares down at the pile of newspapers with very suspicious eyes, but since he has been careful to leave them even more tidily arranged than they were when brought out to him, she can surely find no fault.

She glares at him. Then, the single word so loud and so sudden that it both hurts his ears and makes him jump, she shouts, '*Douglas!*' and, in a moment, the red-haired youth reappears.

Silently she points at Felix. 'He wants fifty more,' she says in tones of stony disapproval.

Douglas grins at Felix. 'Coming right up! Done with these, are you?' Felix nods. 'Won't be a minute, then.'

An hour or so later, Felix has finished and, having thanked Miss Mundy with subtle irony for 'all her help' and slipped the obliging Douglas sixpence for his trouble, Felix is heading back to World's End Passage and the Bureau.

But he walks straight past the entrance to Hob's Court and on out to the Embankment. He turns left and strides along to Battersea Bridge, walking out across it until he is halfway over, where he stops and, facing upstream, leans against the railing, watching the Thames moving powerfully beneath him.

He knows he should be concentrating on what he has found

out about George Sutherland, for he cannot see how this new knowledge can possibly constitute a motive for harming Albertina Stibbins and so George can now be crossed off the list.

But his mind is on the other headline that caught his eye: the one for the *King's Road Chronicle and Gazette* of August last year that read *FIFTH WOMAN MISSING FROM BATTERSEA BRIDGE AREA.*

The article, which went on to describe how a young woman who worked part-time in a bar (and, the implication is, the rest of the time on the streets) had been reported missing by other women who shared her lowly lodgings. Some desultory enquiries had been made, but it was assumed the young woman had left and gone back to Yorkshire, where she was born. 'It is a tendency among such women not to stay long in a place', a police spokesman was quoted as saying.

The trouble is that the smug little phrase got under Felix's skin. It is a generalization, he thinks, and surely neither a fair nor an accurate one. It piqued his interest, and he worked through the back numbers of the newspaper until he found details of some of the earlier cases. Not all, for it seems that the disappearance of one prostitute is not newsworthy beyond the briefest mention, and that a report only becomes worth-while to a paper once several women have suffered the same mysterious fate.

Felix glances over to his left, to the south side of the river. It is here that most of the missing women lived; only the fifth one was from the Chelsea side, which might, Felix reasons, be why the newspaper did not report the mystery in any depth or detail until someone more local was involved.

He is still thinking hard. He has heard a reference to missing women, or some such inference, quite recently, and he cannot recall where it was.

He goes on standing there, staring down at the great powerful surge of the water, until the fading light suggests it is time to move.

ELEVEN

ily is seated at her desk, deep in thought, thinking how to phrase what she must write, when she hears Felix come in. She half-welcomes the distraction, but the other half knows she should ignore his presence and get on with the task before her.

Felix takes the choice out of her hands.

'I know what George Sutherland is so worried and guilty about,' he announces, coming to stand in the doorway to her inner office.

She looks up. 'What?'

He tells her about a court case involving an accusation of negligence, a desperately wounded man, and what his distressed, furious mother might or might not have heard from the accused man afterwards, once he had been safely acquitted.

'And George Sutherland was the briefing solicitor!' he finishes triumphantly, although she has already guessed as much. She looks at him, frowning. Then she says, 'So why does George feel so bad?'

'Because, presumably, it was he who persuaded the barrister – who was William Fleurival Hart, by the way – that Granville Roberts was a decent, considerate employer who treated his staff with respect, consideration and kindness, and couldn't possibly be guilty of negligence leading to such dreadful injuries as those suffered by Gregory Amberley.'

Slowly she nods. It makes good sense, and Felix has argued well. She respects George Sutherland for his decency in having responded as he has; for feeling so ashamed of having allowed himself to have been so thoroughly hoodwinked by a man like Granville Roberts. 'I think we may now disregard George from our list of people who might be ill-wishing Albertina, and his son as well,' she says.

He nods. 'So do I.' He pauses. 'There's something else I'd like to talk over with you, if you can spare a moment?'

Reluctantly she shakes her head. 'I would like to hear about it, whatever it is, but it will have to be another time.' She glances down at the writing paper before her upon her desk. 'I must get on with my report, which I admit is proving challenging.'

'Of course,' he says. Then: 'What's the report about? Can I help?'

She hesitates. This is really something she should do alone, given that she is quite sure he doesn't see it as she does. But then, considering he has done much more work on the case than she has, it seems unfair to exclude him, so she says, 'It's for Lord Berwick.'

Felix's expression changes. 'And what are you going to tell him?' he asks quietly.

'The truth, of course,' she says with some asperity. 'He engaged me to find out certain facts, I – we, or mainly you – have found out at least some of the facts, and now I must pass on these findings to the man who is paying us.'

'Yes, I understand all that –' there is an ominous note of patience in his tone – 'but what will you *say*?'

She has had enough. 'I shall write my report and then show you what I have written.' His expression has lightened but instantly she goes on, 'Not in order that you may suggest the leaving out or the disguising of any of the content, but to ensure that I have represented accurately what you have discovered.'

He looks as if he is bursting to say something; to yell at her, perhaps, to leap in with his defence of Violetta da Rosa. He manages to keep his mouth shut. After a short, tense pause, he turns and says, 'I have some notes to write up,' and walks into the outer office, pulling her door closed behind him.

In all the time he has worked here they have never closed that door.

Feeling inexplicably sad, she picks up her pen, dips it in the inkwell and begins to write.

Some time later, she calls him into the inner office and silently hands him four sheets of paper covered with her neat, small writing. She turns away while he reads them.

Presently he says, 'So you are allowing Violetta no chance to marry her young swain without the protestations and interference of his father.'

'Julian is over twenty-one, he can do as he likes.'

'He can't marry against his father's wishes with any hope of preserving his inheritance!' he protests.

'And since that is obviously why Violetta is planning to marry him, then maybe she'll call it off!' Lily retorts.

'She hasn't done anything wrong!' he cries. 'She married a man who already had a wife, but she—'

'She was pregnant when she married him,' Lily points put relentlessly.

'Yes, but so are hundreds of women, and the children are legitimate provided the parents are man and wife at the time of birth.'

'Violetta – Violet and Archie were never legally married.'

'*But that's not her fault!*' Felix shouts.

Lily hears the echoes of his loud voice ring in the office. She is quite taken aback by his vehemence. 'She—' she begins.

But he doesn't let her finish. 'Violetta's career won't last for ever,' he says roughly. 'Her sort of looks are fine when a woman is young, but soon she'll begin to put on too much weight, her hair will start to go grey and she'll no longer be invited to play the sort of roles that she's made her own. Is she then to fall into poverty? Become destitute? Starve, unless she takes to earning her living by less honest means?'

Once again his angry words echo in the small space. When they have died down, Lily says, as calmly as she can, 'These are not our concerns, Mr Wilbraham. Our duty is to report the facts to the man who is paying us to find them out. And now, if you have no comment to make on the accuracy of what I have written –' *which is the only element upon which I am inviting your comments*, hangs frosty and unspoken between them – 'I shall put it in an envelope and take it to the post.'

After a tense moment, he shakes his head.

She is coming back from the post box when she sees him standing on the front step, waiting for her.

'I want to apologize,' he says disarmingly. 'You were quite

right in what you said. Furthermore, you're my employer and I had no right to shout at you.'

She ushers him back inside and closes the door. They go into the office. 'I admire you for speaking your mind, even if it was a little on the loud side.' He manages a smile 'And there is nothing wrong with becoming involved with a case, or, indeed, with developing sympathy for the participants. But we have to be professional, and we have to report what we find without bias.'

'I know,' he says quietly.

'We cannot—'

'Please, Miss Raynor, don't decide that this makes me unsuitable for the job of your clerical assistant,' he says urgently. 'I applied for this job because I was all but out of funds, and I had no expectation whatever that I would come to enjoy it as much as I do. I want to go on working for the World's End Bureau, and I believe I can be of use.'

She watches him steadily. Clerical assistant, she thinks. Well, he is already considerably more than that, even after such a short time, and so far he has generally done well. But, as he reminded her, she is his employer and he has just been apologizing for shouting at her, so perhaps it is not the moment to share this with him.

So she just says, 'I believe you can, too,' then, smiling, goes on into her own office.

In the morning there is a hand-delivered note waiting on the doormat, addressed to L. G. Raynor. Opening it, Lily finds that it is from Lord Berwick. He has received her report and wishes to discuss it with her. *I shall be at my small town house in Bloomsbury this morning*, he goes on, *if this time and place are convenient. I shall expect you at ten o'clock unless I hear otherwise.* It is signed *Berwick*.

She looks at the address, printed at the top of the single sheet of writing paper. She knows the square in which the house is situated; it is behind the British Museum. She glances at her half-hunter: it is a quarter to nine. She can be in Bloomsbury in plenty of time.

She hurries back up to the top floor and, in front of her

cheval mirror, tries on one or two different outfits. But this, she reflects, is not an occasion like the invitation to the Rose Tea Rooms; this is a serious, not to say sad, meeting. She puts her severe office shirt, skirt and waistcoat on again, adds the matching jacket and a totally unfrivolous hat, then goes downstairs. She writes a quick note to Felix, who will be arriving any moment, then picks up her bag and her own copy of the report and sets out.

Lord Berwick's house in Bloomsbury is small but it is an exquisite little gem, set in a square of similar houses around a well-tended, iron-railed garden where there are trees, flowers and even a modest-sized fountain. It is very exclusive and, for all that it is only a street or two away from main thoroughfares with their bustle of traffic, extremely quiet.

Lily walks up to the door and rings the bell.

It is opened by Lord Berwick. He wishes her good morning, then stands back to let her enter. 'I hope the early hour does not inconvenience you,' he says.

'Not at all.'

'And forgive my having answered the door myself: I do not keep staff in residence, for neither my wife nor my son visits the house and I prefer to look after myself when I am here.'

Lily would not dream of questioning him. She mutters, 'I quite understand.'

He leads the way down the short, narrow hall, past an elegant staircase with shining mahogany banisters and into a bright and sunny room at the rear of the house. He invites her to sit down in the chair placed on one side of the small and well-buffed walnut table, and he takes his seat opposite. Her report is before him.

'I will come straight to the point, Miss Raynor,' he says. 'Your Agent A observed the woman who my son insists is his fiancée in a box at a rather dubious music hall in the company of a man simply referred to as Billy, and saw them engaging in certain . . . intimacies. Your Agent B saw her with the same man at the Glass Slipper Theatre, where she is currently in rehearsals for a new play, and the conversation between them strongly suggested they were going that evening to visit the

house on the edge of Tunbridge Wells where a young girl
believed to be her daughter resides, with an older woman who
is apparently a relation-in-law.' He pauses. 'Is there information suggesting whether or not the woman and this Billy
stayed away overnight together?'

'No,' Lily replies.

'And did either Agent A or Agent B speculate as to the
likelihood of this?'

'The Bureau's agents try not to speculate, my lord. Their
job is to observe and record.'

'Quite, quite,' he mutters. Then he says briskly, 'I believe
my son is being a fool over this woman. I believe that as an
ageing actress –' she can only be in her late thirties, early
forties at most! Lily wants to protest – 'she is all too aware
that her future on the stage is uncertain, and she sees my son's
devotion, and his insistence on making her his wife, as a promise
of security when her career comes, as it soon surely must, to
an end.' He looks at Lily, his eyes hard. 'Upon my death my
son inherits a title, a considerable amount of property, several
houses and what a woman of Miss da Rosa's sort would probably term a fortune,' he goes on. 'I am prepared to believe he
really does love her, Miss Raynor; I am even prepared to believe
she loves him.' It is, Lily appreciates, quite a concession. 'But
what I cannot believe is that Violetta da Rosa, or indeed any
actress with her – ah, her somewhat *colourful* past, is the right
woman to become the next Lady Berwick.'

Lily, who well remembers what he had to say about his
wife, the present Lady Berwick, keeps quiet.

But as if he has read her mind, he says softly, 'You think
me hard, I dare say.' She doesn't reply. 'Well, perhaps I am.
But if I may be frank, Miss Raynor – for I know this will
remain between ourselves – what is guiding me through this
sad situation is my fervent wish that my son does not make
the mistake I made. Not that Lady Berwick was an actress,
or had a bigamous first marriage and an illegitimate child!'
He laughs as if to highlight the absurdity of either scenario.

'Of course not,' Lily murmurs.

He is looking penetratingly at her. '*Do* you think me hard,
Miss Raynor?'

It is, she senses, a moment for honesty. 'I believe your son will interpret your actions so, although for myself, I appreciate that, aware perhaps of his youth and relative lack of sophistication, you are within your rights as his father to try to steer him towards a sensible – er, a mature decision.'

He laughs softly. 'Diplomatically put,' he remarks.

Silence falls, and he looks down at her report. 'She was pregnant when she married Archibald Twort,' he observes.

'So the parish records suggest.'

'And the vicar was certain she had no idea that the man already had a wife.'

'That is so.'

'Hmm. Then little or no blame can attach to her in respect of the bigamous marriage, perhaps, although the conception out of wedlock is, of course, another matter.' He pauses, once again studying the report. 'And the child, this Florence, is well provided for?'

'Adequately, it appears, although the work she does is hard.' But she is loved, Lily could have added. Felix keeps pointing out how much Violetta must love her daughter, to go on visiting her, making her a part of her life, even with the bright prospect of marriage to Julian and all that goes with him in the offing.

She wonders suddenly what Violetta proposes to do about Florence once she is married. Since it seems this happy outcome is unlikely to materialize, she dismisses the thought.

Lord Berwick is tidying the sheets of her report and she takes this as a signal that it is time to go.

'I will have your cheque put in the post,' he says. 'Thank you for this.' He waves the report. 'Lord Dunorlan was right to recommend your Bureau, and I shall put in a good word for you if ever it is appropriate.'

'Thank you, my lord.' She is tempted to offer him a handful of her cards but nerves get the better of her and she doesn't.

He sees her to the door. His hand on the latch, he says, 'I shall find as kind a way as I can to inform my son of the truth about his lady love.'

She meets his cool, determined eyes.

'Kindness would be right, my lord,' she says softly. 'He will not, I think, see that these discoveries discredit her, and will argue that there is no reason to call off the engagement.'

Lord Berwick sighs. 'I fear you are right,' he agrees. Then, more formally and with a crystal-clear note of polite but ruthless dismissal, 'I will take care of it from now on. Thank you, Miss Raynor, and good day.'

Then she is out on the street, the door has been closed quietly but firmly, and she has been ejected from Lord Berwick's and young Julian's life.

She hopes she has done the right thing. She shudders suddenly, although the day is warm and she isn't cold. What else could I have done? she asks herself. I had to tell him what Felix discovered; what I observed with my own eyes.

She sets off along the attractive, shady street with its air of privacy and privilege.

Despite its charms, its beauty, its restful air of calm and the sky-high value of its beautiful dwellings, she is profoundly glad to leave it.

She knows she will not go on foot all the way back to World's End, for it is a long way and will take precious time out of her day. But she resolves to walk the first mile or so, for the exercise is doing her good, releasing some of the pent-up emotions.

She strides down Bedford Way, around Russell Square and along Montague Street, turning to the right down Great Russell Street. The British Museum looms up on the right.

And she sees a familiar figure crossing the large open space in front of it. Walking at a determined pace, shoulders back, arms swinging, and, if only she could see his face, undoubtedly smiling to himself, is Ernest Stibbins.

Very early that morning, a long time before it is fully day, Felix wakes in his too short, too narrow and thoroughly uncomfortable bed, shaken out of a light sleep. He has remembered who had spoken to him of missing women. It was the Reverend Mr James Jellicote. They, or rather he, had been talking about how Albertina's situation had been temporarily precarious, or potentially so, after the death of her great-aunt, when she found herself very much alone in a city where she knew hardly

a soul. James Jellicote had been saying that it was fortunate
for her to have found a kind, dependable husband in Ernest
Stibbins, going on to remark that marriage had saved her from
the perils into which she might otherwise have fallen. Even
there in his own parish, he had told Felix, girls and young
women had gone missing, and he feared that some, at least,
had probably taken their own lives.

There is after all, Felix now thinks, a very ready source of
death for the suicide running close by, its strong tidal flow
giving very little, if any, chance of survival to someone who
falls, or throws themselves, in.

He relaxes against the meagre and rather smelly pillow. He
has not slept well throughout this night, for he has been trying
to remember who mentioned missing women even when he
was semi-unconscious. Now, having answered his own question, he knows he will sleep like an innocent child until he is
woken at a quarter to six by the regular fanfare of deep-chested
coughing, hawking and spitting, and its accompaniment of
thunderous flatulence, that is the daily reveille performed by
his neighbour.

Felix hates this room, but when he was almost out of money,
it was all he could afford. It is small, dark, dank and, even
now in late spring when the weather is warm and sunny, it
smells of mould and there are ominous black fungal growths
creeping down from the junction of walls and ceiling. The
single window only opens a crack, and Felix usually leaves it
shut because it is situated over the yard, and in the yard is the
deeply noisome privy.

For a man like Felix, who loves the fresh air and all his life
has slept with at least a crack of open window, even in the bitterest
weather, it is a slow torment.

He thumps the lumpy pillow, draws up the blanket and,
turning on his side, falls asleep.

Lily is not in the office when he arrives at Hob's Court just
before nine o'clock. There is a note from her on his desk: she
has been summoned to speak to Lord Berwick. Felix doesn't
want to think about that.

He sits at his desk. He has evolved a plan for today, but he feels he should discuss it with Lily before putting it into action. There are quite a few clerical jobs he can be getting on with, however, so with a will he settles down to some report-copying, some letter-writing and some filing.

It is an hour and a half later that Lily returns. She looks distressed, and tactfully he holds back the question he was about to ask. She meets his eyes. 'Shall we have a cup of coffee?' she suggests.

He leaps up and goes into the scullery to make it. It is not a Mrs Clapper day, and he is quite glad. Her hostility towards him has lessened by a few degrees, but there is still some way to go before he can even begin to believe that she likes him. The mood in the Hob's Court kitchen area is definitely more congenial when she isn't there.

The Little Ballerina's undergarments are, as usual, soaking in a bowl of greyish water. As usual, he ignores them.

He returns to the outer office to find Lily has drawn up the visitor's chair and is sitting on the opposite side of his desk. She takes her cup and saucer from him with a word of thanks.

She doesn't initiate any sort of conversation, so he does. 'The matter I wished to discuss with you yesterday, and which you asked me to postpone, concerns something I came across when I was looking for details of whatever is troubling George Sutherland. It concerns a succession of women who have gone missing over the past year or two. You're probably going to ask me why it attracted my attention and what it's got to do with us and the business of the Bureau, and I'd have to answer that I can't really explain, other than to say I have the strongest sense that I ought to follow it up. Someone ought to, anyway,' he adds in a mutter.

'Go on,' Lily says.

'I'd like to go and speak to somebody on the *Battersea Illustrated News*,' he says.

'Yes?'

Taking the brief response as an invitation to proceed and elaborate, he says, 'I had a vague memory of somebody else having spoken to me about missing women, and after a night's sleep I remembered who it was.' He repeats his conversation with James Jellicote. 'Now I've seen what the *King's Road*

Chronicle and Gazette has to say, which isn't much and barely amounted to more than a brief mention until one of the missing came from their side of the river. What I'm thinking is that—'

'The *Battersea Illustrated News* may have made more of a feature of the story since the women went missing there,' she finishes. Her eyes have just a little of their usual sparkle, and he is relieved to have stimulated her out of her despondency.

'That's right,' he says. 'I'm hoping I can do the same trawl through back numbers that I did on the north side of the river, and with any luck find some keen-eyed journalist who has taken a personal interest in the story and has all the details at his fingertips.'

'A man can hope,' she mutters. He sees a thin smile on her lips.

'I've a feeling I'm going to have that luck,' he says firmly. Then, for her face has fallen again and now she also looks slightly anxious, 'What's the matter?'

She stirs from her brief reverie. 'This is rather odd,' she says quietly.

'What is?' He senses it is somehow important.

'I've remembered something, prompted, no doubt, by what you have just told me.'

'What?'

There is a short pause, as if she is having to concentrate hard to bring the details to mind. Then: 'I believe I have it. When I left Albertina's seance, Mrs Sullivan was anxious about my setting off for home by myself. She said—' She frowns. 'Yes. She said it wasn't safe for a young woman on her own because there have been far too many . . . something.'

'Too many something?'

'She didn't finish the sentence,' Lily says with slight impatience. 'Perhaps she thought it would only frighten me if she told me what there had been far too many of.'

'Cases of women going missing?' Felix suggests.

'Undoubtedly,' Lily agrees. 'So, perhaps I should go and visit Mrs Sullivan, say I've been worried about what she said and please could she elucidate?'

'Good idea,' he says.

She gulps down the rest of her coffee and stands up. 'I don't know how long I shall be,' she says.

'Well, I'll be setting off too and nor do I,' he replies. 'We'll compare notes later, shall we?'

Dorothy Sullivan lives in a neat double-fronted terraced house with a small front garden, a privet hedge and a low gate. She opens the door to Lily's knock and her slightly anxious expression turns into a beam of delight.

'Miss Garrett! How very pleasant! I have just made a pot of tea, so will you come in and take a cup?'

'I do not wish to disturb you, Mrs Sullivan.'

'You're not disturbing me! Please, step inside and go through into the front room – in there, yes, that's right!' Lily enters the room to the right of the front door. 'I will bring a tray – make yourself comfortable, please!'

Faced with such an effusive welcome, Lily obeys. The room into which Mrs Sullivan has ushered her is square and spacious, but it is so crammed with furniture, shelves, little tables and what-nots, pot plants, vases of flowers, cushions, bits of embroidery, ornaments, magazine and newspaper racks, photographs in heavy frames, landscape paintings in even heavier frames and piles of books that the eye is deceived into thinking it is in fact tiny. It is, however, clean, warm, homely and welcoming.

Lily edges her way very carefully to a chair to the right of the fireplace; the chair opposite has a shawl draped over one arm and an open book on the other arm, a pair of spectacles placed in the angle between the pages, and is clearly where Mrs Sullivan has been sitting. She glances around, but there is far too much to take in; she would need a couple of days to do everything justice.

Her eye is drawn to one of the photographs. It has pride of place in the centre of the mantelshelf, between two tall candles in brass holders. Before each candle is a posy of flowers in a small cut-glass vase. The photograph, a professional portrait, is of a handsome man with a twinkle in his eyes. Unusually for a studio photograph, he is smiling. Lily takes an instant liking to him.

'You're looking at my Rodney,' says Mrs Sullivan, returning with the tea tray.

'I am,' Lily agrees. 'I was just thinking that I'm quite sure I would have liked him.'

Mrs Sullivan pauses in her setting-out of cups, saucers, milk jug and sugar bowl, silver teaspoons and sugar tongs. 'You would, Miss Garrett. He was a dear, dear man.'

Tea is poured, and Lily takes a sip. It is strong with just the right amount of milk. She takes another sip, framing her next remark. 'I hope Albertina helps you?' she asks, very tentatively. 'In reassuring you about him, I mean – I'm sorry, I couldn't help but hear what she said to you.'

'No need for apologies, dear,' Mrs Sullivan says. 'Albertina, bless her, offers private sessions for those who require privacy, but I've always felt it's a help to be with others who grieve for lost loved ones. And as for reassuring me . . .' She sighs. 'Yes, I suppose she does. She *means* well, bless her, and I always tell myself that she may very well be hearing my Rodney's voice, and that the comforting things she tells me don't just come from her own kind heart and her wish to help.'

Lily, taken aback, mutters something about Albertina certainly appearing to be a very kind person. But she is thinking about what Tamáz said; thinking that the words Albertina Stibbins says to Mrs Sullivan could very easily stem from the fact that she senses the old woman's pain and hurt and so very badly wants to assuage them . . .

'. . . such a dear, dear young woman,' Dorothy Sullivan is saying, 'and a *good* wife to Ernest, who was lonely and with-drawn after the loss of his first wife – why, there were times when he didn't even come to church, and we were all so worried about him. But then along came Albertina, and they fell in love, and now there they are, happy as sandboys in that house that has become a home again, and Albertina so full of plans to open up and improve the areas not presently in use and—' She stops, then, leaning towards Lily, says in a whisper, 'Of course, I and some of the other ladies at church hope very much that perhaps a little addition to the family may be coming along in the not too distant future.' She smiles roguishly. 'After all, that is the usual explanation for a wife asking her husband to arrange for some more space in the house!'

'How delightful!' Lily says. 'Albertina is still a young woman, so there is no reason why not, is there?'

'No indeed, dear, and Ernest, although of course considerably the elder, is a very vigorous man, is he not?'

It's not the first word that springs to mind when Lily thinks about him, but nevertheless she agrees.

Mrs Sullivan is topping up the cups. It is time, Lily realizes, to raise the matter that she's come for. 'Mrs Sullivan, when we all left the Circle meeting last Sunday you asked if I was going to be home by dusk and you told me it wasn't safe for women on their own. You said there had been many instances of something, but you did not say what.'

Mrs Sullivan's cheery face has fallen and she is looking, or so Lily thinks, a little guilty. 'Oh, I'm *so* sorry, Miss Garrett! I've thought it over many times since and I see now how foolish and inconsiderate I was to warn you of a danger and then not go on to explain! Oh, my dear, have you been *very* worried?'

'Not really, no,' Lily replies. 'But I would very much like to hear what this is all about. I intend to visit Circle again, and I'm planning to do so this week in fact, and I'm wondering if I should take a cab home next time?' She turns it into a question, pretending a tremulousness she doesn't really feel.

'Yes, yes, perhaps that would be wise,' Mrs Sullivan says anxiously. 'I myself am very lucky, for George Sutherland and his son always walk me home. Although it is not a little out of their way, they insist, and I am too cowardly to protest!' She gives a short and slightly hysterical laugh. Then, her expression steadily tightening into firm resolution, finally she says, 'Women have gone missing, Miss Garrett. Five or six, I am not sure, and those are just the cases reported in the newspaper, and for all we know there may be more.'

'Missing?' Lily repeats invitingly.

'Yes, dear, and our vicar, the Reverend Mr Jellicote, ventures the opinion that they may very well be – er, women who have been unfortunate enough to, to encounter *troubles* that they cannot – that society does not – well, you know what I mean, I'm sure.' She has flushed a rosy pink.

'Of course,' Lily says. Deciding to be frank, she goes on, 'They have been seduced, perhaps, by a man promising marriage, only to find that they are with child and the man nowhere to be seen.'

'Quite so!' says Mrs Sullivan, her relief at being understood and not having to venture more in the way of explanation palpable.

'Or I suppose they could be street women,' Lily goes on, 'in poverty, desperate, finding life no longer endurable.'

Mrs Sullivan sighs. 'Yes, I suppose so.' But there is something else she wants to say; Lily can sense it. She waits.

'But, you see, there are also the rumours,' she says after a moment.

'The rumours?'

'Oh, dear, dear, I'm not at all sure I should be repeating them, for Mr Jellicote does so disapprove of what he calls inflammatory talk . . .' She eyes Lily, but it seems the naughty pleasure of sharing the rumours with a new and interested audience quickly overcomes the prospect of the vicar's disapproval. 'Some of us believe that the truth is even more wicked,' she begins in a confidential tone, 'that the missing women are snatched from the streets and taken to low dives to entertain the Chinamen who smoke opiates, or that they are imprisoned for the use of wealthy men, or even put aboard ships and taken far away to become slaves to men with flashing black eyes and dark skins who dwell in the desert in silken tents!' She sits back, and her expression seems to say, *Now what do you think of that!*

Lily, momentarily speechless, is both amazed and impressed by Mrs Sullivan's vivid imagination. Whatever has she been reading, to put such ideas into her innocent head? Surely her life as a suburban housewife in a modest home in an ordinary street has not permitted any glimpses behind the murky veil of sin and vice?

'I – I have heard tell of such dreadful happenings,' she says. 'To think that women could have been abducted from these very streets for such purposes is –' Totally unbelievable, is what she wants to say, but it would be far too crushing – 'horrifying,' she says instead.

'Isn't it?' agrees Mrs Sullivan.

'Thank you for telling me,' Lily says, putting her empty cup down on the table beside her chair. 'And for the tea, which was most welcome. Now I must be on my way, and leave you in peace.'

Mrs Sullivan gets up to see her out. 'You are most welcome, Miss Garrett, and it was my pleasure to help,' she assures her. 'And how glad I am that you are to come to Circle again!'

'I wouldn't miss it,' Lily says. 'Good day, now!'

Mrs Sullivan stands in her doorway waving until Lily turns the corner.

TWELVE

F elix finds the staff of the *Battersea Illustrated News* to be altogether more welcoming and friendly than Miss Mundy of the *King's Road Chronicle and Gazette*. The fat young woman who sits behind the reception desk waves cheerfully at the large cabinets of back numbers and tells him to help himself, and when he's been searching for half an hour – and already found several very pertinent articles – comes over to the desk where he sits reading and offers him a cup of tea and a bun. He says yes to both, and she comes to join him as she too eats and drinks.

'I shouldn't eat these,' she says ruefully, waving her current-filled iced bun in his direction, 'but I can't help myself.'

Felix, who after a couple of bites has found the bun so teeth-achingly sweet that he's not sure he'll be able to finish it, doesn't want to hurt her feelings by insulting a favourite delicacy, so just nods and agrees that they are good, aren't they? She glances over his shoulder at his notebook. 'You interested in anything in particular? Oh, the women!' She answers her own question before he can either do so himself or prevaricate. 'You want to talk to Marm Smithers,' she says, nodding. 'Well, he's Marmaduke really, but he hates it and we all call him Marm, or even Marmie. He's the reporter who's been doing the pieces on those poor women, well, I say women but quite a lot of them were not much more than girls, which in a way makes it worse, only it's hard to see how it can be worse, and—'

Very gently Felix interrupts. 'That's very helpful, thank you so much!' he says. 'Could you, do you think, tell me where I might find Marm Smithers?'

'Of course I can!' She glances at the large clock on the wall, whose hands read 12:05. 'He'll be either on his way to or already installed in the Cow Jumped Over the Moon, which is the pub at the top of World's End Passage where it comes out into the King's Road.'

'I know it,' Felix says. Know it and have pretty often had a drink in it, he might have added. 'Why does he drink over there if the newspaper's this side of the river?' he asks, curiosity getting the better of him.

The fat young woman smiles. 'For one thing, he's not really attached just to the *Battersea Illustrated*, he writes for quite a lot of other papers too, and some magazines as well, so there's no reason his local should be here in Battersea. For another –' her smile widens – 'he's been banned from quite a lot of the pubs round here. Gets a bit argumentative, does Marmie, once he has a drink or two inside him.'

Felix is putting away his notebook and pencil, picking up his hat. 'I'll go and look for him straight away. Thanks very much for your help, Mrs? Miss?'

'Alderton, Polly Alderton, and it's Miss,' says his new friend, who, from the way she's eyeing him and the lascivious ring she gave to *Miss*, could well be implying she would rather like to be more than a friend. 'Tell him Pol sent you!'

Felix hurries back across the bridge, up World's End Passage and is outside the Cow Jumped Over the Moon – the Cow, as locals call it – some twenty minutes later. He has realized, as he paced along, that he should have asked Polly Alderton how he was to recognize Marm Smithers, but as he enters the smoky saloon bar (which seems the right option out of it or the public bar to try first) he appreciates that it wasn't necessary. Marm Smithers sits on a stool at a small, round table in a far corner, the dregs of a pint of bitter to hand and a pork pie on a plate waiting to be broached, a cigarette between his fingers, and he has a notebook, two pencils and an edition of one of the broadsheets before him on which his attention is fixed to the exclusion of everything else, including, apparently, the racket going on all around him.

Felix grabs a second stool and sits down opposite him. 'Are you Marm Smithers?' he asks.

'Who wants to know and why should I tell him?' the man says truculently.

Suspecting that this isn't the first pint and recalling what the fat young woman said, Felix says pacifically, 'I've just

come from the *Battersea Illustrated News*'s offices, and Polly
Alderton told me where to find you. She said to tell you she
sent me,' he adds as Marm Smither's expression softens.

'Pol,' he says, a smile on his handsome but dissipated face;
the skin is reddened as if by overexposure to wind and weather,
the lines are surely too deep for a man who can only be in
his late thirties, at most, and the intelligent blue eyes have
pinkish lids and quite a lot of broken veins. His brown hair
is a little too long and streaked with grey and his jacket, shirt
and trousers all look as if they need a good clean, as do his
well-worn shoes.

Despite all these drawbacks, Felix warms to the smile, and
to the way Marm goes on to say, 'She's a sweetheart, is Pol.
A woman to warm a man's bed at night, and no bony hips or
knees to dig in to your tender parts.'

'You speak from experience?' Felix asks with a grin.

'Wish I could say I did,' Marm replies. 'No, she's about to
be married, and utterly faithful to her young man.'

So much, Felix thinks, reproving himself, for Polly wanting
to be more than his friend.

'What can I do for you?' Marm asks. 'Got a story for me?'
His eyes gleam hungrily.

'No. Well, I don't think so,' Felix replies. 'It's more that I
want to ask you about a story of yours.' He takes out his
notebook. 'Missing women. Five in the Battersea area, one in
Chelsea.'

Marm's expression has sobered and he nods slowly. 'Six in
Battersea, not five,' he says quietly. 'And I'd stake my pension,
if I had one, that there are more.'

Felix glances down at his notes. 'You postulate in one of
your articles that the reason nobody is taking these disappear-
ances seriously enough, or perhaps seriously at all, is that the
women were prostitutes.'

'Too bloody right I do,' Marm says, a spasm of anger
creasing his face. 'Does that make them no longer human?
Does it make their deaths – for don't you go believing they've
simply decided to leave the area and try their luck elsewhere
– does it make their deaths unimportant? Not worthy of a
proper investigation? At least seven women, one of them only

sixteen, one a year older, and who cares? Nobody fucking cares.'

Felix waits for a moment, then says, 'You obviously do.'

'Yes, and I get told to cut my articles by half and leave out all the speculation and the tub-thumping because it's *not what our readers want to hear about*.' His fury is evident in the way he almost spits out the last words.

'Yet you persist.' Felix looks at his notes again. 'The last piece was only a fortnight ago.'

Marm nods. 'Yes, that's right, although it wasn't occasioned by another woman going missing.'

'No, you were trying yet again to get something done about the ones who already have.'

Marm looks at him, interested now. 'You bothered to read the article,' he remarks. 'Wish more people did. What did you say your name was?'

'I didn't but it's Felix Wilbraham.' He takes out a card. 'I'm with the World's End Bureau.'

Marm takes the card, glancing down. 'I've heard of it,' he says. 'Your chief's a woman.'

'Yes,' Felix confirms. He feels it would be insulting to Lily to qualify the answer.

And also insulting to Marm, as it turns out, because, 'I like the thought of a woman boss,' he says.

Felix grins. 'It's different.'

'I also hear she's had not a few successes,' Marm goes on. 'Good for her. Now, Mr Wilbraham, I suggest you go and buy me another pint, and one for yourself and maybe a pork pie too as they're uncommonly good here, and then tell me what your interest is in my missing women.'

Felix stands up, feeling in his pocket for coins, and does as he's told.

An hour and three more pints later, Felix has greatly enlarged the list of names and the sparse details that he has managed to glean from the back editions of the *King's Road Chronicle and Gazette* and the *Battersea Illustrated News*. Now after each name is an age, a description, a brief account of where last seen and a summary of the speculations, if any, as to what became of the missing woman. In some cases there is also a last known address, although for quite a few this information, indeed any address, is absent. 'Some of them don't live anywhere,' Marm says when Felix asks about this. 'They define precisely and brutally what's meant by a hand to mouth existence. They earn a few pennies and it's enough for a few drinks and something to eat. Then they earn a few more and can afford a bed for the night in some rooming house. They carry everything they own on them, and that's made easy because most of them own bugger-all. A broken comb, a handkerchief, a bit of ribbon for their bonnet.'

'And, having no place where they're expected to come home to, nobody notices when they don't.' Felix, feeling the effects of three – or was it four? – pints of best bitter on a stomach containing nothing in the way of solid food but a pork pie, isn't sure his utterance makes sense, but Marm understands anyway.

'That's right,' he agrees. 'That's what I meant earlier when I said there's probably many more gone missing. Of course,' he adds charitably, 'what the disinterested majority have to say about street women moving on is right, as far as it goes, and that may well account for some of them. But it's *no reason not even to fucking investigate*!'

The last words are shouted, which is unfortunate as one of them is a swear word, but happily the noise level in the Cow is so high now that nobody minds, and anyway Felix is quite sure Marm isn't the only one using bad language.

'What do we do?' he asks when Marm stops shouting.

'Do?' Marm pretends to think about it. 'We could stop men using women for paid sex, but that'd mean most of the women starved because that's their only income, so that's no good. We could take away nine-tenths of the wealth of the ruling classes and distribute it among the poorest in the land, but that's not going to happen because the wealthy hold the reins. We could make sure girls get an education approaching that of boys and encourage them to work and put some money by so that they become independent. We could give them the vote, God help us, so that the sex who make up half the population actually have a voice.' Abruptly he runs out of steam, folding his arms on the table and dropping his head on to them. 'I'm tired, Felix Wilbraham, and I'm more than a little drunk,' he says, his voice muffled. Then, raising his head again, he adds, 'But I would like to talk to you again.'

Felix gets uncertainly to his feet and holds out his hand, which Marm takes and grips. 'I would like that too,' he says.

Then, the world revolving a little, he makes for the door.

Back at Hob's Court, Lily charitably overlooks the fact that he is unsteady on his feet and probably reeks of beer and tobacco smoke. She watches him sit down behind his desk, and presently she reappears with a cup of tea and a ham sandwich.

'Blotting paper,' she remarks, indicating the sandwich.

He eats, drinks, suppresses a beery burp or two. She takes away his cup and brings it back full again. He drinks that too and starts to feel more alert. But his bladder is bursting and he really can't ignore it any longer. Muttering an apology, he goes out to the lavatory by the back door. After the exquisite relief of passing a very long stream of urine, he straightens his clothing, runs his fingers through his hair, pauses in the scullery to wash his hands and splash cold water over his face and goes back into the office.

She takes one look at him and instantly struggles to suppress laughter.

'*What?*' he demands. He is still too tipsy for diplomatic reticence.

'Your shirt's all wet,' she replies. 'Did you miss your face when you were trying to wash it?'

She disappears, returning with a hand towel. It is clean, ironed, fragrant from washing soap. 'Mrs Clapper,' he murmurs.

'If you are commenting upon my help's laundering skills, then you are absolutely right. If you are declaring a secret passion for her, as I am tempted to conclude by the fervour in your voice when you speak her name, then sadly I must inform you that she is married.'

He looks up at her. He's not sure he's ever seen her laugh before, or even smile for this long at a stretch. 'You look very, very lovely when you laugh,' he mutters.

She pretends she didn't hear.

*   *   *

She leaves him in peace for half an hour or so, then comes back into the outer office and says, 'Now, if you feel up to it, shall we talk about what we have found out?'

'I most certainly do feel up to it,' he assures her. 'I apologize for my state of slight inebriation, but I was in deep and very relevant conversation with a journalist and he was encouraging me.' He frowns. 'Or possibly it was the other way round,' he adds honestly. 'But you go first: what did Mrs Sullivan have to say?'

She tells him, listing her discoveries as a series of main points. One: there have definitely been cases of women going missing and the general view seems to be that they are women of the street whose movements are not easy to trace. Two: there is, however, a persistent rumour that something very sinister is happening, with suggestions of women being snatched for unspeakable purposes.

'Did Mrs Sullivan elaborate?' Felix interrupts, his eyes alight. 'Did she speculate about white slavers and women sold into eastern harems to satisfy men's lusts?'

'She skirted very carefully round the subject, but in essence yes she did. I gather there has been a lot of gossip among the parishioners of St Cyprian's Church, which brings me to my third point: James Jellicote doesn't like this gossip, which he condemns as inflammatory.'

'He's probably quite right,' Felix says fairly.

'Yes, perhaps.' But there is something on her mind; something that has been nagging at her for a while now. She says tentatively, 'What do you think of the Reverend Mr Jellicote?'

Felix sits back in his chair, narrowing his eyes in thought. 'Former curate at St Albans, took a fancy to young Albertina Goodchild, moved to Battersea to take up his first incumbency and was, presumably, delighted when the same young lady came seeking him out when her elderly great-aunt died and left her alone in a city full of strangers. Introduced her to— Oh!' He sits forward again, alert suddenly. 'Yes, I believe I can see what you mean. If he was sweet on Albertina, why did he not begin to pay court to her himself when she turned up? Why did he make a gift of her to Ernest Stibbins?'

'Well, I'm not sure I would quite put it like that,' Lily says.

'I do feel that we must consider Albertina's feelings. Perhaps James Jellicote did indeed pay court, as you say, but Albertina, not having the same attraction to him as he had to her, looking upon him more as a source of help and support than a potential husband and therefore turned him down.'

'"Whilst not unaware of the great compliment you pay me, Mr Jellicote, I very much regret that I do not reciprocate your sentiments,"' Felix says in a prim falsetto.

'Yes, quite.' Lily suppresses a smile. 'So, with his own suit unsuccessful but still aware that Albertina needed someone to take care of her, he guided her towards the kindly, decent, respectable and lonely widower, Ernest Stibbins. She wants a baby,' she adds.

'Albertina?'

'Yes of course Albertina! Mrs Sullivan told me she's been suggesting some home improvements to Ernest, and all the old ladies of St Cyprian's think that must be why.'

Felix nods. Then, after a pause, says, 'Is that all?'

'Hm? Yes. That was my last point: that Albertina and Ernest may be thinking about starting a family.'

'And why is that relevant to our missing women?'

'It isn't,' she replies. 'It was simply something I learned from Dorothy Sullivan, and I thought I'd share it. I'm going to Circle tomorrow, by the way.'

'Yes, good,' he says absently. But he already has his note-book out, and she suspects his mind has leapt ahead to how he plans to share his own discoveries with her. 'Well, here's what I've found out,' he announces, and proceeds to talk pretty much non-stop for the next ten minutes.

'Your Marm Smithers seems to be a man with a conscience,' she remarks when he has finished. 'It sounds as if he's on the point of embarking upon a one-man crusade concerning the wretched conditions of the women he describes.'

'He's certainly angry that their apparent disappearance is met with little more than a shrug of the shoulders,' Felix agrees.

'So, what next?' she asks.

'I think I'll go along and speak to one of the guardians of the law,' he says.

'If by that you mean the police,' she replies, 'I'd suggest you leave it until tomorrow.'

He grins. 'When I no longer smell of beer. Yes, that's what I thought.'

Lily is alone in the office the following morning. Felix, she knows, planned to call in at the police on his way in, so she knows not to expect him yet.

She wishes she had a similar mission. She is going to the Thursday seance this afternoon and, although she is reluctant to admit it, she is nervous and would welcome something to distract her. It's not only the prospect of sitting in the dark with Albertina and the spirits that is worrying her; it's this tale of missing women. It's not as if I was unaware these things happen, Lily thinks to herself. It's simply that I've never had occasion before to dwell on them, and now it seems I have.

She pictures the dark power of the river, running down there at the bottom of the road. So close. So ancient. What secrets does it keep in its cold, swift depths?

And she recalls her visit to Alf Wilson and his Disciples in the river station at Wapping. She had gone, she recalls, with some vague plan of finding out about the drowned Enid Stibbins, Ernest's first wife, and inadvertently let herself in for a discourse on bodies in the Thames in general.

She decides to pay Alf Wilson another visit. She isn't sure why, other than to get her out of the office, and tells herself vaguely that it'll undoubtedly be helpful. A little under an hour later, she is back in Alf's snug little office on its pier overlooking the river, the scent of the water strong in the air, the Thames powering past only a few feet beneath her boots.

Alf is flatteringly pleased to see her – it seems to be a quiet day – and he puts the kettle on for tea, talking all the time about the weather, the tide, the antics of one of the Disciples and how he missed his footing and almost fell in the water, 'Only *almost* doesn't count, miss, and he'll be a sight more careful next time!'

She explains, when she can get a word in, that having been warned by a friend about the dangers of being out alone after dark, she was prompted to search through the newspapers and came across a dreadful story of missing women – 'From right where I live, Mr Wilson, beside the river at Chelsea!' – and, remembering her earlier visit and his exceptional knowledge of such matters, has come back hoping she might ask him some more—

'Course you may, miss!' he cries even before she can finish. 'Like I told you before, bodies in the river is my job!' He fumbles in a pocket and removes a pair of spectacles – she has her notebook on her lap – and says, 'Got a list of dates and locations and what-not there, have you? Give it here, then, and I'll see what I can do.'

Some quarter of an hour later, he shakes his head and says with obvious reluctance, 'Well, miss, I don't see as how there's much to say.' He raises his head, removes his spectacles and, looking at her worriedly, goes on, 'See, it's not as if those poor women have anything to identity them. If someone has a missing relative or friend, of course, it's different, because very often they can spot a facial feature or a birthmark, or a wedding ring or some item of clothing or whatever, and then it's easy. I'm not saying it's *nice*,' he adds reprovingly as if she has suggested it was, 'but at least it provides an answer. But the other way round, when there's a body and we're trying to find out who it is, well, that's another matter entirely.'

He leans forward confidingly. 'I mean to say, some are naked, some are broken, some are taken from the water in bits and pieces, a head here, a bit of a torso there, a leg or two.' He shakes his head again. 'Course, bodies can get broken by the action of the water. That's a powerful old current out there –' he nods reverentially down at the river – 'and when a corpse gets thrown against a jetty or a pier, a moving or a moored boat or even a big enough bit of rubbish, it's the corpse that's always going to come off worse. So, you see, miss, it's not always right to suppose that the beheading and the dismemberment got done *before* the body went in the water.'

'Yes, I do see,' Lily agrees. 'But sometimes it did?'

'Oh, yes, no doubt about it,' Alf agrees. 'It's a cleaner sort of cut, see, when someone's taken an axe to 'em.'

'I suppose it would be,' Lily murmurs.

Absently Alf refills her cup and offers her a biscuit. 'We do see some strange old things, mind,' he says, and she can tell by his expression that he has gone back into his memories. 'One in particular turned up last autumn, and we never did get to the bottom of it.' He makes a wry face.

'What did it involve?' she prompts. She is hoping very much he won't suddenly remember he's talking to a weak and feeble woman, to quote an earlier queen, and, deciding this conversation really isn't fit for female ears, clam up. But it seems he is well into his stride now.

'Well, I don't rightly know how to describe it,' he muses. 'It was the naked body of a woman, and a very young woman at that. Lovely long hair she had, down below her waist, reddish-brown, and a nice figure. Generous curves, tiny little waist.' He puts down his cup and sketches a figure of eight between his hands, then, perhaps appreciating that these somewhat lascivious reflections are not suitable in front of a respectable woman, gives her a sheepish grin. 'Sorry, miss.'

'That's perfectly all right,' Lily says grandly. 'Please go on.'

After a moment, he does. 'Strange thing was that there was very little damage. Well, there was, because there was one deep laceration down between her – er, down her front and it turned out the internal organs had been eaten away, but that wasn't apparent on first sight. But the corpse was intact, with both arms, both legs and the head, and the skin looked as if it had been . . . well, *cooked* is the best way I can describe it.' He pauses, lost in thought. 'Yes. It was as if someone had basted that poor girl in a very hot oven, and her skin looked just like the Christmas goose when you take it out to carve it.'

The image is vivid, and Lily takes a hasty and restorative sip of tea. 'Goodness,' she says softly. 'The things you see, Mr Wilson!'

'Alf,' he says with a bashful grin. Discussions of roasted bodies, it seems, have prompted a new degree of intimacy. 'Call me Alf, miss.'

He talks some more, and Lily's mind is filled with death by drowning, with helpless victims fighting the force of the water till their strength runs out, of human flesh and human bone hurled against stone bridges and wooden hulls.

And among those victims, so many unidentified, she thinks as she gets up to leave, are possibly some, or all, of the seven women on Felix's list.

THIRTEEN

Felix presents himself at the police station on the road leading from Battersea Bridge just after nine o'clock the next morning. He feels bright and fresh; 'brand-new!' as a friend from his hard-drinking youth used to say. Felix doesn't think he is in the hard drinker category any more, for the four (possibly five) pints he imbibed yesterday over a very long lunchtime with Marm Smithers have had some surprisingly powerful effects on his physiology: he was still passing copious amounts of water well into the evening; he slept deeply for five hours and then all of a sudden was wide awake; he managed to sleep again but subsequently woke himself up with a tumultuous fart, although he thinks that might have been an after-effect of the pork pie. But today he is blessedly free of hangover symptoms, other than a nippy head which he hopes will dissipate as the morning progresses.

He used a lot of toothpowder as he cleaned his teeth earlier and is confident he no longer smells of beer. The superior sneer of the young constable who reluctantly comes out from behind the sturdy oak counter to see what he wants must thus be for another reason.

And quite soon this reason becomes clear.

Felix kicks himself for not having been forewarned by Marm Smithers' remarks about the police's lack of interest. As soon as Felix tells the spotty youngster in his uniform with its shiny buttons why he is there, the constable takes a small step back and tries to look down his nose at him. Not too successfully, because Felix is almost a head taller.

He flicks the piece of paper on which Felix has listed the names of the seven missing women. Felix keeps his notebook, in which are written many more details about each one, in his pocket. 'What do you expect *us* to do about it?' the constable demands. The emphasis on *us* suggests to Felix that the young man is a relative newcomer to the police force and still derives a proud pleasure from simply belonging to such an august body of fine men.

'May I know your name, constable?' Felix asks politely. He has already noted the number on the man's shoulder.

The constable shoots him a shifty look and says reluctantly, 'Police Constable Bullock.'

'Thank you. I would like to know, please, if any of these missing women have been found, and what has been discovered in the course of your investigations into their disappearance.'

'She's not one of ours, she's Chelsea.' A forefinger with a savagely bitten nail stabs at the piece of paper, and Felix reads his own writing: Rebecca Jones.

She was known as Beckie, he thinks, visualizing the notes he wrote down as Marm Smithers talked. Twenty-one, no known address, worked the Chelsea streets and paid her pennies for a night's lodging when she had the money. Black hair and dark brown eyes, and she came from Cardiff. Short, with a slim, petite figure and tiny hands and feet. Spoke grandly of going 'up West' to try her luck with the late-night men spilling out of the theatres and the private clubs.

'Well, what of the others?' Felix persists. He is already finding it difficult to hold on to his temper. 'Are you quite sure they are still missing?'

Constable Bullock shrugs. 'Dunno,' he says with a singular lack of helpfulness. 'As far as I know they are. It's like this, see,' he goes on, 'they don't register any sort of details with anybody, least of all us, because what they do is against the law.' His voice takes on a self-righteous tone. 'They come to London because they think they'll make easy money, then when they don't, they bugger off again. How are we to know who's meant to be here and who isn't?'

'I thought that as policemen your duty was to protect the general public,' Felix says, striving to keep his tone calm.

'Yeah, but not whores,' the young constable mutters.

Felix proffers his list again. 'Please?' he says, and the word almost catches in his throat.

The constable sighs and has another look. 'I knew her.' He indicates a name towards the foot of the page. He nods, turning to give Felix a faint smile. 'Oh, yes, I believe I may reveal to you some important information about *her*.'

Cicely Baker, Felix reads. Known as Ciss, he adds from memory, twenty-three years old, worked part-time in a pub, lived in lodgings with some other women, two of whom reported her missing. Brown eyes, brown hair with reddish tints, comely. Came from Yorkshire and assumed by the police to have returned there.

He waits to see what important information Constable Bullock is about to divulge.

'She was a barmaid,' the young constable says in a whisper, as if he is imparting state secrets. He nods in a self-congratulatory way. 'And my sergeant and me reckon she's gone home to Yorkshire.'

It costs Felix quite a lot to manage not to shout, *I already know what she did for a living and I no more believe that she's gone back to Yorkshire than that you have a brain or even an original thought in your thick head!*

After a moment or two he says with admirable calm, 'And it's not any concern of yours that none of these seven women has been found? That there is a total dearth of news concerning them?'

The constable doesn't answer in words. But his uninterested eyes and the faint shrug of his shoulders tell Felix all he needs to know. He folds and pockets his piece of paper, thanks Constable Bullock for his time and wishes him a good day – it's wise, he feels, particularly for an investigative agent, to maintain cordial relations with the police – and walks swiftly out onto the street.

Lily is feeling increasingly nervous as the time for the seance approaches. She dresses carefully, wearing what she wore to the previous Circle except for a different shirt. Downstairs, she is about to put on her smart shoes but at the last minute selects her boots, with the knife in its secret pocket inside the left one.

Felix is in the outer office, sitting at his desk and deep in his notes on the missing women. She calls out softly, 'I'm off now,' and he looks up.

Across the four or five paces between them it is as if he picks up her anxiety. And he doesn't even know she has just made quite sure she has her knife . . .

'You don't have to do this,' he says.

'I do,' she replies shortly. 'I admit I'm uneasy –' *uneasy* is an understatement – 'but I am taking that as an indication that there is indeed a dangerous threat to Albertina, which is all the more reason why I must be there.'

'I understand that,' he says. Then: 'Shall I come to meet you afterwards?'

It is a lovely thought and for a moment she almost says yes. Then, practicality overtaking emotion, she says, 'Better not. Albertina and Ernest would become suspicious if they saw Maud Garrett walking away with the inquiry agent they believe to be L. G. Raynor.'

He frowns briefly. 'G?'

'Hm?'

'What does the G stand for? I've been wondering.'

'Gertrude,' she says shortly.

'Gertie,' he murmurs, grinning.

She pretends she didn't hear.

He nods in a businesslike way. 'Very well, I won't meet you.' Then he adds in a jocular tone, 'I'll come looking for you if you're not back by six o'clock.'

It is the only element of this afternoon's enterprise to provide any comfort.

Several people Lily recognizes are being ushered inside the house on Parkside Road: George Sullivan stands back to let Dorothy Sullivan precede him, and the two elderly ladies whom Lily observed leaving the house the previous Thursday come hurrying up as Lily approaches. The one with the gauzy veil lifts it, looking nervously at Lily, and says, 'Are you coming in with us?' Lily nods, and she smiles and says, 'It's nice to see a new face!'

Ernest Stibbins greets Lily with a pleasant smile and a gentle touch on her elbow as he stands back to admit her. He looks up and down the road to see if there are any more Circle members coming along and, seeing there aren't, he closes the door.

As she stands in the hall Lily has a swift glimpse into a room leading off it further down the passage from the room in which the seance will be held. It is dimly lit – the curtains are half drawn across the window – and she makes out little more than big, bulky shapes where a desk and an upholstered chair stand. She notices a bookshelf. She can't somehow see Albertina as a bookish, learned sort of person and concludes the books belong to Ernest and this room is probably his study. Her eyes are drawn back to the shelves, and she sees that there are a pair of bookends supporting a short row of books on the top one. They are decorated with intriguing figures that remind Lily of illustrations in her childhood book of myths. The little statuettes represent some sort of hybrid, with human faces and animal bodies. She sees wings, clawed feet, long hair . . . are they harpies? Rocs? Manticores? Sphinxes? Minotaurs? No, the minotaur was the other way round, with the head of a bull and the body of a man. She tries to recall the details of the various beasts illustrated in the book of myths that Aunt Eliza gave her when she was seven and which they used to read together, Aunt Eliza telling her so much more than the rather basic little book ever did about the gods and goddesses of Greece, Rome and Egypt . . .

Then, with a very courteous gesture of apology, Ernest gently closes the door and ushers Lily, along with the other Circle members, into the seance room.

Lily, feeling slightly guilty at having been caught staring so blatantly into his study, feels a sense of kinship with him, for here undoubtedly is a fellow devotee of the myths of the ancient world. And, suddenly recalling having seen him outside the British Museum, she now understands why he was there. She looks at him with a smile, which he instantly returns.

She takes a seat between Dorothy Sullivan – who greets her like an old friend – and the woman in the veil, which she has now removed, along with her hat. 'I am Mrs Finchcock,' she mutters to Lily, breathing out a scent of liquorice cachou, 'Alice Finchcock, and this –' she indicates the woman on her other side – 'is my friend Mrs Margaret Tees.'

'Maud Garrett,' Lily whispers back.

When they have all settled themselves and are sitting, still

and expectant, in the dimness, Ernest leads Albertina into
the room and she takes her seat. She looks around the Circle,
murmuring greetings, and then nods to Ernest, who lowers the
gas so that the illumination in the heavily curtained room
dwindles further.

At first, it is as it was on Sunday. Albertina has a message
for Mrs Finchcock's friend Mrs Tees, to do with some uncle or
other who seems to have been in the army and had an unfortunate experience in Afghanistan. Dorothy Sullivan receives a
kindly word from Rodney – Lily thinks she feels an almost
imperceptible nudge in the ribs from Dorothy as Albertina
addresses her, but she could have been mistaken – and then the
room falls silent.

Lily wonders whether this is a common occurrence during
a seance, which wouldn't surprise her as it seems unreasonable
to expect Albertina or her spirit guides, depending on one's
opinion as to the origins of the messages, to carry on for an
hour or more without pausing for breath.

But then she becomes aware that the air has changed.

That is the only way she can describe it to herself.

And how inadequate a description it is, for suddenly Lily
is filled with dread, and she is so cold that she starts to shiver.

She looks from face to face around the table. Are the others
feeling it too? Does Mrs Margaret Tees's expression of vague
anticipation hide the fear that is crawling through her? Does
George Sutherland's quiet clearing of his throat suggest a
sudden urge to vomit in terror?

For Lily is beset with both these deeply unpleasant sensa-
tions, and it is only the warm, plump and comforting body of
Dorothy Sullivan close beside her that prevents her from crying
out her protest.

She sits very still, trying to deepen her breathing.

And then she makes herself look at Albertina.

Oh, oh, something is badly amiss, for Albertina doesn't look
well. No, it is much worse than that; Albertina looks dreadful.
She is deathly pale, there is a faint sheen of sweat on her
forehead and cheeks, and her wide eyes stare round the room
as if she is expecting to see the terror that she senses insinu-
ating itself all around her in tangible form.

Lily tries to keep a sense of proportion. Can it be that Albertina is pregnant – Dorothy Sullivan, after all, implied that a baby in the Stibbins household is a much-desired event – and all at once feeling sick? Lily has nursed many pregnant women through the distress of sickness and she is well aware how suddenly it can come on.

But then she thinks, if Albertina was pregnant, that would be an occasion for happiness.

And this new, horrible mood in the dark, shadowy room is so far from happiness that Lily can't come up with a word that adequately describes it.

The silence goes on.

Lily, her fear rising and her breathing slowly speeding up again, tries to analyse what is frightening her so much. She senses blackness; she can almost see it creeping through the air, a darker shade against the dim light. She remembers the thick veil she thought she saw descend over the window when Albertina was drawing the curtains, that day she watched the Circle members leave the house after the seance.

She had suspected that Albertina might be in danger even then. Now she is a long way past suspicion: she *knows* the threat is truly there, and it's suddenly become a great deal more powerful.

Whatever it is, it's imminent.

She is about to speak – she doesn't think she can bear the awful silence a moment longer – but then George Sutherland clears his throat again and Ernest Stibbins steps forward from his customary place behind Albertina's chair, proffering a glass of water which George takes with an apologetic smile.

The sheer normality of this small, considerate gesture seems to break the black terror. Lily feels Dorothy Sullivan's plump body relax, and Mrs Tees gives a little laugh, although for the life of her Lily cannot think what could possibly be funny.

Then Albertina says – and is it only Lily who hears the tremor in her voice? – 'I believe, dear friends, that the spirits may have withdrawn, for I do not sense any presence.'

And thank God for that, Lily thinks fervently.

Where did it come from? she thinks wildly. Was it a spirit? But no, she doesn't believe in spirits, does she? Even if everyone else in the room does, she will not accept that it was some disembodied force that made that ominous, threatening, terrifying black shadow.

Some outside agency, then, acting through someone in the room? This is possible, Lily feels, and surely more likely than to believe that gentlemanly, courteous George Sutherland, or kind Dorothy Sullivan or Mrs Finchcock or her friend Mrs Tees could want to impose such fear and dread upon the little gathering.

She glances at Albertina. Even if the other Circle members haven't noticed her discomfiture, Ernest has, and now he stands by her side, holding her hand, bending down and murmuring to her with such loving concern on his face that Lily is touched.

Yes, she thinks. There *was* something dark here just now, and I am not the only one who sensed it.

She discovers that she is saying the Lord's Prayer in her head. Especially the line *Deliver us from evil*, which she silently repeats again and again. She also feels a strong urge to hold Tamáz Edey's witch's bottle, and raises a subtle hand to clutch it through her clothes.

Then the dread has gone, and she begins to feel like herself again.

Her suspicion that Ernest has also felt his wife's distress is confirmed now, for tea and biscuits are served rather perfunctorily, and it seems to Lily that Ernest is a little hasty in his ushering-out of the Circle members, although as always he is courteous and mannerly, holding out George Sutherland's light coat for him to put on, helping Mrs Finchcock with her veil.

And then they are all out on the street, and George Sutherland is inviting Dorothy Sullivan to take his arm so he can escort her home, and the two elderly women are trotting away, and Dorothy, looking at Lily with anxious eyes, is saying, 'Will you be all right, dear? Won't you walk with us until Mr Sutherland may summon a cab for you?'

But Lily shakes her head. She has made a sudden decision, and she says, 'Thank you but no, for I am going to visit St Cyprian's before I go home.'

'You wish to pray, no doubt.' Dorothy nods understandingly. No, Lily thinks. I have no idea how I'm going to accomplish it, but I intend to find out from the vicar why, if he was in love with Albertina Goodchild as everyone seems to think, he encouraged her to marry Ernest Stibbins. 'Then give my regards to the Reverend Jellicote,' Dorothy is saying, 'and *please*, Miss Garrett, when you've finished, get him to call a cab!'

'Yes, I will, of course I will,' Lily replies. Then, before Dorothy can think of any other way to detain her, she strides away.

She thinks she knows where to find St Cyprian's Church, but the mental stress of the past hour must have thrown her more than she realizes and she takes a wrong turn, having to retrace her steps before eventually the big mass of the Victorian edifice looms up ahead of her. In contrast to its frowning grey bulk, a large and cheerily colourful sign has been put up on the small patch of grass in front of it, the bright yellow of the background and the vivid scarlet letters shining through the gloom: APRIL BAZAAR NEXT SATURDAY! it says, and a list of enticing activities ranging from a spring bonnet competition to coconut ice and candy floss are listed beneath. COME ALONG AND BRING ALL THE FAMILY! 2PM ONWARDS! ALL PROCEEDS TO THE MISSION!

She hurries through the porch, taking in but not really studying the big noticeboard for parish announcements and another, smaller one beside it that seems to be associated with some mission in the East End. She opens the inner door into the church and stands still, searching for the Reverent James Jellicote.

But the church is empty. Unless he is hiding under a pew or busy in the vestry, the vicar is not there.

Slowly Lily walks up the aisle. As the sharp disappointment of finding that her quarry is not where she expected him to be slowly recedes, she looks properly at the interior of St Cyprian's.

It looks from the outside like the sort of barn of a building so beloved by the architects of the age, and, indeed, there is space within for row upon row of pews. But as Lily walks through the shadowy space, she senses a whisper of something a great deal more ancient. The stone flags beneath her feet are deeply worn and she knows even without thinking that these sorts of indentations in such hard material cannot have been made by a mere few decades of wear. The floor, and therefore also the original building, has been here for centuries.

The last of the day's light shines suddenly through a window high up at the west end of the church. The day has been cloudy, so perhaps the falling sun has found a small gap as it sinks below the horizon. Lily stops, caught up in the little drama.

But then the light goes out and instantly the shadows spring forward. The side aisles on the far side of the long walls with their high arched openings become places of deep mystery. The high-backed pews whisper of spirits and strange beings who lie concealed, waiting to spring. Lily feels the thumping of her heart, fast, high in her throat.

And in the utter silence she hears a small noise.

She calls out, 'Mr Jellicote? Are you there?'

She thought she would sound strong and confident; she thought her words would banish the fear and the darkness. But her feeble little voice is like that of a child scared by a nightmare calling for her mother.

There is no answer.

She stands perfectly still, waiting, listening.

Nothing.

To distract her mind from the growing fear, she tries to think what could be the source of that noise. A mouse, perhaps. The settling of an ancient timber. The wind, rattling a window frame.

But none of these possibilities even begins to convince her, because she knows exactly what made that little sound: a foot, in a leather-soled shoe, striking the church's stone floor.

She senses a change in the air and she knows that whoever came in, whoever made that one mistake and let her hear a footstep, has gone as silently as he – she? – came in.

Lily is alone.

And then the panic overcomes her.

She walks swiftly back up the aisle and pushes open the heavy door. It is, she notes, soundless. In the porch she catches the faint hint of a scent . . . sandalwood? Perhaps it's incense. She catches a flash of gold writing on the smaller noticeboard

and reads *LADY VENETIA THEOBALD'S MISSION TO
LIMEHOUSE*, and her eyes light upon a piece of paper bearing
a banner headline that commands *All Good Christian Men
and Women Unite Against the Scourges of Lustful Practices,
Illegitimate Births and Disease!*

She catches the name James Jellicote: it is at the foot of
this piece, and he is its author.

On a little table beneath the noticeboard there is a small
stack of pamphlets about Lady Venetia's mission, priced at
fourpence each, and a small brass-bound wooden box with a
slot for the pennies, chained to a ring in the wall. Lily reaches
in her little bag for her purse, puts fourpence into the box and
takes a leaflet.

Then she emerges from the porch door into the murk and
the gloom of the advancing evening.

She is not afraid to begin with; indeed, she is ashamed of her
sudden terror inside St Cyprian's. It may be a relatively modern
church, she tells herself, but it is very deeply rooted in the
past, and undoubtedly it bears many scars. But there is nothing
there that can hurt me, she tells herself; nothing to be afraid
of! She lifts her chin and steadies her pace, walking easily
now, her courage surging back.

She is halfway along a long street of terraced houses, lit
only faintly by gas lamps that are too widely spaced, when
she finally has to admit that somebody is following her.

At first she puts it down to her imagination. Or to some other
solitary walker hurrying home. And she cannot be sure, for it
sounds less like another set of footfalls and more like an echo
of her own, so nearly perfect is the synchronization.

As if someone was deliberately matching his pace to hers . . .

She stops dead.

For a second or two the other footfalls carry on. Then they
too stop.

She hurries on. She is not running, *will not* run, but she
knows in her bones that she must get as quickly as she can
to a place where there is light and the presence of other people.

Thump, thump, thump, go her feet on the pavement, faster,
faster.

Thump, thump, thump go the other feet. Always, each time she increases her pace, they copy her.

The street seems endless. No lights show in the windows, the curtains are tightly drawn, the doors no doubt locked and barred against her, and nobody will help her. She knows with some small and still-logical part of her mind that this is nonsense but panic is rising again, too swift and too strong to be stopped.

The street ends in a T-junction, and the road that runs across it is wide, with the park on the far side. Lily has no idea how she ended up here, for it is not the right way home and she is some way from the road up to Battersea Bridge. But she is encouraged by the sight of this wider, surely more important, road, and she increases her pace again.

As if her pursuer has realized time is running out, his footsteps accelerate to a trot.

Lily strides out onto the wider road and looks frantically right and left. To the right there is nobody – *nobody!* How can it be? Is some malevolence working against her, making sure that she is all alone? – but to the left – oh, thank God! – a hansom cab has just drawn up outside a large house set back a little from the road and the occupant is climbing down, making some remark to the cabbie. The cabbie replies, already clicking to his horse, encouraging him to turn round and set off again.

Lily yells at the top of her voice, '*WAIT!*'

She gathers her skirts in her hand and runs down the wide road beside the park as if demons with red fire-filled eyes were after her. Her workman's boots are sturdy and strong, and she is grateful to the depths of her soul that she elected to wear them and not the fashionable shoes with their constricting toes and their elegant little heels.

The cabbie speaks a calm word to his horse and the horse stands still. Lily, panting, gasping for air – her stays prevent a good, deep breath – comes dashing up to the cab and the cabbie says pleasantly, 'Steady on there, miss! I heard you, and I wasn't going to go without you!'

'Thank you,' she manages. She tries to climb up into the cab but her legs are jelly and she slumps for a moment against the left-hand shaft.

'You all right down there?' comes the cabbie's voice from above.

'Yes!' It comes out as a squeak. She tries again to get into the cab, this time succeeding, and calls out, 'Hob's Court, please. It's across the river, at the end of—'

'I know where it is, miss,' the cabbie says easily. 'You just relax, now, and I'll have you home in two shakes.'

Lily sinks back against the leather upholstered seat. Her heartbeat gradually returns to normal and her terror recedes.

She has lost track of the time. As she says goodbye to her saviour the cabbie and hurries into Hob's Court it is quite dark, and she cannot see her watch. She goes up the steps to number 3 and is just about to put her key in the door when it opens.

Felix stands there, his face pale and drawn with anxiety. He steps aside so that she can go in, then closes the door with quite a forceful slam.

She takes off her hat as she walks through to her own office. 'What's the matter?' she asks.

He doesn't answer and so she turns round to look at him.

He meets her eyes, and she can't read the expression in his.

After a moment or two he says, 'I was worried about you. I've been – I came out to meet you.'

And she remembers him saying, *I'll come looking for you if you're not back by six o'clock.*

Now she can see her little watch. It reads ten minutes past seven.

She stares at him, and it seems to her that he is fighting to maintain his bland, innocent expression. She says, 'I am sorry that you were worried. I went to St Cyprian's after the seance to speak to the Reverent Jellicote, but in fact he wasn't there. I've been thinking about what you said regarding why he'd have encouraged her to marry Ernest if he—'

Felix's voice, low and controlled, says, 'Miss Raynor, it's a cloudy evening which means an early darkness. There's someone about in this area who is making women go missing, and whether this means he kills them or whether your friend Mrs Sullivan is correct in her belief that they are spirited away to deserts or harems just doesn't seem very relevant.' He is no longer sounding so controlled. 'And you decide you're going to go off all by yourself, wandering in the very streets from which women have disappeared, and you come home over an hour late and say *I am sorry that you were worried*!' His mimicry of her voice is cruel. He takes a step towards her and now she can see how angry he is. '*What did you fucking well expect?*'

His furious words echo in the room. Then abruptly he moves away, turning so that she can't see his face. 'I apologize,' he says. 'It is not my place to question what you do and I had absolutely no right to speak to you in such crude and vulgar terms.'

She waits until her heart isn't beating quite so fast. She is shocked, but not by his language. She has worked as a nurse with soldiers in far-flung parts of the world, after all, and is well used to the words men use when their emotions are heightened.

What has shocked her is that, beneath the anger, she sees fear: he really was worried about her, and the thought that she might have come to harm seems to have distressed him very much.

She says calmly, 'Your apology is accepted, Mr Wilbraham. You're right, I probably shouldn't have gone to St Cyprian's on my own when it was getting dark, but I didn't realize how late it was. Something happened at the seance that rather drove such sensible considerations out of my mind but, if you don't mind, I'd rather not talk about it now.'

He draws a sharp breath and she senses he very much wants to ask her, despite her reluctance. But he controls himself.

He goes back into the outer office. 'I'll see you tomorrow,' he says neutrally. 'Make sure to lock up after me.'

'I will,' she replies.

'Good night, Miss Raynor.'

'Good night, Mr Wilbraham.'

She hears the door close – much more gently this time – and he is gone.

FOURTEEN

In the morning, Lily shows Felix the leaflet. She finds herself standing very straight, face a blank mask, shoulders back, as if to demonstrate that she is firmly in control once more now and has forgotten all about the wild passions coursing through the office late yesterday. Felix's stiff expression suggests he is equally keen to put the incident behind him.

It is just as well, Lily thinks, that they have something so positive upon which to concentrate their minds.

'So the Reverend James Jellicote is interested in the prostitutes of Limehouse,' Felix says, slowly turning the dozen or so pages of the pamphlet. The written content, Lily has already noticed, does not fill all of it, for there are several half-page advertisements. James Jellicote, it appears, has offset the costs of producing his publication by suggesting others pay to advertise in it. Images inviting readers to buy Fry's Cocoa Powder, a patent ointment for saddle sores, ear trumpets, an anti-fat remedy and Pears' Soap thus are interspersed with earnest articles about the moral danger of prostitution to both the participants and those who have to witness women enticing their customers, and reminders that it is Christ's message that we love one another, and not to judge lest we be judged. 'Hmm,' Felix goes on. 'He writes with great authority on the life of a whore.' He points to an article with a heading in bold upper-case letters, A DAY AND A NIGHT IN LIMEHOUSE. 'How, I wonder, does he know about several women taking their customers to the one bed? Not at the same time, I presume . . .' He reads on. 'No, they take it in turns. And there's this section about the problems of staying clean for the more fastidious clients when the only washing facilities comprise a cold tap in a communal yard.'

'No doubt he has made it his business to meet and talk to the women he is trying to help,' Lily replies. Felix raises his head and gives her a long, slow look. 'He's a vicar!' She is stung to protest, even though he hasn't said a word. 'Isn't it his job to concern himself with those less fortunate than the well-fed householders who sit in his pews every Sunday?'

'Yes, of course,' Felix says shortly. 'But isn't it at least possible that he uses Christian charity and good works as a cover to mingle with women of loose morals because he enjoys it? Because he finds it exciting and daring?'

'Like Gladstone,' she says, acknowledging his point. 'He did his rescue work, as he called it, and *trod the path of danger*, by which it was taken to mean that he was tempted to do rather more than talk the women out of their sinful ways.'

'I read once that he liked to look at pornography,' Felix says. 'Both his reading matter and the company of prostitutes stimulated him, apparently, and he used to scourge himself to – er, to maintain self-control.'

'Quite,' Lily says. 'So, are you suggesting our James Jellicote has similar tendencies? That his interest in and support of this mission –' she points at the Lady Venetia Theobald brochure – 'has an ulterior motive?'

Felix shrugs. 'I wouldn't like to say. But he's a man, isn't he? He's unmarried, he's in love with Albertina, or at least he was, so we're told. Maybe the company of women of easy virtue satisfies his – er, his urges.'

But Lily hardly hears the last few words, for she has been thinking of something else. Catching Felix's eye, she is sure he is too. 'You don't think he could have anything to do with the missing women, do you?'

And instead of a robust denial, Felix says, 'I don't know.'

For a moment neither of them speaks. Then Lily thumps her desk, quite hard, and says, 'I cannot think why we have allowed ourselves to be distracted by these seven women! Oh, I'm not saying they don't matter – of course they do! – but we are running a business, we have paying clients to think of, and it is high time we gave them priority!'

'But suppose we are right about the Reverent Jellicote,' Felix says swiftly, 'and suppose he is taking women off the streets and doing something dark and evil with them? Isn't this just the sort of thing that someone with Albertina's sensitivity might pick up? Might his activities, whatever they consist of, be precisely the threat she perceives? He lives close by, doesn't he? And she goes to his church – it's where she met her husband!'

Lily looks at him in silence for a few seconds. Then she says, 'I believe you may be right.'

The remainder of Friday somehow passes.

Felix meets Marm Smithers for a few beers at lunchtime and Marm tells him glumly that he's feeling very guilty, having worked out that it's going to be nigh on impossible to get any lead on why the women are going missing and who is responsible unless and until it happens to another one.

Which, Felix reflects as he stumbles back to Hob's Court after several beers too many in the Cow Jumped Over the Moon, is enough to make anyone glum and guilty.

On Saturday, Lily announces her intention of going to the April Bazaar at St Cyprian's Church.

She manages to ignore Felix's not-very-well-suppressed amusement at her spring bonnet. It once belonged to her grandmother, and the vast circle of straw that pokes forward from the close-fitting crown effectively cuts off virtually all her peripheral vision. It is in a soft gold shade, and Lily has decorated it with swathes of lilac, purple, pink and blue ribbons and a bunch of pansies.

As she reaches St Cyprian's Church and goes through the gates to join the modest crowd enjoying the delights of the fair, she is glad she bothered. Her headgear is relatively modest, although walking over Battersea Bridge beneath its huge, sweeping brim attracted several interested looks, a snigger or two and considerable embarrassment to herself. Other women from the Reverend James Jellicote's congregation have been considerably more daring: one wears a wobbly cardboard structure in the form of a giant cup and saucer; another has fashioned a sailing ship complete with scraps of cotton for the sails; several sport extravagant coronets of foliage – usually laurel – with ribbons and some pretty spring blooms to brighten them up.

Lily tries her hand at the coconut shy and buys a poke of

fudge, which is delicious and melts in the mouth. She sees
James Jellicote lobbing the wooden hoops at the hoopla stand,
and notices in passing what a strong man he is (he has removed
his dark coat and throws the hoops in his rolled-up shirtsleeves
and waistcoat). She observes some of the Circle members:
George and Robert Sutherland, who both tip their hats to her;
Miss Hobson and Mrs Philpott, who are behind the White
Elephant stall trying valiantly to sell mismatched china and
chipped glassware and fail to notice her.

And then there is a gentle hand on her arm and a cheery
voice says, 'Miss Garrett! How good of you to come to our
little fair, and what a beautiful bonnet!'

It is Dorothy Sullivan, and her pleasant face is rosy with
the excitements of the day.

'I am enjoying it very much,' Lily assures her. 'And what
a lot of people!'

'Yes, it's quite a good turn out,' Dorothy agrees. She leans
closer and adds in a confiding whisper, 'I do not see Mr and
Mrs Stibbins, however.' She gives a knowing nod and Lily
guesses she is just longing to be asked for elucidation.

Lily willingly provides it. 'Oh?' she says. 'And do you have
an idea as to why they are absent?'

'W-e-l-l,' Dorothy replies, drawing out the word, 'I saw her
yesterday, in the late afternoon, and I thought she looked a
little peaky. She was tired, she said, for she had been to Pearson
and Mitchell – that's the department store where dear Ernest
has his employment – and she was carrying some large books
of wallpaper samples and some paint charts. Seeing that they
must surely weigh heavy, I helped her carry them for the last
part of the walk to her house.'

'Could Ernest not have brought them home?'

'That's what I said, dear, and Albertina was a little *evasive*,
but I had the impression that Ernest might not be quite as keen
on these home improvements as she is!' She gives a light little
laugh. 'I know how husbands are, my dear! They become
accustomed to their homes exactly as they are, and the prospect
of all the upheaval and the inconvenience of altering rooms
and moving walls, and repapering and painting, really doesn't
seem worth it! My dear Rodney was just the same! I had to

work quite hard to convince him when it was time for even quite modest amounts of redecorating, and I understand that Albertina has rather more in mind.'

It is Lily's turn to lean over and whisper. 'And so you suspect that they have absented themselves from the church fair to begin on the decorating?'

But Dorothy looks faintly shocked, and it becomes apparent that she didn't mean this at all. 'Oh, *no,* dear, no! Dear Ernest is such a dependable member of our congregation, and always such a support to Mr Jellicote, that I am quite sure he would never even consider missing such an occasion as this for purely personal reasons.'

And coming to the fair would mean he could postpone beginning on the home improvements a day longer, Lily thinks cynically. 'What is your suspicion, then?' she asks.

Dorothy Sullivan looks at her for moment, her eyes rather bright. 'Albertina looked a little pale on Thursday, did she not?' Lily agrees that she did. 'Then I am wondering if . . .' Dorothy doesn't finish her sentence, but the tiny gesture she makes towards her own plump little belly does it for her.

'Oh, I see!' Lily exclaims. 'Yes indeed, perhaps you are right.'

And later, walking thoughtfully home to Hob's Court, Lily finds herself saying a quiet little prayer: please let it be true, and Albertina really is pregnant, because perhaps something so good, so pure and positive as a baby on the way for a loving husband and wife will have the force to drive away evil.

The next day is Sunday, and Lily sets off in the afternoon for the seance. Other Circle members stand on the little path outside as she approaches, and Ernest, a slight frown on his face, is standing in the doorway, the door all but closed behind him.

'I am so sorry to say that there will not be a gathering of Circle today,' he says, his eyes full of anguish. 'You have all had a wasted journey for which I deeply apologize –' he looks very embarrassed, Lily notices – 'and I regret the inconvenience very much.'

'What has happened, Ernest?' asks Mrs Sullivan in a hushed tone.

'My dear wife—' Ernest stops, then tries again. 'Albertina is indisposed,' he says.

There are various murmurs of sympathy and commiseration, and a general shuffling as the assembled Circle members bid Ernest farewell, turn and prepare to depart. The prevailing mood, Lily thinks, is a mixture of disappointment and fascinated speculation.

And it is not long before the latter gains expression.

Dorothy Sullivan hurries to Lily's side as they stroll away. Looking back towards the Stibbins house with knowing eyes, she leans in close and says quietly, 'They weren't at church this morning.' She nods, her eyes sparkling. 'And women in a *delicate condition* tend to feel unwell in the mornings, do they not, Miss Garrett?'

But before Lily can reply, George Sullivan calls out – 'Mrs Sullivan, Robert and I will happily see you home!' – and, with obvious reluctance, she tears herself away from Lily and trots off to join the two men.

Discussing it on Monday morning, however, Lily and Felix explore the possibility that Albertina's 'indisposition' may have a very different cause.

'She's afraid,' Lily says flatly. 'That's why she couldn't face another seance: the fear is overcoming her.'

'I wish I could say I disagree, but I don't,' Felix replies. 'Do you think that whoever is threatening her is turning up the pressure?'

Slowly Lily shakes her head. It is precisely what she fears – her mental image of poor, terrified Albertina at last Thursday's seance is still far too vivid – but somehow putting it into words is a step too far.

After a moment, during which she can almost *see* Felix's mounting anxiety, she says, 'I'll make us a cup of coffee. It might—'

But abruptly Felix stands up and heads towards the door.

'Where are you going?' Lily cries.

'I'm going to speak to James bloody Jellicote,' he replies.

*   *   *

Felix makes the journey down to the river, across Battersea Bridge and on to St Cyprian's Church in record time, his long legs eating up the distance. The gaudy poster advertising Saturday's fete is still there, although one corner has been torn and is flapping in the breeze. Ignoring it, Felix strides on towards the church, flings open the door and bursts inside.

James Jellicote is not there.

He's not in the body of his church, nor in the vestry, nor the graveyard, nor, when Felix marches over to it, the vicarage. The door is opened to his thunderous knocking by a small, aproned woman with tightly curled gingery hair who says she hasn't seen him that morning.

'I don't live in, see,' she says, 'for all that I'm his house-keeper, since he always tells me he doesn't need more than I can provide in a day's work. Me,' she adds confidingly, 'I reckon as how he likes his privacy, but then he's a single man, dedicated to his living and his flock, so why not, I say?'

'Quite,' Felix says tersely. 'Do you know where he is?'

'Well, like I say, he wasn't in when I got here, so I'm only guessing, see, but if you want my opinion, I'd say he's prob-ably out walking, which is something he often does while he works out what to say in the next week's sermon.'

'What time will he—'

But the garrulous housekeeper hasn't finished. Raising her voice to drown out Felix's interruption, she goes on, 'He delivered ever such a good one yesterday, all about hating the sin and not the sinner. Brought in three or four references to Fallen Women –' the capital letters are audible – 'and not a few of the congregation didn't like it, which you could tell from the clearing of throats and the shuffling of feet.' She chuckles. 'Quite carried away, he was! He—'

'Thank you,' Felix interrupts. 'I'll call again later.'

But as he walks away, his pace slower now that his urgent objective has been foiled, Felix wonders. Is it not, he thinks, a little early in the week to be working on next Sunday's sermon?

He wonders again when he returns half an hour later and Jellicote still isn't there. There is no answer to his knock on the door, and he has a strong suspicion that the housekeeper knows full well who it is and, in the vicar's continued absence, has no intention of picking up the earlier conversation where it was left off.

Walking away, Felix spots a man cutting back forsythia next door to the vicarage. He nods to Felix and calls out, 'After his reverence, are you?'

'Yes,' Felix replies.

'He's out,' the man says helpfully.

'So I observe.' Felix tries not to sound caustic but fears he may have failed.

'I can tell you where he is, though,' the man goes on.

'I'd be most grateful,' Felix says meekly.

'He's gone up the East End to that charity house,' the man says smugly, evidently proud to be the one with knowledge of the vicar's whereabouts. 'He's delivering the takings from Saturday's bazaar to that mission place he goes on about, the one for women who are no better than they should be.' He gives an affronted little shudder, as if the very mention of such women is too much. 'No saying how long he'll be,' he adds over his shoulder, going back to his forsythia. 'Once he's up there giving them what for, he often stays away all day.'

And, walking thoughtfully away, once again Felix wonders . . .

It is late on Monday afternoon.

Felix is at his desk in the front office and Lily has just gone through to the back to make a cup of tea. He can hear her chatting to Mrs Clapper.

The outer door opens and he hears a tentative footfall, and then several more. Then Ernest Stibbins's head peers round the door to the office.

He looks ashen.

Felix rushes towards him, takes his elbow and guides him to a chair, positioning him on the opposite side of the desk. 'Mr Stibbins,' he says, far too loudly, for he wants to make sure that Lily realizes who their visitor is and doesn't appear; Miss Maud Garrett has no place in the offices of the World's End Bureau. He resumes his own seat. 'My dear Mr Stibbins, whatever has happened?'

Ernest, who jumped slightly as Felix shouted his name, subsides into a crouching heap, his spine bent in a curve, his hands up to his face. Through them he mumbles, 'It's my wife, my Albertina.'

A sick feeling spreads through Felix. 'Is she unwell?' Please, let it be that and nothing worse than that, Felix prays. Let her be sick with something temporary and not too serious, such as the effects of the early stages of pregnancy.

But Ernest drops his hands and reveals his anguished face. Felix is horrified at his expression. 'No, oh, no, no, no, Mr Raynor! She is not unwell, she is – oh, I can hardly bear to put it into words!'

'You must!' Felix urges. 'Come on, Mr Stibbins!'

Ernest Stibbins meets his eyes. 'Oh, Mr Raynor, she is *missing!*'

The last word emerges as a howl of anguish.

Felix waits, silent and still, for Ernest to recover himself. Then, opening his notebook and filling his nib with ink, he says calmly, 'Tell me everything you can think of.' Realizing immediately that this is far too wide a command for a man in Ernest's highly distressed state, he breaks it down to specifics. 'Let us begin with when you last saw her.'

Ernest frowns, the effort to concentrate and speak in words that make sense obviously costing him dear. 'Well, let me see . . .' He clears his throat, sniffs, pats his nose and eyes with an immaculate handkerchief. 'Let me see, now. She has been feeling a little unwell over the past few days – Thursday, I believe it was, when she first complained of an unusual lassitude and a slight headache – and on Friday she somewhat unwisely insisted on struggling home from Pearson and Mitchell – that's the department store where I work, as I believe I told you?'

'You did indeed,' Felix agrees.

'Where was I?' Ernest's eyes fill with renewed panic.

'Explaining that Mrs Stibbins had been to your department store,' Felix supplies, remembering not to add the details that he already knows, Lily having reported her conversation with Dorothy Sullivan.

'Yes, yes, yes,' mutters Ernest, frowning in anguish. 'I said

I would bring the samples of wallpaper and curtain fabric and the cards with paint colours home with me when I returned, and not to burden herself with them when she wasn't feeling quite herself, but she was impatient, Mr Raynor, and so excited at the prospect of brightening up our little house, and she said she could not bear to wait!' Once more his hands come up to cover his face, and his shoulders shake as he sobs.

Sensing that a comforting word or hand would only undermine him further, Felix sits silent and still.

'And then on Saturday we had fully intended to go to the St Cyprian's April Bazaar. Albertina had made a very fetching hat, and I had undertaken to help Mr Jellicote by manning the second-hand book stall, but as the morning progressed it became clear to me that she really wasn't up to it, and I persuaded her to lie down on the sofa with her feet up under a rug, and I made her a cup of tea, which she enjoyed.' His expression as he recounts these small domestic attentions is pitiful. 'Then on Sunday – yes, of course, Sunday was yesterday – she wanted to go to church and to see Mr Jellicote afterwards to apologize for our absence the day before, but once again she wasn't strong enough, and we rested and I read out snippets from the local paper to her, only then she seemed to doze off, and so I tiptoed away.' He pauses, looking down at his hands clenched together in his lap, the now-crumpled and damp handkerchief between them.

He takes a deep breath.

'This morning I left for work at seven forty-five, as I always do,' he continues, 'and I was allowed to leave a little earlier than usual – in the middle of the afternoon, in fact – because I have been doing many hours of overtime recently, and my superior said I had earned a little leave. And then when I opened the door and called out, "Albertina my dear, here I am, nice and early!" there was *no answer*.' His voice breaks on the words. 'Mr Raynor, I *knew* she had gone, the moment I walked in!'

'And what did you find as you hurried through the house searching for her?' Felix asks quietly.

'Oh . . .' Ernest's eyes focus on the far side of the room and Felix senses he is seeing the empty house again. 'Everything was neat and tidy, just as it always is. I believe she must have been there at midday, for her plate, cutlery and glass were on the draining board, washed up, of course, but not put away. Which isn't really like her . . .' He frowns.

This is all very well, thinks Felix, and these small details may prove useful, but now it's time to push on to the main point. 'Mr Stibbins, you have notified the police, haven't you?'

Ernest's mournful eyes with their reddened lids stare at him. 'Naturally, Mr Raynor. But—' He cannot go on.

'But?' Felix prompts, controlling his impatience with some difficulty.

'I was taken through to speak to a sergeant,' Ernest says, 'and he took down Albertina's name and our address, and, like you, he asked when I had last seen her. But, Mr Raynor, it was the same man to whom I spoke when I tried to make them help me because Albertina was being threatened! I said – and I fear I may have become a little belligerent – "I *told* you she was in danger and you did nothing, and now she has gone missing! *Now* do you believe me?"'

'And what was the response?'

Ernest sighs heavily. 'The sergeant ordered his constable to come back to the house with me and I had to stand and watch as he went through Albertina's chest of drawers and her cupboard, and then he said that there appeared to be garments missing, and what about a suitcase, and I had to admit that a suitcase was indeed not in its normal place on top of the wardrobe, and that some articles of clothing and some personal items such as her hairbrush and hand mirror were not in their accustomed places, and then –' he smothers another sob – 'and then the constable said it looked very much as if she had left of her own accord and there wasn't anything they could do, she being over twenty-one and free to come and go as she pleased.' He folds his arms on Felix's desk and drops his head onto them.

It is a dreadful, stark tale. Felix can understand the reaction of the policeman – he wonders if it is Constable Bullock – but nevertheless he has enormous sympathy for Ernest Stibbins.

Again, he waits.

As Ernest straightens up, Felix expects to see tears in his

eyes. They are there, but just for an instant something else is there as well, an expression far too fleeting to pin down. All the same, it astonishes Felix, and he has the sudden thought that he wouldn't like to be the man who has taken Albertina Stibbins – if, indeed, she has been taken – when Ernest catches him.

Such, he reflects, is the power of love.

After a moment, Felix says quietly, 'Mr Stibbins, I suggest you go home.'

'But I—'

'I know that returning to your empty house is the last thing you want to do, but there is always the possibility that your wife may return,' Felix goes on.

'What if the police constable is right? What if she's left me?' Ernest mumbles, his voice breaking and cracking with pain.

But Felix, who is trying hard not to envisage something far, far worse, doesn't know how to reply.

Eventually, when Ernest Stibbins doesn't move, Felix gets to his feet and gently takes hold of his arm. 'You must go home,' he says. He wants to make wild promises, such as *I'll set out right away and start looking for her*, or *I have an idea who may have taken her and I'll do for him myself if I beat you to it.*

He manages to hold his peace.

Lily comes out of the kitchen when Ernest has gone. She is wide eyed. 'Where is she?' she whispers. 'Oh, dear God, what's happened? What should we do?'

'I'm going back to St Cyprian's and I—' Felix begins to say.

But abruptly he stops, because Mrs Clapper, who usually remains firmly in the kitchen domain all the time, and especially when there are visitors to the Bureau, has emerged and is crouched down just inside the front door.

'Such goings-on as I never heard!' her voice floats back to them. 'People going missing and packing their bags, wives leaving good husbands, grown men sitting sobbing like babies, and now this, whatever it is, on the mat!' She is tutting, wiping at the small patch with a cloth. 'Smells like perfume, but it's tacky and I'll be lucky if I ever get it off.'

The muttering degenerates into a low rumble.

Lily looks at Felix, who has turned to go.

He waits for some sort of protest, but it is not forthcoming. All she says is, 'Be careful.'

A little under an hour later he is back.

He goes into the outer office and slumps into his chair. He closes his eyes. He senses Lily, coming to stand beside him. He says dully, 'He wasn't there and there's no sign of Albertina.'

FIFTEEN

In the morning, Lily is in the office very early.

She has barely slept. She lay awake until well after midnight – more like one or even two o'clock – and just as she was at last beginning to feel drowsy and thinking she might actually drop off, the front door opened with a scrape and a clatter, closed with a resounding bang and the Little Ballerina's elephantine tread in her diver's boots went echoing down the passage to the lavatory, where shortly afterwards the roar of the flush began and seemed to go on for ever. Then came the crash, crash, crash as she made her way upstairs to the first floor, followed by the opening and even louder closing of her own door and the pattering to and fro as she went about the interminable process of preparing for bed. As if all that were not enough for Lily's frayed nerves, the Little Ballerina was humming, loudly and totally tunelessly, what appeared to be one of the better-known melodies from *Sleeping Beauty*, a rough approximation of the same little phrase over, over, over and over again.

And Lily, losing her patience and her temper at last, banged on the floor with the heel of her boot and yelled, '*SHUT UP!*'

To her surprise, it worked.

Now, though, the all but sleepless night is catching up with her, and she feels scratchy-eyed and fraught, as well as desperately anxious about Albertina Stibbins. She and Felix managed to come up with one or two ideas about what they should do next last night before he left, but, thinking about them now, they seem petty and ineffectual.

Lily hopes very much that Felix will arrive with good news. He promised to call at the police station on his way in, and who's to say the constable, or the sergeant, won't greet him with the cheerful tidings that Albertina is safe and well and restored to her loving husband? Failing that – and Lily has to admit she is not over-optimistic – then perhaps Felix will have some better ideas as to how to go about looking for her.

Lily admits to herself that she has none whatsoever.

The street door opens and closes, and she hears his step in the hall.

Why doesn't he come bounding in like he always does?

He crosses the hall and comes in through the open door to the outer office.

'Is there any—' she begins.

She stops, for she has caught sight of his face.

Felix is holding a rolled-up newspaper as if he would prefer it to be a machete. Unfurling it – he has been clutching it so tightly that it resists being smoothed out – he flings it down before her on his desk.

'Look at this!' he shouts, the suddenness and the volume combining to make her jump violently.

She looks.

And the awful words fill her mind.

PEER'S SON'S SUICIDE! shouts the headline.

And, below, in slightly smaller print: *SON AND HEIR OF LORD BERWICK FOUND HANGING IN OUTBUILDING ON FAMILY ESTATE.*

Struck dumb, Lily reads on.

The body of the Honourable Julian Willoughby, only son of Lord Berwick, was found early yesterday morning at the rear of a disused stable block by a groom hunting for a lost hound, the story begins. *He was hanging by the neck from a beam and the state of the corpse suggested he had been dead for some time. According to local sources, he had come down to the family estate, Willowdene, the day before to dine with his parents and stay overnight in his childhood home. It is believed that a matter of grave import was on his mind and that he discussed it over dinner with his father. There are reports of heated words, and the young man was observed to fling himself out of the dining room, upsetting a tray of crystal glassware and a brandy decanter. Asked to comment upon what had upset his only son, Lord Berwick said merely that it was a private matter. Our social correspondent, however, is able to report that of late the Honourable Julian Willoughby has been seen about town in the company of an actress, Miss Violetta da Rosa, at present preparing for a starring role in* Miss Sanderson's Fortune, *the new production at the Glass Slipper Theatre off Drury Lane; Miss da Rosa has been playing the ingenue lead for many years and is beloved of theatre-goers both in London and the provinces.*

Oh, the cruelty of that little dig, thinks Lily. *Playing the ingenue lead for many years*; the journalist who came up with that might just as well have said Violetta was getting on in years and considerably older than her young suitor . . .

But she knows she is concentrating on the sharp and unkind little details when it is the terrible whole picture that she should be absorbing.

She forces herself to go on.

Although Miss da Rosa was said to be too distraught for comment yesterday, friends of the actress report that marriage between her and young Julian was a likely and happily anticipated event. It is left to the reader's own conjecture as to what Lord Berwick might have had to say on the matter, and it cannot be assumed with any degree of certainty that his son's dreadful deed in taking his own life comes in reaction to a possible refusal on the part of Lord Berwick to countenance Miss da Rosa as a daughter-in-law and the future Lady Berwick.

The present holder of that august title is—

Lily stops reading.

She forces herself to look up and meet Felix's furious eyes. She would like to tell herself that his fierce anger is at the journalist and his horrible story, but she doesn't believe it.

Gathering her courage, she says quietly, 'Go on, then.'

He raises his eyebrows. 'Go on?'

'You are bursting to tell me this is all my fault; that I should have told Lord Berwick that Violetta da Rosa was a woman of exemplary reputation with not a single thing in her past that could possibly make her unsuitable as a wife for his son. You want to say that I was wrong not to emphasize how hard she has worked all her life, what a fine and reliable actress she has always been. You think I should have advised him to let Julian go ahead with his wedding plans, and give his son his blessing!'

She too feels her temper rising. She stands up, swinging round the desk towards Felix until she is standing right in front of him. 'In short, you believe I should have fudged the truth; *lied*, not to put too fine a point on it! Dear *God*, Felix –' the words explode out of her and she has called him by his Christian name without thinking – 'you have *no idea* what I've had to do to get the World's End Bureau established as a viable business! You don't know what my life was like before, what happened to me in India—' But she cannot bear even to think about that and she shuts off the sentence long before it has come to its end. 'This means so much to me, and I have to succeed, I *have* to! If I begin altering the facts, amending the truth so as not to hurt people and to save them suffering, what is that going to do to our reputation? Can you really see men and women who want to be told the stark facts bothering even to *ask* a bureau with a reputation for lying to work for them?' She is panting now, trying to draw a deep breath and feeling her stays cutting painfully into her ribs. 'If you can –' she is shouting now – 'then you're a bigger fool than I think you are!'

'A fool, am I?' he shouts back. His face is scarlet with fury. 'It's foolish, then, is it, to care about a young man driven to suicide? To feel remorse and grief because it didn't have to happen?'

'*YES IT IS!*' Lily screams. 'We have to tell people the truth, and that's just what we did! There wasn't a word of a lie in the report I presented to Lord Berwick! If he chose to forbid Julian to marry Violetta, and if Julian couldn't take the disappointment, if he was too feeble to envisage life without her, then it's his—'

But she hears inside her head what she is about to say and she knows she can't.

And with a nasty smile, Felix finishes the thought for her: 'It's his own fault for not being as strong as you?'

She can hardly believe she's heard right. Yes, she was about to say it was a failing within Julian that led him to take his own life, but just in time she stopped herself.

But that Felix believes she is strong . . . Oh, that is astonishing.

He is still looking at her, and she doesn't like what she sees in his face.

Before he can speak she gets in first. 'I can't be in the same room with you,' she says very coldly. 'Furthermore, if this dreadful news has shown up the irreconcilable differences between us that I fear it has done, then I shall have to consider carefully whether you have a future with the World's End Bureau.'

Then she goes out into the hall, picks up her light jacket, puts on her hat and climbs into her boots. She collects her little bag from its hook, makes sure her keys are inside and, opening the door, steps out into the street. The temptation to slam the door very hard is all but irresistible, and she only just manages not to.

She flies out of Hob's Court and emerges onto World's End Passage, turning to her right without even thinking about it and towards the Embankment and the river.

She walks as swiftly as she can to Battersea Bridge, climbing the steps and striding out until she is at a spot midstream, where she stops, leaning her forearms on the rail and catching her breath.

She feels awful.

The Honourable Julian Willoughby is dead. He has hanged himself in a disused stable on his ancestral estate. Poor Little Jack Horner, forever in his corner, his dreamy-eyed plan to make a wife and a titled Lady out of a glamorous actress a little past her prime, and with an illegitimate daughter into the bargain, blown to pieces. Suddenly Lily wonders if there is anyone to comfort Violetta, and immediately thinks, of course there is, there's Billy.

It all seems unspeakably tragic.

We – *I* – should have done better, Lily realizes.

And then there's Albertina Stibbins, she thinks wildly, whose deeply anxious husband appealed to the World's End Bureau for help because he didn't feel he could protect her alone, and now she's missing, and God knows what has happened to her – what's happening to her even as I stand here above the great surge of the river – and so *that's* a failure too, and now I've had the most dreadful row with Felix, who might be quite wrong in his passionate declaration that I shouldn't have told Lord Berwick the bald truth about Violetta but dressed it up and hidden it behind mitigating circumstances and a general approval of Julian's would-be bride, but, even if he was wrong, had a perfect right to express his opinion – and to criticize me – and now I've told him he may not have a job with my Bureau any more and *oh I don't want him to go!*

Her thoughts swirl up with a force that feels like a whirlwind and then abruptly subside, leaving her weak and shaky.

She goes on standing there, quite still now.

Presently she thinks, what should I do now? Go back? But Felix will be there and I am not ready to confront him yet.

You are not ready to admit to him that he may be right, says her conscience censoriously.

Where else could she go? Who else can she seek out?

And it dawns on her, as she watches the Thames flow powerfully past beneath her, that she has nobody.

She lets the dismal realization sink in.

Before it can depress her totally, she makes up her mind. *When troubled, work* has long been her motto. It served her when she lost her father and was abandoned by her flighty mother, far too preoccupied with trying to make her lover marry her before her pregnancy showed to spare a thought for her grieving daughter. Then Lily had thrown herself with renewed determination into her studies, first with Aunt Eliza, then at Miss Heale's School. The same motto served her when, struggling with the demands of her five years' training with St Walburga's Nursing Service, the pangs of homesickness for the pharmacy in Hob's Court and the beloved people who lived there became too much to bear. It served her in India, when news of the deaths of her grandparents reached her and she was so far away that there was not a hope of getting home for the funerals. It served her when The Incident shocked her to her very core and ended the career and the life she loved.

Well, it can damned well serve me now, Lily thinks.

Work.

What, then, should she do?

Felix – oh, Felix! – failed yesterday in his attempts to see the Reverend Jellicote. And surely he had good reason to seek the man out, for at best he may be able to help in the search for Albertina and at worse—

But she can't bring herself to think about *at worse*.

Felix didn't find James Jellicote. Well, Lily will see what she can do.

She turns towards the south and strides off the bridge.

But on the way to St Cyprian's she finds herself walking along Parkside Road.

The door to Albertina and Ernest's house is ajar . . .

She walks up the little path and pushes it wider, calling out, 'Mr Stibbins? Are you there? Is there—'

She had been just about to say, Is there any news? Just in time she remembers she is Maud Garrett, and has no way of knowing that Albertina has gone missing.

She stands just inside the door, irresolute. She can smell something that is familiar . . . Yes. It's the scent she thought was sandalwood, and she detected it in the porch at St Cyprian's. James Jellicote must be here, she thinks, he'll know about Albertina, of course he will, and he'll have come round to offer his support and his help, and he and Ernest will be in the back parlour sharing a pot of tea and the vicar will be suggesting they say a prayer to ask God to keep Albertina safe until she can be restored to her home and her loving husband.

Of course Mr Jellicote isn't responsible for Albertina's disappearance!

For a moment or two, she believes it.

'Mr Stibbins?' Lily calls again. 'Mr Jellicote?'

No answer.

She advances into the hall. The spicy, woody smell intensifies. The door on the right to the seance room is closed, as is the one to the room just beyond it. Ernest's study, she recalls, with the desk and the bookshelves and the bookends with the mythological figures.

A shadowy little passage leads on to the rear of the house. So convinced is Lily by her mental image of the desperately worried husband and the kindly minister who has come to help him sitting sipping at their cups of tea that she follows the course of the passage, into the dimness.

Here is the kitchen, with the scullery leading off it. Kitchen sink, dresser with cheerful blue and white plates, a table, chairs.

Empty chairs, and no sign of tea.

Another door is tucked away beneath the stairs, which rise up on Lily's left. The door is open, just a crack, and the scent of sandalwood seems to be coming from whatever cupboard, or room, lies beyond.

She walks over to it on tiptoe. She pushes it further open. Stone steps lead steeply down into the fragrant cellar below. It is utterly dark down there, but an oil lamp hangs on a hook beside the door, vestas in their case on a little shelf beside it. Lily takes out a vesta and strikes it on the side of the case, then puts the flame to the lamp's wick. Very carefully, holding the lamp with one hand and the other on the wall to steady herself, she descends.

The cellar is quite small: a stone-floored space some two paces by three, containing shelves on one wall on which there are a meat safe, a bottle of milk, a covered plate of cheese and a muslin-wrapped slab of butter, three bottles of stout set on the floor below the bottom shelf. It's cold down there, Lily realizes, and, like everyone lucky enough to have a cellar, Albertina and Ernest use it to keep perishable food fresh and beer cold.

She jumps down off the bottom step and stands on the stone floor. There is a neat pile of boxes against the wall to her right, and she is just wondering why the cellar doesn't extend for the whole width of the house – it's quite clear that it doesn't – when there is movement in the shadows and before Lily's amazed and frightened eyes the boxes begin to come towards her. And with a shrill meow, the small cat that must have been hiding on top of them leaps down and, flicking its neat little body round Lily's ankles, flies away up the steps.

The boxes must have been stuck together, she thinks frantically, for as they were disturbed by the little cat's movements they didn't topple over one by one but fell as a single mass. Straight onto the floor, so that she has to jump back. They all seem to be empty.

In the space against which the boxes stood she can make out the wall, featureless, blank.

Lily steps round the boxes and looks at it. She taps it. It sounds just like a wall should. She taps again, then curls her hand into a fist and hits it.

And she hears, very faintly, a soft moan.

Now she is acting with no thought except to find a way in. She feels all round the wall, left edge, right edge, as high as she can reach. And there is a brick that is recessed slightly and that moves when she hits it. She finds a corner, feeling a fingernail break as she does so, and pulls it out. There is, as she knew there would be, a handle behind the brick. She turns it, a catch is released, and that portion of the wall reveals itself to be a door. She opens it and steps inside the concealed space beyond.

She has no idea what to expect. She is in a dream now, and the strong scents in the cellar are intensifying powerfully as the hidden door opens. Is it a drug? she wonders. Do they keep something dangerous hidden in there, well away from nosy visitors so that nobody gets hurt?

But I *am* getting hurt . . .

For her head is pounding as painfully as if a sudden migraine has struck.

Her eyes take in what is before her but the images mean nothing to her brain. She steps further into the hidden cellar, trying to force herself to think. *Think.*

A workbench runs all along the left-hand wall. A cupboard with a narrow door is built into the corner. A row of trestle tables stand before the rear wall facing towards her, close together, only inches between them. On them are statues, some enclosed in wrappings, some covered with what look like shells. The three at the right-hand end have rather beautiful masks over where the faces would be. Images stir inside Lily's sluggish mind: the little figures on Ernest Stibbins's bookends; the wonderful, beautiful statues from the ancient world in the British Museum. Is this how Ernest spends his spare time, then? Making these lifelike figures, wrapping them, varnishing them, decorating them with those gorgeous masks with their vivid colours?

Count them, a voice says in Lily's head. COUNT THEM. *COUNT THEM!*

One, two, three, four, five, six . . . seven.

Oh, God.

She has no idea what she's looking at, what is going on down here.

What Ernest Stibbins has done.

Then she hears the moan again, softer now, helpless, hopeless. Spinning round – for it comes from behind her – she sees another trestle table in a recess beneath the steps. On it, deathly white, naked, the smooth flesh innocent of every scrap of body hair, flawless, perfect, lies Albertina Stibbins.

Her wide, frantic eyes meet Lily's. And she mouths, *Help me.*

Lily doesn't know what to do. She puts down the lamp and lunges forward, taking Albertina's hand. It is cold, it is slippery with oils. The fragrance is very strong here and it is centred around the still body on the table.

'What has happened?' Lily whispers.

But it seems that Albertina cannot speak. Her eyelashes flutter; her eyes close for a few moments, then open again, very slowly, as if her eyelids were made of lead. She mouths something, but Lily cannot make out what it is. Then her eyes widen, she tries to shake her head, terror fills her face and, right behind Lily, a courteous voice says, 'Miss Garrett! How very pleasant that you have come to see us!'

Lily turns round and finds herself face to face with Ernest Stibbins.

He has moved in utter silence down the steps and across the cellar floor, and now he is standing inches away. He has a cloth in his hand, and from it comes a strong chemical smell. His smiling mouth turns down in apology and, quick as a cobra, his hand flies up and he presses the cloth hard against Lily's nose and mouth. She struggles, she kicks, she flails her arms and feels her fist connect with some bony part of his face – he grunts in pain – but whatever impregnates the cloth is far too powerful and she can feel it overcoming her. She has time to think, *Felix, I'm sorry, I didn't mean it, I need you*, and then it is as if the dreamlike state that has affected her since she walked back into the rear of the house finally takes her over. Almost with relief, she lets go and feels herself slump against him.

She wakes up.

Straight away she wishes she hadn't.

Her headache is fifty times worse. She is in total darkness, standing up very straight. Her back and her shoulders ache. When she tries to relax, to slump a little from her stiff posture, she finds she can't. There is a brick wall behind her – she can feel its hard contours against the back of her head – and wooden planks in front of her; she smells the wood and presses the tip of her nose against it. The space from front to back is barely enough for her body. Her hands are by her sides and very tentatively, for she has no idea what she will find, she extends them outwards. Once more she touches brickwork.

She thinks, at least I can breathe, and indeed there seems to be a steady air flow through the tight space.

Where am I?

She closes her eyes – not that there is any need for she is in pitch darkness – and visualizes the cellar. The trestles with the statues, Albertina's table, the workbench, the narrow little cupboard.

She is in the cupboard.

He has drugged her, put her in this horrible space and shut her in. She tries to feel round the door: which side are the hinges and which side does it open? She explores with her fingers up the right-hand side and yes, there are the hinges. The means of closing the door, then, the latch – for undoubtedly there must be a latch – is on the left.

Is it a single latch? She stares at her mental image and it seems to her she can see the one iron latch, the bar sitting snug inside its hook. Very gently she begins pushing at the left-hand edge of the door, feeling for resistance. As far as she can tell, there is just the one fastening.

But it could just as well be a dozen, she realizes, for she is on the inside and the latch on the outside.

She forces herself to relax.

I have my knife, she thinks.

For what seems the next hour or more, but is probably nowhere near as long, she occupies herself with trying to force her right hand and arm across her body and down, down towards and beyond her knees, until she can reach inside her left boot. For much of the time she doesn't think she will do it. The space is so tight, and to get her arm in front of her she has to draw in her body so tightly that soon every muscle is aching and beginning to cramp. And in order to reach so low, she has to bend sideways. There is so little room, and already she can feel blood on the side of her forehead where her flesh has rasped repeatedly against the bricks.

I have to get my knife, she thinks over and over. I have to get my knife.

And at last, her agonized body screaming at her to stop, her hand is up under her skirt and her fingers grasp the end of the red leather-bound brass handle, and she draws her grandmother's boning knife out of its sheath.

She is still in desperate straits. She is still in great pain – the headache is the worst she has ever known, and that is saying something – terrified, dizzy and nauseous with the after-effects of whatever he used to drug her, with no idea what is happening or what the intentions of her captor may be. But having a knife in her hand makes her feel quite a lot better.

She stands very still for some time, recovering.

And very suddenly, shocking a small scream out of her, a light appears right in front of her face.

It takes a few moments for her eyes to adjust from the total darkness. When they have done so, she sees the mild and kindly right eye of Ernest Stibbins peering at her through a peephole.

'I apologize for dazzling you, Miss Garrett,' he says politely.

'Indeed, the light is not bright out here; merely a couple of oil lamps, for although they are old-fashioned now, I do love the glow they give, don't you?'

His eye is right there before her, with no glass insert to form a barrier, and she would flinch away if she had the space. He must have twisted aside whatever was covering the spyhole, she thinks.

'Why am I in here?' she asks. She hopes she sounds calm. Unafraid. If she does, she reflects, it's a miracle. A feat of acting worthy of Violetta da Rosa.

'Why, you are in my drying-out cupboard, Miss Garrett!' Ernest exclaims, as if it should have been obvious. 'To aid the process, normally a body placed in there would be packed round very firmly with a mixture of sodium carbonate and sodium bicarbonate, which you may know as salt and baking powder, and which once upon a time, long ago, was referred to as natron.' He pauses to think. 'Of course, the process does not begin with the drying-out, for first, as soon as possible after death, the internal organs are removed and the brain is drawn out down the nostrils. This matter, strictly speaking, should be stored in canopic jars, for that is what the ancients did, and I am trying to ascertain if I can find a source of these beautiful objects. In the meantime, however, I dispose of it in the river.' He pauses, then says, 'I have been thinking of acquiring a little dog, Miss Garrett. It could potentially serve two purposes: the consumption of the offal, until such time as I manage to find some canopic jars, and, were that to prove impractical – although I would imagine, wouldn't you, that a dog would eat human brains and organs? – the affording of the perfect excuse for late-night walks to the water, my package of body parts under my arm!' He laughs.

'The heart is replaced with a replica made from a carved scarab,' he continues. 'I cannot of course obtain the real thing in Battersea, or indeed anywhere in London, and so I make my own, out of wood.'

He sounds so self-satisfied, so proud of his resourcefulness, that Lily imagines he expects her to applaud.

'Then the body cavity is thoroughly rinsed out with wine, which should, to be precise, be palm wine,' he says, 'although of course I have to use a substitute. Aromatic substances are placed within the space and the body is carefully and neatly sewn up. Only then does the drying process commence.'

He pauses again, and she hears him humming as he thinks.

Then he says, 'Until my dear Albertina breathes her last and I can begin to deal with her body, you will not be able to replace her on the table, Miss Garrett, so in the cupboard is, I'm afraid, where you'll stay. But don't worry,' he adds cheerfully, 'for it will not be long now.'

Lily tries to swallow her nausea and her horror.

'What are you giving her?' she says, the voice that emerges nothing like her own. 'Laudanum?'

'Yes!' he says. 'Well done, Miss Garrett! Not unpleasant, I assure you, as you will discover when your time comes, for it relaxes the body and brings about an increasingly deep sleep that turns into a coma and, eventually, death.' It seems to Lily that he leans closer. 'The bodies must be perfect, you see. No marks of violence, no unpleasant staining or contortions of the face such as might be brought about by poison. And, naturally, I have no wish to make my ladies suffer – oh, no, I'm not a sadist!'

For a moment there is the shadow of something very dark in the eye peering in at her. Then it is gone.

'And then—' Lily swallows and tries again. 'And then you turn the bodies into statues, with those beautiful masks over their faces?'

'You like them, do you?' The eye crinkles and she guesses he is smiling. 'I'm so glad. The first ones were not so good, but then I was learning my art then. As indeed I was with the process itself, for I did make mistakes and sometimes a body would be despoiled. I even had to throw one that was too far gone into the river.' He falls silent and the eye stares at her unblinking for several seconds. 'But they are not statues, Miss Garrett. They are mummies.'

'*No!*' The horrified whisper forces its way out of her, yet even as she utters it she is thinking, I should have known! As soon as he described that terrible process, I ought to have realized! 'You can't,' she cries, 'you—'

But the light goes out as abruptly as it appeared, and Lily is left in the darkness.

She knows now how silently he moves and she has no idea whether he is still in the cellar or whether he has gone upstairs, or even out of the house. She waits, hardly breathing. Then, very faintly, she thinks she hears the front door close.

She gets to work.

She has had an idea, but it is an unlikely, desperate idea, and she is very doubtful whether it will work. First she will ascertain if she can open the door. She is almost certain she can't, but it seems foolish not at least to try.

She tries to work the tip of the knife blade into the gap between the left-hand edge of the door and the door frame. In some places – at the lowest place she can reach, for example – it just about goes in. Elsewhere – such as at the spot where the latch holds the door closed – the gap is too small.

For some time, despair overwhelms her.

I am stuck in here, entirely at his mercy, she thinks. He will come back when Albertina is dead, and he will push his drugged cloth into my face as he opens the door, and I will not be able to fight him as he drags me out, puts Albertina's despoiled, mutilated body in here in my place, packs it out with natron – she is mildly surprised that she seems to have memorized the word – and puts me on the table under the stairs. Then he will begin to feed me laudanum in increasingly large doses until I too am dead and my emptied body replaces Albertina's here in the cupboard.

Can I stab him as he opens the door?

Is there a chance I can surprise him and stick my knife in his heart before his drug overcomes me?

Of course there's a chance, she tells herself robustly.

But it is a slim one, and equally likely that he will be on his guard. After all – she is forced to admit it – he has had plenty of practice.

She returns to the unlikely idea.

Slowly, painfully slowly, she gets her hand up, the knife held firmly, and tries to angle it so that the tip of the blade presses against the inside of whatever covers the spy hole.

But there are two problems: first, the knife is too long to

be easily manipulated in the space between the front and the back of her imprisoning cupboard. It will just about fit, but she is left with no room to manoeuvre and she has to hold the blade up right next to her face. It is far too sharp for such proximity; there will be little purpose in escaping from the cupboard if she slices off her face in doing so.

And I *will* escape, she tells herself.

But the other problem with the knife, even if she were prepared to risk using it, is that she doesn't think the blade will extend far enough through the spyhole to do any good. Or any *harm*, from his point of view, she corrects herself. How, she wonders, can she be thinking such a thought at such a time?

She stands still again, resting. She breathes as deeply as her stays and the confining space allow, and makes herself relax.

Her ribs ache. She puts up a hand to rub at them.

And feels her salvation under her fingers.

When at last he comes back she is ready. Has been ready for a very long time, in fact.

She still has not worked out how to open the cupboard, but that, she tells herself severely, is the next problem.

She knows he will appear as suddenly as he did the first time, and her hand is aching from clutching so hard, her arm from being held up in front of her chest.

Her ears strain. Was that a sound? Was that?

And then the spyhole cover is swung away and there is the eye.

Lily strikes, and the great roaring howl of surprise and agony tells her she has struck true.

She waits, hardly daring to breathe. The adrenaline soars through her, making her heart beat too fast, up in her throat so that for a moment or two she thinks she will be sick.

She can hear him sobbing in pain. He sounds like a child.

Time passes. His sobs turn to gurgles, interspersed with long silences.

She pushes at the door, a careful, controlled movement at first, but quickly escalating to wild panic and she begins to scream, 'Let me out! Let me OUT! *LET ME OUT!*'

And suddenly the door is open.

Albertina stands there, supporting herself with a hand on the wall. Her naked body glows softly in the gentle light. He was right, Lily thinks, about the beauty of oil lamps.

She stares beyond Albertina.

Ernest Stibbins lies on the cellar floor, a pool of blood beneath his head and spreading out round it like a red halo.

Sticking out of his right eye is a very long nail.

SIXTEEN

ily knows she needs some time away from the World's End Bureau. Away from Hob's Court; away from the never-ending stream of journalists, policemen and the perpetually nosy general public; away from London.

She knows Felix is trying so hard to help her, but he is not who she wants just now.

They have worked without ceasing over the past week, both alone, the two of them bent over her desk together until late at night, and with the police.

The full details of what Ernest Stibbins has done are slowly emerging.

He has killed seven women, he almost killed his wife Albertina and he planned to kill Lily.

The police have been unable to identify every mummified body, for in some cases nobody could be found to look at one of the embalmed faces, freed from their masks and their cloth wrappings and say, *Yes, that is my mother*, or *my daughter*, or *my friend*, or even *my wife*. The poignant moments when a friend or a relative is able to make a positive identification have apparently been even more harrowing.

The ones whose names are now known are Gladys Hatcher, Henrietta Oakley and Rebecca Jones. The three who remain anonymous will be buried in a communal paupers' grave with no headstone. What is the point of a headstone when nobody knows the name to inscribe on it?

Gladys Hatcher was twenty-eight, she regularly rented a room for the night in Battersea and a discarded and much-mended stocking was found there, believed to have belonged to her. Her body was identified by a man who had once been married to her. Henrietta Oakley, known as Ettie, was sixteen. Tall, of an athletic build, she had frequently slept on the floor of another woman's room in Battersea, and it was this woman who identified her. She had shed not a few tears over the corpse, and remarked that Ettie had said she was homesick (although the older woman didn't know where home was) and that when Ettie went missing, she had assumed her to have gone back there. Rebecca Jones – Beckie – worked the Chelsea streets. Twenty-one years old, she came from Cardiff, whence her elder brother, his mood a mixture of rigorous disapproval of what his sister had become tempered with a flash of true grief, came to identify her body.

Cicely Baker – the barmaid Ciss – is not among the victims. As news of the killings hit the headlines and the newspapers spread the terrible tale, she contacted the police to tell them she left London some months ago and, just as had been suggested, has indeed gone home to Yorkshire.

There has been one more confirmed identification; rather a surprising one.

The first body, the one at the end of the sinister row of trestle tables and the first that Ernest worked upon, lay in wrappings of the finest linen and was embalmed with a rich mix of perfumed oils, the face covered with a mask on which the features and the hair were painted with such lifelike skill that there was no doubt as to the woman's identity.

She was Enid Stibbins, Ernest's first wife. She didn't drown in the Thames when she fell from Chelsea Bridge, and it appears that Ernest must have identified the ruined corpse of some other poor unfortunate woman and claimed it was the woman for whom he mourned. She had to die, it transpired, because Ernest needed her modest inheritance to fund his obsession with the Egyptians and their mummification process. He also needed her body, of course, and he had the secret room in the cellar all ready for the moment when he took her life by holding a pillow over her face. Subduing his victims with chloroform and slowly killing them with ever-larger doses of laudanum was a refinement, for Ernest had been distressed to discover that Enid's face bore slight damage from the pressure of the pillow.

Albertina invited her own death by her insistence on home improvements.

'The cellar must surely extend beyond that wall,' she had said to Ernest, 'for the house is deeper than the existing room down there, and we could make good use of the extra space!'

Ernest is not dead.

The nail from the witch's bottle that Lily drove into his eye blinded him on that side, but he survived. On his arrest, he preened as he described his skill at making mummies, and there is no record that he ever showed a moment's remorse. He refuses utterly to consider madness as a defence, and his legal team despair of being able to keep him from the gallows.

He has made mutterings about suing Lily for the harm she has done to him, but nobody seems to take this very seriously. She was, after all, in terror of her life, and it was her right under the law to defend herself.

Lily is aware she will have to give evidence at Ernest's trial. This one of the reasons why she knows she must get away for a short while; her experiences in Ernest's drying-out cupboard haunt her waking and sleeping, and she fears that she will break down utterly in court unless she can recover herself. Breaking down will not do, for she is, as the prosecution barrister will keep telling her, a key witness.

For the sake of seven dead women, not to mention Albertina, Lily must hold firm and do what is expected of her.

One person to benefit from the affair is Marmaduke Smithers. Now his crusade to stop prostitutes and destitute women being ignored by the forces of law and order and being dismissed as unimportant has received all the attention he could ask for, and he has responded with a coruscating series of articles which have appeared in the most famous and infamous newspapers of the day. Questions have been asked in the House of Commons, and there is to be a debate. The conscience of the nation, as one of Marm's more sensational headlines says, has been awakened.

Lily wanders through into the front office, where Felix is tidying away a huge stack of papers. It is early evening, and the house is empty but for themselves. Mrs Clapper, who at first refused to leave Lily's side and virtually camped in the kitchen, promising to guard the doors all night and not let any murderers ever threaten Miss Lily again, has, thankfully, reverted to her normal routine, and went home after having set Lily's supper tray. (She appears to think that one of the results of Lily's ordeal is that she was half-starved, and insists on feeding her up 'to put the roses back in your cheeks!' Lily, however, knows what it will take to do that, and it has nothing to do with monumental portions of pies and puddings.) The Little Ballerina, whose dark eyes widened so much that they almost took over all the upper part of her face when she heard what had happened, was agog to know every single detail, and it was to Lily's and Felix's enormous relief when she was given a part in a tour of *Sleeping Beauty* and disappeared to the Midlands for a month.

Felix looks up as Lily stops before his desk. She notices how tired he is, his face drawn, his eyes red-rimmed and bloodshot.

She will never forget how he looked when he came thundering up Parkside Road, summoned by the police to take her home. She does not let herself think about what his expression might mean. He is far too good and valuable an employee to allow personal feelings between the two of them any manoeuvre room whatsoever.

'You're really going?' he asks gruffly.

'I am. Later this evening.'

He stands up abruptly, knocking his carefully arranged stack of papers to the floor. Neither of them makes any move to pick them up.

'Are you sure?'

'Yes.' She must be resolute. It would be unfair to give him any hint that part of her would quite like to stay here with him. She has made up her mind, and she knows, deep down, that what she is going to do is the right – the only – thing that will cure her. That will drive away the sudden paralysing, sweat-inducing terrors and the awful nightmares.

He nods.

Then, after quite a long pause, says, 'I'm going away too. Only for a few days,' he adds hurriedly.

'Where will you go?'

'Out of London, to stay with some old friends.'

'Very well.' She pauses. 'But you will come back?'

'Yes.'

'How – er, will I be able to let you know when I have returned to the office?'

'Of course.' He takes a blank piece of paper and writes a few lines. Peering over his shoulder, she sees that it is an address in Cambridge. 'Send a telegram telling me when to come back to work. I'll be here.' Just for a moment he meets her eyes. 'I promise,' he adds softly.

Then he gives her an odd little bow, turns and heads out. She hears the street door close behind him.

But Felix does not go far.

He knows what Lily is going to do, for she has told him. Very briefly; just that she has a friend who is taking her away on his boat. He understands both that she has to do it, and that she will be safe; something in the way she refers to this friend tells him that. Safe once she is on the boat, he amends to himself.

He is her guardian until then, and he will watch from the shadows all the time there is the faintest possibility of danger.

He finds a hiding place, creeps into it. Watches out over the river.

And, perhaps an hour later, she emerges from the rear door of 3, Hob's Court; the one that opens out of her grandfather's shed and workroom. He watches as she carefully turns the key in the lock and secures a couple of padlocks. He goes on watching as she hurries down onto the path along the riverbank, a carpet bag swinging by her side. She is dressed in a simple cotton gown, her hair in a long plait down her back, a soft white bonnet on her head.

She looks quite unlike herself; not in the least the Lily Raynor he knows.

And then a big, broad figure emerges from beneath the shadow of a wall and strolls to meet her. They fall into step and side by side they walk away to the basin where the river craft moor up.

She'll be all right now, Felix tells himself. You can go, for she is in safe hands.

Suppressing the thought that his hands too would have been safe – suppressing, in fact, almost every thought – he turns and strides away.

For want of anything better to do, he returns to his horrible digs. He would quite like to seek out some rowdy and vulgar pub where he could drink several pints of strong beer in the hope that it might cheer him up, but he recognizes that the more likely outcome is a bad head and a sick stomach, so forces himself to do the sensible thing.

He may not have to be in the digs much longer – that is the one cheering thought amid so many depressing ones – because there are plans afoot for him and Marm Smithers to take lodgings together. Marm is all at once considerably more affluent, thanks to the nationwide hunger for his story and his electrifying pieces on the filthy underbelly of London, and he is moving to a new address. It is a modest first-floor apartment in a tall, narrow old house in Kinver Street, one of a network of similar little streets between Royal Hospital Road and the King's Road. It is more than a little run down but full of charm, with high-ceilinged rooms, cornices and mouldings, an elaborately elegant staircase and black and white tiles in the entrance hall. There is a small second bedroom at the back which, Marm suggests, would be a great deal better than the accommodation Felix presently occupies. He has told Marm bluntly that he can't afford much by way of rent, but Marm is perfectly certain Felix's penury will soon be a thing of the past. 'You've done well, my old son,' Marm said when the subject of the new apartment first came up. 'That smart and astute lady boss of yours won't want to lose you now, and what's the one certain way to hang on to an employee? Give him a pay rise!'

The two of them were in the Cow Jumped Over the Moon at the time of this conversation, and on the strength of it Marm suggested it was Felix's round.

Now Felix packs a small bag, for he has decided he cannot stay in London a moment longer (now that Lily has gone, says a voice inside his head that he tries to suppress, along with some lurid and disturbing images of what she and her burly boatman might be getting up to) and he will take a train to Cambridge tonight. His friends know he'll be arriving some time soon and they won't mind if he's a day early. They keep late hours and will undoubtedly still be up when he reaches their house. They know all about what has happened, as indeed does virtually everyone in the country who is not senile, still in infancy, deaf or terminally stupid.

Before he heads to the station, there is something he must do.

He goes back to the Glass Slipper Theatre. *Miss Sanderson's Fortune* has opened, and he hopes he has timed it right. The crowd around the stage door suggests he has.

Violetta da Rosa emerges. She waves, acknowledges the generous praise and the cheers, she blows a kiss here and there. No hired conveyance or expensive private carriage awaits her tonight.

On the edge of the crowd Felix spies Billy, shouldering people out of the way. Violetta has seen him too, and a small, private signal passes between them.

Now or never, Felix thinks.

He edges between two men in evening dress and pushes forward until he is just behind Violetta. Leaning close towards her, he says quietly, 'Miss da Rosa, please may I speak to you? It's about Julian, but I'm not a journalist, you have my word.'

She spins round as he says *Julian*, and, now that he is right beside her, he can see the pallor beneath the makeup, the panic in the eyes, the beads of sweat above her eyebrows and on her upper lip.

'Why should I believe you?' she hisses furiously. 'You scavenging bastards, you won't leave me alone!'

Out of the corner of his eye Felix can see Billy, face like thunder, pushing towards them. He hasn't got long.

'I am employed by an investigation bureau,' he says, right in Violetta's ear. 'Lord Berwick employed the office I work for to find out about you. Please, I really think you should hear what I have to say to you!'

She stares right into his eyes for what seems a long time. Then she gives a curt nod. 'Come with me,' she says coldly.

The crowd make way for her and she sweeps through the massed men and boys (and a handful of women) until Billy steps forward to take her hands. She mutters something to him, and he frowns at Felix and shakes his head. Violetta speaks again, her tone more insistent, and eventually, with a shrug, he turns and walks away.

Violetta leads the way along the road a short way and into a side street, where a very much more modest carriage sits beside the pavement, its driver on the box. Violetta opens the door and climbs inside, beckoning to Felix to follow.

'You've got fifteen minutes,' she says baldly. 'After that, Billy will be here, and he's spoiling for an altercation and would like nothing better than to pick you up by your collar and chuck you out into the gutter. Until he gets here, I might add, Davor up on the box –' she nods to where the coachman sits – 'will hear if I shout out. He's from Belgrade, he doesn't speak much English and he's not very bright, but he's big, he's loyal, he works hard and he has fists like stones.'

'I very much hope you won't shout out,' Felix says. 'Please believe me when I say that I've come here to seek you out because there are things I believe you should know.'

She gives him a shrewd look.

'Your employer doesn't know you're here.'

'No,' he agrees.

She gives him a long, assessing look. Then she says, 'Go on, then. What are these things you think I should know?'

Felix takes a deep and he hopes unobtrusive breath. Then he says, 'I was the agent assigned to watching and reporting on you and your relationship with Julian Willoughby. I observed the two of you together, and I did some research into your professional life. I found out about your fondness for Tunbridge Wells. I went to the Dippers' Steps Theatre and I discovered your connection with the house in Marlpits Lane. I saw a very beautiful young woman there who I took to be your daughter, and I found out that you had been married to her father, but that, although you acted entirely in innocence, the marriage was bigamous since he already had a wife.'

She is looking at him very intently. All she says is, 'My, what a busy little bee you have been.' The caustic tone is, however, unmistakable.

'All of the above went into my report, which was submitted to Lord Berwick, and—'

'No doubt you included the fact that my daughter was born six months after Archie and I tied the knot,' she says.

'Yes. I'm afraid I did.' She makes no response, and after a moment he goes on, 'It appears that Lord Berwick confronted his son with these facts, and made it clear that you would not, in his opinion, be a suitable wife nor right for the role of the next Lady Berwick. Nobody has actually said as much, but the general view seems to be that Julian hanged himself because he couldn't bear the thought of life without you.'

The silence this time is even longer. Then Violetta gives a great sigh and says, 'You're here to appease your conscience, are you? To confess it all to me in the hope that it makes you feel better?'

'I'm here because I think it's only fair that you know what's been happening,' he replies. 'But I admit that the young man's death is indeed on my conscience, and I'd very much like to feel better, although I don't imagine there's anything you can do about *that*.' His voice has got louder as his anger rises.

She is looking at him with a different expression now. 'So you feel it's important that the truth be known?'

'Yes,' he says shortly.

She sighs again, and it is a sound full of sadness. 'Then perhaps it is time for me to tell you the truth, too. It wasn't Lord Berwick who told Julian there wasn't going to be a wedding, it was me.'

'*You.*' He is amazed. 'But I thought you were making sure of a secure future once you no longer appear on the stage?'

'Yes, you and everybody else in London,' she replies sharply. 'Which is fair enough, I admit, since it was pretty much the main reason.' She has been gazing out of the window at the softly lit street outside but now she turns to face him again. 'I couldn't do it. I thought I could, and I told myself that a life of luxury with maids for this and servants for that, and never having to worry about money again, would make marrying that dear, fond boy worthwhile. For he *was* a dear boy, make no mistake, and he needed love like nobody I've ever met.' She pauses, and when she resumes her voice has a different quality. 'His mother is a selfish piece of work, for all that she overindulged him with gifts and money and was always helping him out when yet again he ran up outlandish debts, but as for loving him, forget it. Packed him off to boarding school when he was only just six, and even when he was sent home for the holidays it was nannies and servants who cared for him, poor little sod. He was so hungry for approval, for softness, for kindness, and—' But her voice breaks and she does not go on.

'He wanted a mother more than a wife,' Felix says.

She shoots him a sharp look. 'You're no fool, are you?' She studies him. 'How old are you?'

'Twenty-seven.'

'Only four years older than Julian, but you're a man and he was a boy,' she says softly. Then, smiling faintly, 'Bet *you* don't need any mothering.'

Felix thinks about this. It is, he concludes, true. 'I did have a long and happy association with a woman many years my senior,' he says.

Her smile broadens. 'Yes, but I'd wager a sovereign to a soiled handkerchief you didn't want her for her maternal qualities.'

'You'd win,' he says briefly.

She leans closer, her voice dropping so that it is a murmur. 'I told myself I could be both wife and mother for Julian. I kept telling myself, but in the end I no longer believed my own words.'

She pauses, and he senses a strong emotion building up. 'He was so needy! Dear Lord above, he was! I felt I could never give him enough of myself. He'd turn up looking for me when he knew I was busy, standing there with some pathetic bunch of flowers and a face like a kicked dog, and when I'd ask what he was doing there he'd say something about thinking I might have wanted him for something, or might like a ride home in his carriage, and all the time I was thinking to myself, you're not telling me the truth, young man, you're here because

you want to make sure I'm behaving myself and not flirting
with my leading man, or having a bit of a giggle with the
stage hands or a good old gossip with my dresser. He didn't
approve of such behaviour.'

She sighs again. 'Then he always used to want to collect
me for a late supper after a long day. It's tiring what I do,
don't you go thinking it isn't, and nine times out of ten I'd
have preferred sitting at home with my corsets off in my
dressing gown with my feet up and a large whisky. Anyway,
I'd do as he wanted, get myself all dressed up in my finery
and set out with him to some restaurant full of chinless braying
toffs, and I'd say to him, "How are you, Julian?" and he'd
look at me out of those great mournful eyes and say, "Not *too*
bad," and I'd know fucking well – sorry – he really meant,
I'm sad and I'm lonely and I worry about what you're up to
all the time, and I'll only be happy if you give up everything
and become one hundred per cent mine.'

'Bloody hell!' Felix exclaims.

Violetta grins briefly. 'Bloody hell indeed,' she agrees.

'So you told him you wouldn't marry him?'

'I did.'

'And then he—' But it is too cruel to go on.

'He did,' Violetta whispers.

They sit without speaking for some minutes. Then there is
a tap on the window and Billy's suspicious face looms up.
Violetta opens the door a crack and says, 'It's all right, ducks,
he's kosher. I'll be a while longer.'

Billy scowls at Felix, then disappears again.

'So what will you do now?' Felix asks presently.

She is looking at him again. 'I shall settle down with old
Billy out there. He's a good man, he knows me inside out,
nothing I do offends or distresses him, and he's happy to
let me live my own life without trying to cut my wings and
shut me up in a jewelled cage. We go back a long way, Billy
and me.'

'Will you marry him?'

'I might, but probably I won't.' All at once her smile is
back, and he sees what a handsome, sexy, attractive woman
she is. 'I've told Billy I'll give up younger men, otherwise I

might have suggested you and I had a swift fling before I settle down with him.'

'I might have agreed,' Felix replies.

She leans forward and kisses him. Right on the mouth, expertly and with a certain degree of passion. He feels himself responding, hard and hot.

Then she pulls away. Glancing down into his lap, she chuckles. 'Thought so,' she remarks.

Considerately, she gives him a few moments to subside. Then Felix, thinking that he really ought to put this strange encounter back on a respectable and proper businesslike footing, reaches into his inside coat pocket and takes out one of the World's End Bureau's cards.

'You did me the courtesy of believing I was who I said I was,' he says, giving it to her, 'but I thought you should have the proof.'

She leans over so that the gas light falls on the card. Then, eyes wide, she looks back at him. 'This is the organization involved in the Battersea murders!' she gasps.

'It is.'

'You work for *her*? That cool-looking blonde who stabbed Stibbins through the eye?'

'Yes. My name's Felix Wilbraham.'

She is nodding slowly. 'My God, but what a case!' she exclaims. 'She's a one, isn't she? That boss of yours?' She nudges him. 'Passion there beneath those tight stays and those prim spectacles, you mark my words.'

But Felix, all too well aware that this secret aspect of Lily probably does indeed exist, can't bear to think about it. Considering where she presently is, and with whom, he really prefers not to. Violetta seems to understand, for she stops teasing him and says kindly, 'But then they always say never get emotionally involved with people you work with, so no doubt best to leave that side of things well alone, eh?'

He thinks how much he likes her.

Something else has occurred to her: 'Do you know that man who's been writing those devastating pieces in the papers?'

'Marmaduke Smithers. Yes, indeed I do.'

Now it is her turn to take out a card. 'I like him,' she says.

'I like what he has to say, and I like the fact that he has the balls to say it. You give him my card, which gives my agent's details, and you tell Mr Smithers that if he ever feels like an interview with a leading actress giving the true story about what really goes on behind the fire curtain, get in touch.'

Felix pockets the card. 'I will.'

Violetta regards him steadily, her eyes warm. 'I like you too, Felix Wilbraham,' she says softly. 'So much so that I think you'd better go now, before I forget myself again.'

He grins, opening the door. He jumps down and is about to close the door again when, waving his card, she says, 'I know where to find you.'

And for the first time in ages, he feels a very small glow of happiness.

AFTERWORD

E rnest Stibbins is tried at the Old Bailey in September 1880 for the murders of seven women and the attempted murder of two more. His defence, such as it is, maintains that he has been seduced by the colour, the vivacity and the ingenuity of the Ancient Egyptian world. He became entranced by it – he uses the very word – when he was quite young, following a school trip to the Egyptian Rooms in the British Museum, and his dearest wish has always been to visit the land of his dreams, only the absence of sufficient spare cash having prevented it. Instead he has satisfied himself with making his own replicas of everything Egyptian; to begin with the art and the architecture, and he describes how he painted scroll after scroll of images copied from illustrations from tomb walls, and made little paper models of temples, and even carved a scaled-down wooden felucca with a sail made from a piece of sheet, working away down in his secret cellar at night while his wife – his wives – slept. But always he was drawn to the Egyptian way of dealing with the dead, and in the end he could not resist the temptation to acquire bodies for himself and emulate the magic and the wonder of their burial practices.

The prosecution barrister makes quite a meal of attacking that particular line of argument.

Lily Raynor of the World's End Bureau gives her evidence calmly and succinctly, according to the subsequent report in *The Times*, and impresses all present by her utter refusal to be intimidated by Mr Stibbins's defence team. The ordeal she describes so succinctly and unemotionally – despite the swirling horror of the memories roaring inside her – moves many in the court to gasps of dismay.

Also giving evidence is the wife of the defendant, Mrs Albertina Stibbins. (Now, in September, it is clear that Dorothy Sullivan and the twittering ladies of St Cyprian's Church were wrong about a happy event being anticipated in the Stibbins household, which is just as well under the circumstances.) Among many other questions posed to Albertina – she is in the witness box for well over an hour and a half in total, even longer than Lily – she is asked to describe how it was that she came to save Miss Raynor's life.

'It was all because of Ernest's impatience,' she replies. 'He came down to the cellar to administer the next dose of laudanum to me, for the time was ripe for it. But he had Lily – Miss Raynor – locked up in the cupboard, and he just couldn't resist having a peek to see how she was doing. So, when she—' There the prosecution barrister gently stops her, explaining that it isn't the moment to describe what Lily did. 'Well,' Albertina resumes, 'I was starting to come round by then, so after she'd—' The prosecution barrister raises his eyebrows. 'Afterwards, I managed to get up off the table and let her – Miss Raynor – out of the cupboard.'

The prosecution barrister commends her for her bravery, and there is quite a loud murmur of approval and agreement in the court.

It is already fairly clear which way the trial is going.

Like Lily, Albertina remains resolute in her refusal to retract her evidence, although in the final phases she becomes very emotional and, as she steps down at last from the witness box, has to be comforted by a very concerned-looking man in a clerical collar.

James Jellicote later describes himself to reporters as Albertina's suitor; it seems he is holding back from claiming to be her fiancé while she has a husband still living, although the due process of the law will soon be taking care of that. The story emerges that they had been acquainted years ago in St Albans, Mrs Stibbins's home town, and that the Reverend Mr Jellicote was overjoyed when later Albertina Goodchild, as she then was, sought him out at his parish, St Cyprian's in Battersea. But he dared not woo her then, being penurious in the extreme and barely able to support himself, let alone a wife. Loving her deeply and truly, wanting the best for her, it was in a rare spirit of philanthropy that he introduced her to Ernest Stibbins, sad widower, whom he believed to be a decent, respectable, hard-working, modestly well-off and devout member of the congregation and a man very ready to give his loyalty and his devotion to a new young wife.

Which, as one of the more gossipy and lurid newspaper stories points out, just goes to show how wrong you can be.

The trial does not last long. The judge's summing-up is a model of impartiality but the facts speak for themselves, and the jury returns after a little over an hour with the guilty verdict that everyone, with the possible exception of Ernest Stibbins himself, anticipated. The judge dons the black cap and, in beautiful, sonorous tones saying terrible words, informs the man in the dock that he will be taken from there to a place of execution and hanged by the neck until he is dead.

He gives the customary final exhortation to God that He may have mercy on the soul of Ernest Stibbins, although most of those who hear him, and in particular such friends and relatives of the seven dead women as the various authorities have managed to locate, fervently hope the good, wise and just God above will see sense and send Ernest down to the everlasting flames.

Afterwards, back at Hob's Court, Felix fetches the bottle of champagne that Lily has set ready in the cool cellar. He opens it and pours out two glasses, handing one to Lily. They raise them, and the toast is not to the successful conclusion of the case.

Felix says simply, 'To Miss Raynor and the World's End Bureau.'

'To its stalwart employee Mr Wilbraham,' Lily adds, 'and to their joint future.'

They drink.

Then, putting down her glass, Lily says rather diffidently, 'I think, don't you, that, considering all we have been through together, perhaps we might consider a slight relaxation in the level of our formality with each other?'

He hesitates. He is pretty sure what she is suggesting, but he doesn't wish to appear presumptuous. 'In what way?' he asks.

'My first name, as you know, is Lily. I should be quite

happy for you to use it, provided, of course, that no clients are present.'

'Of course,' he echoes. There is a faint but detectable note of irony in his voice. 'And I, as *you* know, am Felix.'

'Felix Parsifal Derek McIvie,' she murmurs. *Her* voice holds a very definite note of irony, not to say amusement.

'Let's dispense with everything except Felix,' Felix says rather firmly.

She picks up her glass again, raises it, clinks it against his. 'Felix.'

'Lily.'

Then they set about finishing the bottle.

Lightning Source UK Ltd.
Milton Keynes UK
UKHW041832270820
368936UK00005B/91